ODE TO A YOUNG LOVE

ODE

TO A YOUNG LOVE

a novel by Basil Davidson

HOUGHTON MIFFLIN COMPANY BOSTON
THE RIVERSIDE PRESS CAMBRIDGE
1959

The Riverside Press
Cambridge, Massachusetts
Printed in the U.S.A.

Like many men today, I am weary of criticism, of belittling, of spite, in a word, of nihilism. That which deserves condemnation must be condemned, but briefly as well as firmly. That which still deserves praise must be praised at great length.

ALBERT CAMUS

All these people are imaginary

PART ONE

ONE

My bedroom window looked out upon an orchard. Beyond the orchard I could see a strip of Jerman's land that was green and gold with corn in summertime; though in winter it was dismal as a ten-mile walk, and all plough. Even then I liked to see it, for even then, beyond the ploughland, I could tell where the edge of the woods swung gently between earth and sky. Our woods were shaped like the curve of a cloud that lies upon the earth: like the frothy sailing curve, chill or sunlit, of our clouds of East Anglia.

I never thought how much I knew and loved all that until I lost it. I found this out during the time I was in court. Now I pretend often that it is still ahead of me instead of behind me.

Even in cold wet winter I liked to see the weather blowing down from Manford Hill, which is not really a hill but a rolling upland, such as we have in our countryside, with Lowton spire pinned on it among slim poplar trees. The clouds at home come westward from the sea. They climb up over Lowton spire like mountains in the sky, and often they are white and gold, gilded by the sun. These clouds of ours were the first thing I remember of the world.

Sometimes I was ill; and Mother thought for a long time that I should never grow up like other girls. 'Haven't you started yet?' she used to say; but I never had. I was ill instead, sick in my stomach and sick at heart, although no one seemed to understand the cause of it. Then I used to lie in bed and watch the sky and the clouds and the joyful treetops sway and blow outside my window; and I loved the safety of my room.

But at night I was afraid of my room. I was frightened of the dark and the shadows, and the faces which might look in through the panes of that window; so that I howled for Mother to let me have my door open. If she happened to be out I used to keep it open and sit for a long time on the stairs. When she was having company she would sometimes come up and say I need not shut it; and then I could go to sleep, safe in hearing their talk and their noises in the parlour below. Now and then she said I should not have it open because I would listen to their talk and the rest of it: then she would shut my door and tell me to keep it shut. That was when there was no drink in the house, and the company had brought none either.

On those bad evenings I lay in bed as rigid as a stick. Over Mother's wardrobe that she kept in my room, so that there was barely space to get into bed and out again, she also kept an old black trunk of a kind which must be out of fashion nowadays, for I never saw another like it. That trunk had a rounded top, with flaps, and frayed leather handles and a brass lock. I doubt if people have such trunks any more. They go about in suitcases now, as though they would like to lock away behind them as much of their lives as they can.

Mother would not tell me what she kept in that trunk, although I saw it afterwards, when Jacob got up there and broke the lock for my sake; and it was only old clothes and stuff. She used to say it was not natural to ask so many questions. I read too much, she said: always with my nose stuck into a newspaper, and frightened of what I read too.

When I remembered all this for Miss Pakeman, the other day, she said it was wrong for children to read newspapers. All these terrible things would never happen, she said, if it weren't for newspapers: they made bad things seem right. But I think myself that she was wrong about this: the newspapers never made bad things seem any less bad to me.

One evening when Mother had shut me in because she was having company and there was no drink in the house to make her happy and forget her troubles, and I lay rigidly in bed, not daring to go to sleep, I guessed what it was in the black trunk on top of the wardrobe. I knew then that it was into this trunk that Mother had put the pieces of my father after she had killed him and cut him up.

When she came in answer to my screaming, and stood over me to comfort me, I asked her if it was true that she had wrapped the pieces of my father in old clothes and newspapers, and put them bloodstained into that trunk.

She did not hit me nor even shout at me; she laughed. But I saw that her laughing was not real: there were shadows under her wide-open dark eyes and lines in her face that everyone said was handsome and that frightened and thrilled me by turns. She said to me: 'You wrong in the head, too?' I remember that her eyes were like dark brown stones when she stood over me then.

Always after that, and even until the time that Jacob and I were living in the woods, I knew that I was not quite right. I used to think about this before saying my prayers, and I often asked God to make me right again. But God's eyes were also like stones; not angry as Mother's were, but only dull. I never thought the Angel Gabriel, who stood on God's right hand, nor the other angel who stood on God's left hand, could even hear me. So I used to sit up and talk into the shadows; and the shadows could hear me. I used to tell them not to hurt me because I was going mad, just like them: I used to wonder why the pieces of my father did not smell. All this was long ago.

It is past and gone. Now I understand many things I never understood before. I think no longer of being wrong in the head; and I am not much afraid. All this I owe to Jacob; and I shall never forget him nor stop loving him as long as I live. He was never afraid and he never let me be; he was much better than other people. It doesn't really matter if you do not think this is true: the magistrate did not think so either, although she was kind or meant to be. She said that only a monster could have gone the way that Jacob did, but we must try and forgive him.

There is time for thinking now; and because I am no longer

afraid, or not very much, I think about what became of us. Whenever I look out of the window, in this place where I am now, it is not these roofs and slates but the countryside at home that I see: the strip of Jerman's land between the apple trees and the briar'd fringe of the woods. I can see them much more clearly now than when I first came here. I shall go back to them. I shall continue with my life. I even imagine, sometimes, that Jacob will forgive me, and I shall forgive myself.

TWO IF I remember how it all began there is a single day that shines out on its own – a day when we pulled bluebells together, so as to sell them to Morton if we could, instead of going to school. It was right at the beginning, soon after Ted and Jacob had come to live among us.

Instead of going down to Jerman's corner at a quarter past eight and catching the bus, we slipped early across the airfield and stayed there, pulling bluebells in Vixen's Wood, until late in the afternoon. It went without saying that Mother should never notice, and besides that she had gone to Rolcaster with an American friend: because the Americans had never gone away although the war was over, or perhaps they had gone away and come back again, I am not sure which. We have always had the Americans here; they add a lot of life to our countryside. Dook, to me, was an especially kind uncle: practically a real one. He also took Mother for comfortable rides in a long motor car with a bashed-in mudguard: except later on, when they had got the business going, and then they went in Ted's car. Even Jacob could be quite friendly with Dook; although he regularly imagined the whole world was against him but for me and perhaps for Morton.

In the land round Jerman's the barley was going up ankle-high; and all this corn, the fastening between earth and sky, was slim and smoky in the blue dawn light while Jacob ran along the green road and I ran after him. We had skirted the fields of corn and reached the green road that runs out past the church – carefully, so that no one should see us, taking care among the hazels that could shelter us here from the upstair windows at Jerman's; but now we were free. Now we ran shouting to the woods.

Blue mist of sky and woods, and glistening green fields: that is how I remember such mornings at home. Through this blue and green gleaming world we ran between the hedges while rooks in Jerman's elms were waking up and roaring like the waves of the sea: far away their roaring always sounded, though if you stopped and craned back your neck you could easily watch them, as they flapped from nest to nest above you at the top of Jerman's elms. Then we heard the Sealyhams at Mannerses, and the crowing of late cocks from our own village and from Chudbury too; and after passing Mannerses we swung off to the airfield and went across it into Vixen's Wood, and burst through all the nettles and the bindweed while Jacob shouted back at me: 'Lindy, come *on*!'

We gathered armfulls of bluebells and wandered in the woods all day with nothing to eat but a slab of chocolate Dook had given us, and late in the afternoon, safely after the returning of the school bus, we took the bluebells over to Morton's and sold them to her.

Morton's cottage stands rather by itself. It is trim and neat and private. She came herself to the door and said in her nervous way, looking sideways at Jacob: 'You have been to school, haven't you?'

She wore tight trousers of a purple colour and a canary-yellow sweater: her lipstick was mauve – I was young enough, then, to think it funny – and her eyebrows were two sharp arches under a pale high forehead. When Morton had first come to our village, a year or so earlier, we had never seen anything quite like it before, because the people at Jerman's, for all their money,

look much like everyone else; and then, what made it stranger'
we noticed that Morton talked always of 'my village' as though
she really belonged here. She made everything her business;
which is why this story is almost as much about her as it is about
us. 'Though how I find time,' I once overheard her saying, 'I
really don't know.' For she was writing a book, and she was
often poorly, and then there was Mr Morton to be seen to every
now and then, and guests who came from London for the weekend, and the garden, and the geese, and half a hundred other
things. 'As though,' Mother said, 'she'd really got something to
do, instead of only pretending it.' But Mother's tongue was
sharp; and it was often unkind as well.

Jacob said: 'We've just come back from school.'

'Then where did you get those bluebells?' But she wasn't
going to press that question, I knew it very well: for she liked
Jacob even if she didn't like me. I do not understand why she
and Jacob liked each other, unless it was because they both hated
Mother: yet they took to one another from the very first. Miss
Pakeman has explained this to me in one of her long explanations by saying that Jacob and Morton had the same problems;
but the fact of the matter is that Morton was rich and respectable. As for me, Morton seldom noticed me, not properly, but
for an occasional sad inspection; and Mother, long ago, had
heard her telling Mrs Chamfrey that I was obviously a little
defective in the head and ought to be sent to a special school.
Yet I never came to hate her for it, as Mother did. I never hated
anybody at that time. I should not have dared.

Jacob told her that we had found the bluebells in a copse near
Jerman's corner on the way home from the bus. Then Morton
gave us a shilling for them, and we walked home. There was
nothing special about that day except the happiness we had.

THREE BUT the story of my life begins a little time before that. It begins when Ted and Jacob first came to our village.

One Saturday afternoon while it was still winter I was walking back from Lowton, from the afternoon pictures, by myself because my friend would not come with me. I do not exactly remember who my friend was then, but I expect it was Mollie Waller whose father had the tenancy of one of Jerman's farms on the road to Lowton. Mollie was rather grown-up for me, or thought she was; and she looked much older. Some of the fellows thought she was sixteen or more, but I know in fact that she was only a year older than I – and I was rising fourteen then, at the time when Jacob came.

Whether I'd had a tiff with Mollie or whether she'd gone out with one of the fellows I do not remember: the end of it, in any case, was that I was coming back from Lowton by myself on a grey and foggy winter's afternoon. Fogs are common enough in our part of the country, towards the end of winter: often, through their grey and clammy mist, you can barely see ten yards ahead of you.

On this winter's afternoon I could see farther than that, but not clearly. This is really worse than not being able to see at all, because trees in half-fog begin to look as though they are walking, and bushes and cows turn into men who are following you. They stop when you stop, and they run when you run.

I was shivering with the wet and the loneliness, and my shoes were damp with the grass of the roadside, by the time I came to the end of the small road from Rolcaster where it loses itself on the airfield they built during the war, almost before I was born. There is nothing so strange, in our part of the world, as the sudden way this small road loses itself on the sea of asphalt where they had the aeroplanes. It loses itself like a wandering river that joins an inland sea: until, far away at the other end, it flows out of the sea again and leads away privately to our village. When the mist is down you cannot trace the edges of this sea of asphalt, and then if you are careless you can wander round and round in the mist and presently lose yourself.

There is a clump of trees at the corner where the road joins the airfield, and a signpost pointing the wrong way since the Lowton fellows turned it round. I felt so wet and so frightened with the loneliness that I stopped for a moment beside the signpost; and this was when I noticed Sawsbry Plum come out of the clump of trees. I knew it was Sawsbry and not his brother Gladstone, though they are much alike to look at, because Sawsbry is the dangerous one who wanders round at nights and goes for women on their own. Sawsbry belongs to our village, just as Gladstone does: but he is really some kind of gentlefolk – they all have those names – only a great deal come down in the world. He always wore a filthy cap on the back of his head, and chewed straws and looked as if he wanted to hurt you. They summonsed him in Chudbury once for showing himself at the back door of a council house.

I shouted back at him: 'Is that you, Mr Sawsbry?' But he only dodged in behind one of the bushes.

I hurried on again, keeping to the left of the road so as not to lose the edge of the airfield and go up the wrong runway; and now and then I glanced back over my shoulder. He was coming after me all right. Through the darkening mist I could see it was Sawsbry by the strange lop-sided shape of his head that his filthy old cap always made. I thought I could see him grinning at me.

I walked faster, but Sawsbry did too. Sometimes I lost sight of him, but then he would bob up in the mist again, a dark blur wandering behind me. Not catching up: just following. I began to run, and I suppose this was when I lost the edge of the airfield. I ran as hard as I could, crying by this time, but I couldn't find the edge of the airfield again. So I ran on and on across the asphalt and the potholes; and it made no difference. I could not seem to shake him off. Sometimes he bobbed up to one side of me, and sometimes to the other: once, when he had somehow got himself in front of me, I turned round and ran back the way I had come.

When I failed to reach our road, after trying for a long time, I realized that I must have taken the wrong runway and perhaps be half-way to Chudbury by now. Ordinarily, of course, you can see where you are because the airfield is as flat as a plate, and unless the corn is high you can walk across the strips of field that separate the runways. I thought I had better go to the left across the fields, so as to get back to our own runway and find the road where it flows out again.

But crossing the plough I could barely move for the weight of clods sticking to my shoes; and now I was sure that Sawsbry would catch me up. I was sobbing, and I lost my head. Not even looking where I went I was stumbling across the plough when a man's voice shouted at me. I screamed with terror. Someone grabbed me by the arm and another voice, a boy's voice, cried close to me: 'You lost, or something?'

I looked up and saw this boy beside me: a tall thin boy with long yellow hair that lopped over his forehead, and a thin long nose and a thin sharp chin, and sharp blue eyes. He looked hungry; but he also looked brave. He took his hand off my arm and asked me where I thought I was going. I could not reply for sobbing with relief.

The other voice shouted again and I saw a man standing a little way off beside one of those small brick sheds they had on our airfield: once upon a time they had kept their stores and things in them. 'That's my father,' the boy said, 'you can come over to our place.'

He went towards his father without waiting for me to reply. His clothes were in rags, I noticed, but he seemed not to feel the cold and the damp. When I walked after him I could see that

17

he wasn't shivering either. His yellow hair grew right down his neck at the back, and glistened wet with the mist: it couldn't have been cut for months, but that too seemed right and natural. Once he half turned and called for me to come on: he was not, I could see, in the least put out.

Now I had stopped being frightened and felt rather silly for it; so I went after him. His father came towards us and said I'd better have a cup of tea if I was lost, and then Jacob could show me the way to Chudbury. I told him that I was not going to Chudbury but to our village.

'Oh, what's your village then?'

When I told him he said they were strangers, but they also wanted to go to our village: they knew a lady there called Wellin.

'That's my mother,' I said: 'over to our village there's no one else called Wellin.'

The man nodded as though he knew this already. 'Poppy Wellin, eh?'

I said yes.

'You Poppy's kid, eh?' He looked at me with a sudden grin, suspiciously, doubtfully, and stuck his hands into his trousers pockets and felt around for something as though he'd lost it: then he nodded again, towards the shed this time, and said: 'Here, come an' have a cupper and tell us all about it, eh?'

Now I had a good look at him. He was different from the boy: not sharp and eager but old and grey and somehow broken in his ways. When we got into the shed he sat down on a blanket, beside a primus stove, and said that I should sit down too. He kept shooting little glances at me as though not wanting to be too curious or surprised; but when I returned his look he shifted his eyes away and remarked that Jacob might as well go back with me as soon as we'd had our tea. Even then it seemed to me, oddly, that Jacob was the elder of the two.

I asked him: 'You a friend of my mother's?' For I could see that he was scarcely an uncle: he was too old and sad for that.

He was also too dirty, and that in an old man's way: from neglect and from not noticing himself, his clothes frayed and little cared for.

'Reckon I used to be,' he said. 'Kind of partner, like. So we was on a tour of the countryside, Jacob an' me, just to get away from the noise and bustle of the big city and the bright lights' – and now he was smiling, nodding his head, his eyes shifting all the while – 'well, an' we thought we'd look up Poppy that I ain't seen in years.' His old eyes seemed to wander this way and that like a dog unsure of its welcome, and not knowing if you will fondle it or kick it out.

'You going to stay here then?'

From the doorway of the shed, standing behind us, the boy said: 'I don't mind if we stay here. It's all right here.'

'You can't,' I said, 'they won't let you.'

The man asked: 'Think we're squatters, that it?'

I nodded, but the boy said they could do as they bloody well liked, nobody was going to turn him off. I looked back at him to see if he was boasting: at the time, I thought he was.

The boy asked: 'Who was you running from?'

When I told them about Sawsbry Plum they said I was imagining things, but they didn't laugh at me. The man said: 'Anyway, Jacob can walk back with you, can't he?'

I began to feel at home with them. I began to feel that I had known them before; although of course it was only imagination. I said: 'What you doing in this hole?'

'It's not a hole,' the boy said. 'We're living in it.'

'They won't let you,' I repeated; and this time they were interested. I told them about the squatters of last fall, the couple from Edmonton who had set up house in one of these airfield sheds, and whom the police had moved on as soon as Jerman's Thompson had spotted them. 'Stands to reason,' I explained, for I hadn't yet learnt another point of view: 'We can't have strangers coming on our airfield and living here. Not anybody, I mean.' This upset them, so I went on quickly that of course

19

it was different with them: if they knew Mother then they were not really strangers.

Only I was sure that Thompson and the rest of them would never allow anyone to stay on the airfield. Even the couple of last fall had been obliged to move, although the woman had given birth to a baby right on the opening of November, with nothing to help her but water taken from the rainpools, for it is a long way to the nearest house from the middle of our airfield. They said if they had a baby here they'd a right to stay, but it didn't help them.

'Besides,' I went on, 'you can't live here in winter. It's cold and wet.'

The man laughed then. 'Long way to winter now, isn't it?'

But I could tell that he was saddened by what I said, for it had made his cheerfulness so very thin. He looked around at nothing in particular and nodded as though agreeing with me. And indeed it was little enough of a place to settle in: just a small brick shed with a floor no wider than would be filled by two or three grown-ups lying side by side, and a window with two panes long since shattered from the fellows shying pebbles through them.

I said to comfort him: 'You'll be all right for a bit, though, if you keep quiet. If you don't go out during the day nobody's going to notice you. We shan't tell Thompson or any of them, and the tractor drivers won't either. They don't like Thompson any more than we do. Then you can come out at night when there's nobody around.' With the summer ahead I thought they could manage for quite a long time. 'Though I don't know what you'll eat,' I said.

And all this time when I talked to his father the boy was standing near the door, sometimes looking at me and sometimes not, as though arguing with himself whether to go or to stay: an eager violent boy such as I had never seen before, although we had several boys in our village and a lot more over to Chudbury; and altogether different from his father. I thought then, yes, you're as different from your father as I am different from my mother.

At last the man said: 'Well, you tell Poppy, will you, that Ted Breldon was askin after her, an's goin to look her up in a day or so, eh?'

But the boy interrupted, almost in a shout: 'Who's this Thompson that's goin to turn us off, or thinks he is?'

'He's the manager at Jerman's.'

'And what's Jerman's?'

'Jerman's,' I said, 'is the biggest farm this side of Cambridge. You're on it now.'

The man stood up then, and went to the door with his hands in his trousers pockets. He nodded into the fog and muttered over his shoulder. 'It's good crops they'll have this summer, Jacob. Maybe we can help to bring 'em in, can't we?'

'It's all right here,' Jacob said. They appeared to have forgotten me.

But I was wrong in that. 'You take her along after she's had a cupper,' the man went on. 'An' you tell Poppy I'll drop over, maybe tomorrow.'

'I'll tell her,' I said. 'She'll be back tonight.'

They both looked inquiringly at me, so I had to tell them about Dook. But when I told them about the Americans being at the big airbase beyond Chudbury, hundreds of them, the man's expression altogether changed, as though I had given him some wonderfully good news. He pulled his hands out of his trousers pockets and seemed to stand up straighter than before, and suddenly was brisk and interested. 'Go on,' he kept saying. 'Tell us, won't you?'

I had to tell him all over again, word for word, about the Americans and their new airbase beyond Chudbury, and the motor cars and the jeeps and the PX and the GIs and everything I could remember, and Dook above all; until his eyes were almost twinkling with delight and he fetched Jacob a friendly cuff on the back of the head, interrupting me: 'You got that, son? Oh, I knew we done the wise thing. Always the girl to be on to summat good, Poppy was.'

He continued asking questions while Jacob poured tea into enamel mugs they had. 'That's the girl,' he kept saying until I was beginning even to think myself quite clever. 'A whole air-base full of 'em, is that right? Aeroplanes an' admin an' all? An' thousands of 'em millin round on a Saturday an' wonderin where to plant their homesick fannies, poor silly sods?' He was jubilant. 'There you are, eh? I knew I done the wise thing.' The questions he asked were not exactly questions so much as things he had guessed, for he knew exactly how they were, those Americans, and he seemed almost out of himself with joy. I couldn't in the least understand why. He never even began to explain why but just went on talking, his eyes twinkling as he glanced at me – slyly, sideways on – while I sipped hot tea. Once he got out a comb and a bit of mirror from his pocket and tugged away at his thick grey hair until it looked almost brown and tidy.

'Must be ten years an' more that Poppy's here?' he asked: 'Ever since she give up the bright lights, eh?'

I told him it was much longer than that.

'An' lived here all the time, eh?'

'That's right.'

'An' now there's all these Yankee-doodles, eh? Is that right, eh?'

'I told you it was.'

'Ah, an' what're they like? Go on, tell us some more.'

I told him for the tenth time that they were good friendly people, like Dook, and I said they were here to help defend us. I knew this was true, because our vicar at Chudbury, Reverend William Williams, often preached about it. But Jacob's father laughed out loud when I said that. 'Here to help defend us, eh? You said that, didn't you? Defend us, eh?' He seemed to find this funny, but he went on: 'Course they're here to help defend us. So we got to defend 'em in return, ain't we? On'y fair, wouldn't you say?' He never seemed to make a remark without ending it in a question. 'Couldn't get on without 'em, could we? Perishin sure we couldn't, eh? So we got to defend 'em in return.' He burst out laughing again and took a great swig of tea, holding his tin mug high in front of him and smacking his lips. 'We got to help defend 'em. That's the ticket. From all them wicked temptations that lonely men fall into. From all them fleecin profiteers. From all them sins they didn't ought to commit. Why, we got to build up their morale, ain't we? We got to cherish 'em and care for 'em, love 'em and tuck 'em up safe at nights, ain't we?' He put down his mug and beat his hands together. 'All right, we'll defend 'em. We'll hold their hands and wipe their noses and make sure they're happy, not half we won't. Just *think* of all the wicked people what'd want to rob them. Oh, they'll thank their lucky stars for Ted Breldon. I tell you, they'll go down on their blessed knees an' thank their lucky stars.'

He was quite out of breath with excitement: it was as though he had suddenly come to believe in himself again. 'Just you tell Poppy, my love, that Ted'll be over to see her, Ted Breldon, just to help defend our Yankee-doodles. Defend 'em, that's the ticket.' He was running on in this way when he stopped again and turned to me: 'Wouldn't know of a house we could get, would you?'

I said: 'There's Mrs Plum's. She wants to sell. But it's dreadfully tumbledown. It's worse than ours.'

'Never you mind, we'll build it up. Jacob an' me 'ull build it up. We're good at buildin up, ain't we, Jake?' He was like a fat-stuffed scarecrow suddenly come to beaming life. 'Oh I tell you, Jake,' he went on, 'if it's rainin in Brummagem it'll be fine in Hull, won't it?' He beat his hands together. 'You got the choice, ain't you? You got the choice.'

Yet through all this Jacob went on standing near the door, sometimes listening to me, sometimes listening to the outside: not speaking a word, just as if he were really making up his mind whether to go or to stay. He seemed not to care what his father might say or think: he seemed not to depend in the least upon his father. I had yet to learn how little he would depend upon anyone.

'You can go to school with me,' I said.

He looked at me as though I was a fool.

Ted interrupted: 'No, you drop that, Jacob. We've had that one. We've had it good 'n plenty.' He seemed to lose heart in saying this, so that he went on at Jacob in a way that was half whine and half threat. 'Have I got to lose my chance again because of you and your tricks?' I saw that Jacob neither looked at his father nor seemed to hear him: he continued to lean against the brickwork lintel and stare into the gathering fog. His father said: 'You'll go to school proper, see?'

Jacob said unexpectedly: 'Never said I wouldn't.'

But this scrap of argument, if that was what it was, had taken the fun out of Jacob's father. After that we drank our tea in silence, and then Jacob, quite of his own, said he would take me home if I'd show him the way.

'You find your way back again?' I asked. But for answer he only made a face at me.

Ted was saying: 'You tell Poppy, eh? I'll be over tomorrow, shouldn't wonder.'

When I glanced back over my shoulder I could see only the humped shadow of the little building. I shivered in the loneliness and reached for Jacob's hand.

We went along hand in hand. It was the first time I ever held a fellow's hand; and I think it was that for Jacob, too, the other way round. Until we reached the place where our small road from Rolcaster turns out of the airfield we scarcely spoke at all: I explained to him how the road crept off the airfield if only you could find it, and he found it straight away. Then I felt happier and talked to him of our village and the people who live there. I told him about our sort of people and about the other sort of people; and Jacob listened to it all as though he really wished to know.

24

When I told him about the other sort of people he asked me how many of them there were. I counted them for him as we walked together through the fog. There was Mr Thornham who lived by himself and used to be a poet from London: there was Miss Wixty who had a gentleman farmer from across the county every weekend he could manage, and was otherwise a quiet person almost never seen outside her gate: there were the two Miss Titherams, one young and one not so young, who lived in Rose Manor and were cousins and would not have a man, it was said, within their door: there was Miss Wint who was in work at Rolcaster and therefore not quite one of them (and yet not quite one of us either): and that was all, except of course for Morton and, whenever he might be there, for Mr Morton.

'But Morton,' I said, 'is the only one who interferes.' Perhaps I said more than that: I don't really remember. I should think we soon stopped talking of them; except for Morton, they were in no way part of our lives, nor we of theirs. They were not like Mr Harold Jerman and his family, who were joined to us because they farmed the land: they were people who lived among us like strangers in a foreign country. Now that I am older and wiser, I know why Mr Thornham had never got married, and I know why the two Miss Titherams could never want a pair of trousers in their house, and I know a great deal more besides: but I do not feel any closer to them. Morton is the only exception.

We went together hand in hand, Jacob and I, and talked about ourselves. I was no longer frightened of the gathering darkness.

Jacob said he was fourteen. He was going to be a pilot when he grew up.

'In one of those screaming things?' They split the sky above our heads all day and every day, those jets; and Mother never stopped cursing them, not even when she'd an American in the house.

Jacob said: 'That old stuff? Not me. Space ships, see. By the time I'm big enough they'll get right out of here. Right off this earth.' He pointed sharply into the darkness above.

I was giggling because we were holding hands, and I used to think you had to giggle if only to show them you knew as much as they did, and perhaps even more; and I said: 'Oo, I wouldn't like to get off this earth.'

'Stupid. I would. Right off it. Never see it again.' And that was very like him. Later on he gave up this idea for a better one, and we chose Australia instead; but for him, I think, it was pretty much the same thing, and perhaps for me too.

'How do you get to be a space pilot?' I was vexed that he thought me stupid. But he changed the subject, and said abruptly that I was all right and we ought to be friends. I said so too; and this was like the first sweet kiss of my life.

But I also said: 'You teasing me?' For I was pale and small and, so far as I could know, miserable; and nothing like grown up. People in our village spoke of me with scornful kindliness; they said I was a poor waif, a sorry scrap of a child; while Morton never stopped trumpeting, in shops or in the post office at Chudbury, that Mother ought to be put in charge for the way she sinfully neglected me. Mr Prother, on the other hand, said I was a clever child and ought to have had the scholarship: as a matter of fact I could read and write a good deal better than most of the grown-ups in our village ever would. For all that, though, I carried about with me this disagreeable picture of a pale and sickly child with frizzly brown hair and rings under the eyes, and a disagreeable yellowish skin; and I naturally hated this picture, and hated myself. Anyone must have hated it. When Jacob said that he wasn't teasing – why should he be teasing? – I think I doubted for the first time if this hateful picture need be true.

I think that Jacob was happy too. Later on I should recognize the mood. He could never bear to have things half way: it had to be everything or nothing. And if he had everything, or thought he had, then he would set it all aside and begin trying for the next thing; and if he had nothing he would practically die of despair. He had no patience.

Walking along in the fog with me, talking of plans for the future, for getting right off this earth, he was certainly in the mood for believing that he had everything; although of course I understood no more just then than that I wanted to be friends with him. I wanted it very much, and I remember every smallest detail of that walk. It was dusk by now, but I remember how early honeysuckle in the blackthorn climbed already towards the summer and primrose leaves were opened tight against the bankside turf. Through white mist the calling of our rooks in Jerman's elms rang like the beating of waves on Clacton beach, and put me in mind of verses from *The Ancient Mariner.* When I first read that poem at school I cried to myself; but nobody minded, for they all believed me not quite right in the head, and I believed that too. Those rooks for me were like the spirits of sailors lost in the painted ocean, except that they never rang quite sad enough or lost enough but when the fog was down: while the Sealyhams at Mannerses yapped for me, I thought, like the souls of horny devils whom the Angel Gabriel had cast from Paradise.

'What did he do that for?' Jacob asked.

'They sinned against the Lord. They would not obey.'

He spat into the darkness, which I thought was shocking in the circumstances. 'Oh that,' he said, and dropped my hand, 'same old stuff.' Suddenly he danced on his toes and struck out with his fists. 'Know what I'd 'a done? Them angels? Formed 'em into a flyin squad, and gone bashin through the skies. *Wheeee...*' And he began to shoot out the snorting whistling noises which all boys make when they are playing cars and jets. 'I'd chase those old Sabres 'n Meteors 'n stuff. I'd tip their wings. I'd scream at their pilots. Know what I'd do! I'd ground 'em. I'd force 'em down. I'd *shoot* 'em down.' He sizzled through his teeth. 'Get it,' he said while I giggled, for I was a little nervous, he was so violent, 'I'd make 'em sweat.' Then he was laughing

27

too; and we were friends again, although I was certainly shocked and I said: 'You coming to church, Sunday?'

When he said that he had never once been to church in his life I was so put out that I could think of nothing to reply. Jacob was surprised. 'Sunday's for sleeping, Dad says. But I like to go tracking and hunting. You can come if you like.'

If I had only said no on this first occasion everything might afterwards have come out right. I have discussed this with Miss Pakeman who says that I ought not to blame myself; but I think that privately she agrees with me. But I could not possibly have said no; and I am quite sure that I should not say it now, if the choice were offered me again. I said yes.

Actually I said: 'I don't mind.' But that was as much as anyone could have said, as Jacob well knew.

'Still,' I added, 'we ought to go to church.'

'Not me.'

'God will be angry.'

'He's another of 'em, isn't he?'

I struggled hard. 'God is over us.'

'Not over me, he isn't. No one's over me.'

'You're showing off.' But I said it more in self-defence than because I really thought so. He had a way of telling me fearful things as though they were the sober truth.

I said: 'Your Dad's over you.'

'Only when he gets his rag out. Then I run away till it's over, and I can run faster, see.' He let out another piercing whistle and caught me by the wrist. 'I can run faster than anyone. Come on an' try.' And we ran like wild cats through the pale darkness with Jacob tugging at my wrist until I thought I should be ill with it. But he stopped when I screamed; and we walked on again hand in hand.

FOUR In this comfortable way we passed the derelict windmill and the house behind the laurel hedge and came to Jerman's corner. This is where you can see the high wall of Jerman's, an old manor house they built in the ancient days of moats and wars; only now in the night we could see only the well-lit windows of the first floor, cosily dim behind their curtains, where the family gathered of an evening, as my aunt Pooley who sometimes worked there had let us know; and looked at television.

'They're in,' I said.

But Jacob said nothing to that; and I understood why, and clasped his hand the tighter. 'I don't feel lonely,' I said. He said nothing to that either but held my hand tightly in his, and I knew that he was thinking the same thought as I was. I was thinking that the whole wide world seems against you, walking home on a dark night; but not if you've someone with you whom you trust. Then you feel stronger for your loneliness.

'Where's your place?' he asked after we had got past Jerman's.

We were coming to it.

When we came quite close and Jacob saw Dook's car standing in the road he almost howled. I knew he was delighted although he said: 'All show and no go, Yankee cars.' He walked up to it and round it, and I could see that he was impressed. 'Can't drive either,' he said at last: 'Look at that wing.'

'It wasn't Dook's fault. He's careful.'

'Telling me. Wait till you see my Dad.'

'Can he drive, then?'

Jacob's eyes gleamed. He caught my arm and twisted it but not so as to hurt. I gave a little scream and he was satisfied with that.

'He's a professional. We got a Buick.'

'A what?'

'Eight cylinder Buick. Best you can get.'

I knew that could not be true; but I did not want to say so because it would surely hurt his feelings to be disbelieved in so large a matter. People who camp on Chudbury airfield do not have motor cars. The most they have are little push carts; unless they're mumpers with a proper caravan like gypsies have, and then I do not really count them, because mumpers like living in that way and would not change it, they *say*, for any other. I disbelieved him in silence. I should think it was the only time I ever disbelieved him.

After he had done with inspecting Dook's car and grumbling about its being no good, we went up the path together. When I found the front door bolted I guessed why and whispered: 'We'll go round the back and wait in the kitchen. They won't be long.'

'There's a light in the front room anyway.'

'Well,' I said, 'don't let Mother catch you looking. It makes her mad.'

That was wrong of me. Of course I know that now: I knew it, in a confused way, even then. I should have taken him straight round to the kitchen. But I understood nothing then except that Mother told me she knew what she was doing and it was none of my business: and I thought then that everything she did was just the same as other people did, and nothing out of the way.

Jacob went up to the window and looked through the panes: they had the paraffin lamp turned low. Then I saw the mistake I had made. He came back to me with a strained white face. He only said: 'She saw me.' But I knew that it was somehow worse than that.

'Come on round the back,' I said.

At first I thought he was going to run away. So I added that he need not be scared. But even then he said nothing: he came round the back with me, and we sat in the kitchen without exchanging a word. He would not even look at me; and I held it against Mother, without really knowing why, for being the cause of this. It was the first time that I had ever had the courage to hold something consciously against her; now that I come to look back on it I see that this was a kind of milestone too.

Mother came out of our front room in a few minutes, they must have been nearly finished anyway; and I saw at once that she was mad with us. She came out storming into the kitchen with her long black hair, so different from mine and so beautiful, flying about her face. 'Who's this?' she burst out, staring at Jacob as though she meant to kick him out. I told her who it was.

She stood in the middle of our kitchen with her arms on her hips and her blouse still not done up, and said to me without looking at Jacob: 'I don't like Peeping Toms, see.' She was in a fair old rage, and only Dook saved us from a row. He came in then to save us, jerking at his trousers and jolly all round, a fair and hairless man with little blue eyes and a skin like uncooked bacon rind; and Mother changed her mind about making a row and shut up instead.

'Here, sit down,' she said to Dook, 'there's something left, I shouldn't wonder.'

'That's the girl,' Dook said mildly, sitting down at table and grinning at Jacob and me. Nothing ever disturbed Dook; he was the quietest uncle we had ever had.

He was also the best for Mother. Whenever Dook was in the house Mother quite lost her savageness. There were times with him when she went as far as seeming to forget how many people she had to hate, or how much she had to hate them. And I really think that she felt, with Dook, the chance and possibility of being an altogether different person: there were moments even when she talked of going away with Dook to America and beginning life all over again. 'Start level,' she would say: 'That's what you can't do in this dump, start level.'

So now she got out little glasses for herself and Dook, and poured brandy into them from the bottle in the cupboard, and was almost cheerful again. You might have thought, if you had known her little, that she had quite forgiven Jacob for seeing her

31

down with Dook; but I was not fooled. Even then it was perfectly clear to me that evil had come between us; and afterwards I remembered this first meeting as the reason why Mother and Jacob came so ferociously to hate each other. Perhaps the horror that befell us all was born in this first meeting, though none of us could possibly have known it then.

Dook was everybody's friend, and soon had us all laughing. He was an airforce sergeant with the stripes on upside down, like they have, who never tired of telling us about his home, which was three days in a train from the sea – we are only an hour or so – among fields a hundred times wider than ours. They must be exceedingly wide, those American fields, for ours are not so small either: the field behind Morton's is all of ninety acres, they've rooted up so many hedgerows. 'Why,' Dook went on, while we laughed with him: 'you could put this whole little country into a couple of fields back home.' Only he didn't call them fields, but another name I do not remember. Then he always had chocolates or candy for me; and he ate a great deal of them himself, which was probably the reason why he was pasty faced and fat, and easy-going. He wanted to give Jacob some at this first meeting; but Jacob would not have it. He stood away across the kitchen table, near the door, and said nothing. He looked at Mother now and then as though she had tried to whip him.

When I told Mother that Jacob's father was Ted Breldon, and Ted was coming over to call on her tomorrow, she was delighted. She had her elbows on the table and now she took up one hand and pushed back her long black hair and looked at Jacob in a kindly way as though she had altogether forgotten her anger against him: he could tell Ted, she said, that she would be very glad to see him any time he liked to come.

'That's right,' she went on, smiling so that she was still more beautiful and thrilling, and even Dook sat up and took notice: 'I've a soft spot for old Ted Breldon.' In a moment she was explaining to Dook how she had known Ted Breldon when serving at table in the *Lancashire Lad*, which is somewhere in London for all its name, in the time before they had evacuated her. 'Ted was a good friend to me,' she explained.

Dook was pleased because Mother was pleased. 'Sure be glad to meet him,' he said in his friendly way, 'just so long's he doesn't want to sell me anything.'

'Don't you worry,' Mother said with a laugh, 'you wouldn't know it till after, not with Ted.'

Dook laughed too, and slapped the hip pocket where he kept his money. 'Keeping that right there, Poppy, less there's something you want me to get you.'

'Tell you when I do,' said Mother easily. And it is true that she was never greedy or grasping; which was perhaps another reason why men put up with her moods and wanted her so much.

I saw that Jacob was growing restless, so I made it easy for him to get away and went with him as far as the gate. I could not bear to have him leaving me with that whipped look on his face, but I had no idea what to say. It was suddenly like having to choose between Mother and someone else. These are the moments, Miss Pakeman says, when children grow up. I said to him at the gate: 'I'm sorry if Mother upset you. I hate her too sometimes.' It may sound little enough to have said; but it closed another door behind me.

At first I thought that after all he would walk off without saying a word. I tried again, a little in despair: 'See you to-morrow, shan't I? Thanks for coming home with me.' He would not look at me. I repeated: 'You'll come tomorrow, won't you?'

He said without looking at me: 'It's all right.'

'Thanks, Jacob.'

'What's your name then?'

'Lindy. Lindy Wellin.'

'Lindy,' he said slowly: 'Short for something?'

'No, just Lindy.'

He went off into the mist-glowing night while I shivered and watched him disappear. I was wonderfully happy.

33

WHEN I consider what came out of all this it appears
FIVE   to me that nothing could have happened differently.
Miss Pakeman says that it was really Mother's fault
and Ted's fault, and Dook's fault too; but fault is the wrong
word. Nobody ever wanted things to happen as they did:
nobody ever meant them to happen as they did.

Now I have nothing left but to sit and wonder why: and there
is no answer, none at all, while the days and weeks go by in this
place so slowly that I sometimes wish those old terrors and
troubles could return again.

Ted came the next day.

He seemed less broken down and tired when Mother opened
the door to him and we saw him standing there in the weak
sunlight. They kissed each other on the cheek. 'For old times'
sake,' he said.

The hour of his calling on us was after Mother had returned
from Jerman's where she worked in the dairy; so it was teatime
and we all three sat down for a cup. Ted explained when I asked
him that Jacob was minding their things: you couldn't lock that
shed on the airfield, and anyone might come and think the
owners had pushed on somewhere else.

'You can't settle there, Ted, Jerman's won't let you,' Mother
said. 'You'd better move in here for a bit. There's a room that
you and the boy can have if you don't mind roughing it.'

'Thanks for that, Poppy.' I thought he was glad to be wanted;
and thinking this made me like him and feel equal with him.
'I might do that. Wouldn't be for long, but it'd suit for a few
weeks, like. Maybe we'll stay here, eh?' He cocked back his
head and looked at Mother with a wink that was part cunning
and part sheer laughter. 'Got the Yankee-doodles here, ain't
you?'

34

Mother said sharply: 'What's the line, Ted?'

'Chauffering.' He went on to explain about having a car, and I knew that Jacob had not lied to me. Mother smiled broadly when Ted explained this. She got up and went over to the mirror and tidied her splendid hair and looked at herself sideways, bending back her head and squaring her shoulders and putting out her chest in a certain critical way she had that generally meant she was pleased about something. She glanced over at Ted from across the room, and she was dazzlingly fine with her wide bold eyes and her figure in curves and her long hair drawn back behind her ears.

'Handsome as ever you was, Poppy.'

Mother laughed with the pleasure of it. She strolled over to him and stood in front of him, very straight with her hands behind her back and her legs a little apart so that they strained against her skirt. 'No pads, no bones, no faking,' she said with a crooked little smile: 'But it doesn't seem to do me much good. Though I might have known you'd land on your feet, Ted.'

He laughed. 'S'what I was sayin about you, Poppy, on'y last night.' I think they'd forgotten about me: they were really pleased to see each other again.

Mother said: 'Oh, I get along, only it's not much, you know. And this place –' she shrugged while Ted sympathetically nodded.

'A girl like you,' Ted went on, 'ought to be coinin money. Ought to have a good time.'

They were sharing some thought; and then they were laughing together but not boisterously as before: privately, as though they had reached some private understanding.

'That right you've got a car, Ted?'

He nodded again, comfortably. There were little screwed-up chinks of comfortable pleasure running out sideways from his eyes. He said easily: 'We could fix up something, you 'n me, couldn't we? Partnership and no nonsense? You know me, don't you, Poppy?'

She gave him a measuring look and said thoughtfully: 'That's right, there was never any nonsense with you, Ted.'

'Well, I got a car, and I got a bit of money, not much but enough to start us off like. You got the on-tray to these Yankee-doodles, ain't you? There's a partnership in that, ain't there?' He leant forward almost eagerly: 'Mind you, we'd need a few good lookers. Not too local, neither.'

Mother was still thoughtful. 'In Rolcaster?'

'Could be. Or further off if you like. Can't make it too close anyway. They got to mind out. They let it happen so long's it don't upset the locals. I seen that before.'

'Well, not local, that's sure,' Mother said.

Ted made a sweeping movement with his hand. 'Course not, Poppy. They got to be careful, but they got to have it too. Local girls all pregnant otherwise. Coppers know that as well's you'n me.'

Mother was smiling her crooked little smile. 'I could do with some money, Ted. A lot of money.'

'Course you could.'

'But it wouldn't tie me down, Ted? I'm not leaving this place. It suits me here.'

Ted said emphatically: 'Now you get it straight, Poppy. You ain't involved, see? You're a partner. You just get the business started, and then you sits back, see?'

Mother was smiling more easily now and glancing at herself, patting at her round hard breasts that gave her such pleasure, and smoothing down her skirt.

'A partnership an' no nonsense, eh?'

She was smiling at him. 'You getting that old, Ted?'

Ted threw up his hands: 'Oh, I'm settlin down. Business first for me. And last too.'

'It's all right with me, Ted.'

Then Ted noticed how hard I was listening. 'Little Miss Big Ears,' he said: 'You go out 'n play, won't you?'

Mother snapped: 'Lindy, you get out of here. And put the

36

kettle on again.' She explained to him as I was going out: 'Nothing but a damn nuisance.'

I could hear Ted saying: 'Mistakes will happen.' He always meant everything for the best.

'It was during the war,' Mother added gloomily, and suddenly stamped her foot and screamed that I should shut the bloody door behind me. But when I returned from the kitchen, to say that the kettle was on the boil again, she was back in a thoroughly good humour.

SIX

TED and Jacob never came to live with us although I am sure that this is what Ted wanted. At that time he would have wanted nothing so much as to be welcome, I think, even if only in a stable.

'Pity, though,' he explained to Mother, a day or so later when he was over in the afternoon, 'I could have done a bit o' clearin up for you.'

He was standing on the earth outside our window, chatting with Mother who was in the sitting-room, and his baggy trouser-legs were deep in tall dry weed. Nobody had touched our garden for weeks or even months because Dook was never one for doing useful work, and Harry Swithin, Mother's regular in wintertime, would not come to our place so long as Mother had someone else. Harry was rather a queer one: never jealous nor put out, so far as anyone could see, while Mother was taken with someone else, but always ready, when winter returned and Mother lay between times, to arrive with plenty of beer on Saturday afternoons and then dig the garden all Sunday, or else patch up the roof where easterly gales had blown the tiles off, or mend the gate and the bit of wooden fence we had, mouldy as it was.

I used to wish Mother would make do with Harry altogether,

37

because Harry was a solid man you could rely on, and comforting because also one of us. On Mother he had a deadening effect: after a while with Harry coming on Saturdays and sometimes on Wednesdays too, and doing odd jobs about the place on Sundays, Mother would grow quite tame and gentle. Harry seemed able to draw the fires within her. A mountain of a man, curved with muscle and capable as I've seen of lifting the fore end of a small tractor and turning it round on itself, Harry stood all Mother's nonsense as though she were a child.

But it never lasted. The least sign of spring weather and Mother would be off again. Then Harry just stopped coming, for he never interfered with the others, and I doubt if he cared to know about them. Besides, he was living away to Chudbury now because his aged mother was ailing; and we seldom saw him but by accident. Mother seemed not to miss him, for Dook came then; but I missed him and the garden missed him even more. Now the weeds were high over the fence, and cow parsley thrust loopy snouts up through our blackthorn hedge until you could barely see the dark green stinging nettles which flourished there. I wondered how Harry would manage it all next winter.

'What's eating that boy?' Mother was shouting to Ted through our front window. 'If he won't come and stay here, then leave him where he is.'

I was playing with my dolls on the front step and saw that Ted was embarrassed. He pushed his old hat down over his forehead so that the crown of it seemed to bump from one gouged line into the next, and scuffed his shoe on the path as though trying to get rid of something on the sole of it. 'Can't do that,' he said; and I was glad for him.

He said to Mother, but staring down into the weeds: 'You didn't hit the boy, did you, Poppy? He's took against you, I don't know why.'

Mother only thumped her iron on the sitting-room table. She must have hated being a child so much that she had come to hate all children. They were, she always said whenever the subject was discussed, a pestilential nuisance: of course meaning me, but not only me. I used to sympathize with her because I also regarded myself as a nuisance, as well as a mistake in the first place.

Now with Jacob it was just the other way round, as I soon found out. He considered that all grown-ups were a pestilential nuisance: he mostly hated or ignored them. He and Mother, who grew to loathe each other so much, were opposite sides of the same coin in this matter of loving and hating: they could never forbear to fight each other over the least thing, stubbornly and meanly, so that it was certain in the end, I suppose, that they would come to fighting over me. This is what Miss Pakeman calls ironical: that Mother, in the end, should have fought Jacob over me, whom Mother otherwise regarded as a pestilential nuisance. Miss Pakeman seems to enjoy this idea of hers, and she is writing a book about it; but I would rather she forgot it.

None of that, in any case, could we see coming; and now Ted would not move into our house because Jacob had refused to move with him. I suppose they might after all have gone away, partnership or no partnership. But Mother knew as well as I did that Mrs Plum wanted to sell her cottage across the way from ours.

'She'll take three hundred,' I heard her telling Ted, 'though I suppose that'll be two hundred and ninety more than you've got?'

'No it isn't,' Ted replied, cheering up and letting his foot rest still: 'As a fact, Poppy, it isn't.'

Mother almost screamed. 'Hey! you come into money or what?'

Ted was gravely serious. 'I done a bit since those days, Poppy. Got out of it in good time, see. Had to think for myself for a change.'

Mother said mockingly: 'You amaze me.'

'I don't see why.' He sounded a bit hurt, and stood twisting

39

up his scraggy brown moustaches as though twisting up his courage to say so. But Mother went on more gently: 'Well, I know when to hold my tongue. And you was never one of the worst. You want to go and see Mrs Plum?'

Ted thought he shouldn't mind, he could see if he was suited.

I knew Mother was longing for someone to goad, for she never wanted to annoy Dook, and Harry was away this long time; and there was Ted, standing by, simply asking for it. She said: 'Go on, then. You can see the cottage from the front gate. Over to the left there.'

He replied that he shouldn't hurry himself, he'd think it over.

'Not much of a partner, are you? Of course, if you're going to dilly dally around, that's that. You suit yourself, Ted. But those fellows at the Base like to get a move on, I can tell you. Hustle, they call it.'

There'd be plenty of time, Ted thought, for organizing all that later on.

'Later on? Next year perhaps? Or the year after? Till you've discovered where you left that money you're telling me about? Forgotten where you put it, I suppose.'

So Ted walked off down the path and pushed through the gate without saying another word; and I watched him go with a tense feeling in my stomach. It was like seeing fate unfold itself.

From where I was I could see Ted standing in the road, looking over to the left at Mrs Plum's; after a long while of standing there and looking he turned round slowly and came back to us. He seemed contented, or perhaps he was only trying to look contented. 'She's let it run down, mind,' he observed to Mother, 'it'll need a lot of work.'

'You were always one for work, Ted.'

He glanced at her through the window, screwing up his eyes. 'I won't say it don't suit me, Poppy. And you're right there.

Me 'n Jacob's a famous pair for buildin things up.' He suddenly swung his arms and beat his hands together: 'Tell you, Poppy, I wouldn't be surprised if 'twasn't the kind of country home I've wanted for a long time now.'

Mother said drily: 'So you think his lordship will agree?'

'Jacob? No trouble about that, Poppy my love. He was only afraid we was coming here.' Now he did not even mind telling her that.

He strolled about among the weeds as though he had already done a clever thing. But Mother was never one for letting well alone: once she caught hold of an idea she liked to worry the life out of it. She said: 'What you waiting for then? Now you're in the money?'

Ted explained that he was for taking things slowly. But Mother was for nagging. 'Have to ask his lordship first, eh?'

'No I don't then,' Ted replied, growing upset again. I was dreadfully sorry for him: you needed to be Harry, and as quiet as an ox, to contend with Mother in a nagging mood.

Now I look back on it this was also the first time that she would try to drive herself between those two, between Ted and Jacob: it was the earliest beginning of that.

Ted was far from being Harry: he soon gave in. 'Plum, did you say? I might as well go an' see her.'

I could tell that he did it to prove himself in Mother's eyes. He would never otherwise have allowed himself to be fooled by Mrs Plum, for Ted was no easy one to fool.

He went off down the path again: and again I had a tightening in my stomach as though we had reached and passed the parting of our ways – the parting between the way that everyone lives and the peculiar way that we were going to live.

NEXT morning I awoke with a start and another
SEVEN   stone rattled in through my window. From beyond
our back hedge Jacob beckoned me out. Quickly
I dressed and slipped downstairs.

A milky dawn shone softly on the garden and the fields. That
is why they say that early dawn is like the beginning of the
world; and why the Bible says that darkness was upon the face
of the deep when God made the world, and the Spirit of God
moved on the waters. Sometimes in the summer dawn at home
you could see the Spirit of God moving on the corn in Jerman's
field behind our house, beyond the dump-heap and the hedge,
in dark mysterious waves of shadow.

I slipped down the garden towards Jacob beside the dump-
heap. He was off as soon as he saw me coming; I failed to catch
up with him until we reached shelter in the hedge opposite
Mrs Plum's.

'Hallo,' I said, 'I'm cold.'

He gave me a good long look and I was thrilled with excitement; then he took off his jacket and put it round my shoulders.

'It's torn,' I said.

'Doesn't matter.'

'I'll mend it for you.'

'All right, you can.' He pointed to Mrs Plum's. 'Is that the one?'
I said it was.

He stood quite still, yet quivering a little like a lean long-
haired dog that sets for game, and stared over the hedge at Mrs
Plum's old cottage.

'She's a witch,' I said.

'Got a dog?' I shook my head. Then he went through that
hedge with the ease that ordinary people cross the road. But he
had to wait for me while I walked round by the gate. I'm not

going through any hedge at five o'clock in the morning, I thought, even if you won't wait for me. But he did wait for me; and I knew that he would. You learn these things as you go along. I found him crouched behind a row of broad beans, inspecting the house.

'Come on,' he said: 'Let's have a look.'

For as long as I could remember I had always gone past Mrs Plum's on the other side of the road. Now I went after Jacob as though Mrs Plum were the most harmless creature in the world. And the strange thing is that I do not even remember being surprised at myself: that came later.

'Proper old ruin,' Jacob whispered when we had got round Mrs Plum's broad beans and found a place among her weeds where we could part the nettle-stalks and see the cottage fairly. And it did look a ruin. Rotten thatch lay on the rafters like mouldering paste, smeared and green and stucco'd with wisps of straw: at least half the roof was bare to the sky, and weather stains made dark damp islands on the dirty plaster wall in front of us. I never remembered it as anything else but like that yet this was the first time I ever really looked at it. Into the whole fabric rats and birds and winter weather had eaten ragged mouthfulls.

I whispered back: 'She's very old, and she's a witch. She never budges out of that downstairs room.' I pointed to the place where everyone believed that Mrs Plum passed all her days and nights. 'She can't.'

'What's she live off?'

'She doesn't eat,' I said: 'She doesn't need to.'

'Bet she does eat. Bet she gets out into her garden.' He pointed to a little row of lettuce in a slightly cleared patch near the door. 'Bet she planted those.'

'She never did,' I said. 'It's Gladstone Plum comes over from Chudbury once a week. She *can't* go out. Not since she broke her legs.'

'You're making things up,' he said.

But I waited for him to let the parted nettles sway still again before I would tell him any more. 'There's Sawsbry and Gladstone,' I said: 'living over to Chudbury now, but they lived here till last year.'

'Don't muddle it all up,' he interrupted. 'Tell it right.'

This was the first time I ever told him a story, although I got into the way of it later on; but Jacob was already good at listening, he'd learnt it from Ted who told everything he knew or thought of as though it were a story. Nothing ever happened to Ted but it turned into a story; usually a funny story, too.

Mrs Plum was very old when she broke her legs, at least ninety I should think. Ours is a village where people do grow old, much older than you would think possible; and Mrs Plum was one of the oldest of them all. She had never lived anywhere else, but for being at Chudbury Manor in the long ago when they kept staff to wait at table and Mrs Chamfrey bossed them, though now it's a club for the American airforce: her father had lived in our village too, all his life, and her grandfather too. This is something I know about because I once overheard Morton telling the Reverend William Williams before he retired after his bicycle accident to live at Felixstowe: Morton said that Mrs Plum's grandfather, just like Mrs Chamfrey's, must have been a little boy when Lord Wellington beat the French at the battle of Waterloo. It was most remarkable, Morton said.

'Get on with it, won't you?' he interrupted again.

Mrs Plum would never move from this family cottage although it was fairly tumbling about her. Gladstone was over at Chudbury, working, and Sawsbry did not really count, for he never worked regularly. Sawsbry was the queer one. You didn't want to leave your door unlatched with Sawsbry about. Even Mother said that, although Mother was certainly not afraid. 'He can wave himself at me as much as he likes,' she had declared to Mrs Chamfrey in my hearing: 'Filthy old beast, he won't scare me.' Mrs Chamfrey had reproved her for speaking so vulgarly.

'Tell it straight through, won't you? You keep muddling it.' He never had any patience.

Gladstone and Sawsbry sometimes agreed together; and now they had agreed to move Mrs Plum to Chudbury, where Gladstone could get one of the new council houses and would no longer need to come over to our village to look after her. But when Mrs Plum had learnt of this she made a terrible scene, and took a stick to Gladstone.

'What did he care? Old woman, isn't she?'

I explained that Gladstone would never have cared to stop Mrs Plum from hitting him if she got within reach, because Gladstone was afraid of her. Everyone was.

'Bet I'm not.'

'I won't tell it to you if you keep interrupting.'

He said rudely: 'You're not telling it anyway.'

This made me cry until I remembered where we were. Then I stopped crying for fear of the noise, and went on with the story as quickly as I could.

One day Gladstone told his mother, shouting in to her from the garden so that a tractor driver who had purposely stopped on the road could overhear, that he was getting the copper from Chudbury to come and shift her. Sawsbry was in the garden, too, though Sawsbry kept quiet and left the hard work to Gladstone as he always did.

Mrs Plum had said nothing to this, so Gladstone went on shouting through the window. But she took him by surprise: she pushed her head out of the upstairs window and began swearing down at him.

When Gladstone asked her what she thought she was doing up there she climbed up on the sill and put her legs outside and jumped down into the garden; and broke her legs.

'How do you know she broke her legs?'

'You're interrupting again,' I said; but I hurried on because of where we were. Before Mrs Plum threw herself down into the garden she screamed at Gladstone and Sawsbry that she

45

would rather die than move. When she fell they must have been frightened, for they simply walked away out through the back, which is a short cut to Chudbury. Then the tractor driver went in and found Mrs Plum lying in the garden. Doctor Bliss was called from Chudbury and came that very day; he said it was very serious, she might have killed herself. He was quite sober too.

Mrs Plum would not hear of going to Rolcaster Infirmary: she declared it was half way to the workhouse, and that was half way too far. She had never been to Rolcaster since seeing off old Mr Plum to the war in France, where they had killed him; and she would never go there again. So they had to lift her down into her front room; and Dr Bliss put her legs in plaster, and said it was a marvel she was still alive.

Jacob said: 'Then why does she want to move now? Why does she want to sell the house?'

'Because Gladstone doesn't want her any more. He doesn't mind coming over once a week, but he's set up house with a lady in Chudbury now. So now Mrs Plum wants to move in with him.'

'He doesn't have to take her, does he?'

I said wearily: 'Yes he does. You don't understand anything, do you?'

He was deep in thought, staring at the house. After a time he said: 'It's not worth three hundred. Let's look inside.'

This was one too many for me, and I said so. But Jacob tossed back his long fair hair and went boldly to Mrs Plum's door. I could hear the rapping of his knuckles on the wood: I watched through the parted nettles and admired his cleverness. For in going to the door instead of to the window he would make her curious: nobody from the village would have gone to the door. If anyone ever had reason to call on Mrs Plum they went to the window and shouted through it, and Mrs Plum shouted back in a terrible deep voice until you could hear her from the road, and even from our own cottage across the road.

Then I heard that voice of Mrs Plum's bawling to know who it was; and saw Jacob walk over to the window. There was a long silence. She might poke a stick at him or throw a crock, for this was how she treated Gladstone when he annoyed her, which he usually did, and once she had emptied the slops in the postman's face. I was worried for Jacob, but far too frightened to go and warn him.

Yet I got up in the end and crept close to the window, for I could not hear what they were saying. And just then Jacob went back to the door, opened it, and disappeared inside. I could scarcely believe my eyes; and wondered for a moment if I should go for Mother until I remembered that it was a Sunday morning and she would certainly hit me if I woke her up.

I stood up and looked in through the window.

That may not sound much; yet it was the first brave action of my life. If a blackbird had fluttered behind me, or a dog yapped in the road, I am sure I should have fled: but nothing happened, and after a time I could see through the shadows of the room. Jacob was standing quite close to Mrs Plum's made-up bed. A foul old smell of dirt and death came out of that place.

Jacob was saying: 'We're not paying three hundred.'

From a huddle of blankets came Mrs Plum's voice: 'Your father said three hundred. Hasn't got the money, eh?'

All I can say about Mrs Plum's voice is that it was not like any other human voice I ever heard: it was deep and growling, like a man's, and yet it sounded like a scream. There are birds which have such voices: birds that call to each other in a croaking growling scream. But there was no other Mrs Plum; nor ever could be, I should think.

'Not for this old ruin,' Jacob said.

When Mrs Plum flourished her stick at him, nipping it out from among the blankets, he caught it from her and laid it beside him on the floor. He was like an elderly and tolerant father, seizing her stick and putting it out of reach: his being

47

able to be like this was one of the reasons, I think, why he seemed so strong.

Suddenly I realized that Mrs Plum was looking straight at me; and I screamed.

'Who's that?' bawled Mrs Plum.

Jacob said: 'It's my friend. You can come on in, Lindy.' He pointed back at Mrs Plum, and nodded to me: 'She can't move, and I've got her stick. I'll crack her one if she tries any thing.'

When I told Mother afterwards she at first disbelieved me; for the fact is that I did as Jacob said. I went in and joined him. That was the second brave action of my life.

Gloomy beyond words was that stuffy room, and packed with things. When I stood beside Jacob he took my hand and went on saying to Mrs Plum that three hundred was regular theft, she wouldn't see half that money. But I was spell-bound and could not follow what they said for looking at the room. To one side of Mrs Plum, and standing on a table, was a glass case with two small white dogs whose stuffing had here and there pushed through rents in their skin, and grew upon their bodies like hideous growths of tissue; yet their bright eyes seemed alive and fixed on me, daring me to be sorry for them. On the other side of Mrs Plum, hanging on the wall, was a big picture in a shabby gilt frame of ladies and gentlemen of long ago, with a catechism text pinned in one corner and a pools form in another corner, but all old and yellow with decay. And decay was the smell and being of that room and of everything about it, strong and sickening so that I choked for breath. Scraps of food lay on filthy plates beside her and around her. On the floor in front of her bed stood a tin jug beside a chamber pot half full of yellow stinking water.

All that was nothing, though, compared with the fact of Mrs Plum herself. Like her sons she was a large woman, even now, and made gigantic by her blankets: all I could see above this mound was her long yellow face and her old winking eyes fixed now on Jacob and now on me. Whenever she looked in my direction I wished we could run away.

But Mrs Plum took me by surprise again. She said almost pleadingly: 'Well, I'm sure we've looked after this place all our lives.' And yet the squalor of it all was grim and sickening: but which was the worse, the squalor or that Mrs Plum had lived here all her life and never noticed it, I do not know. 'It's a seemly place to own,' she was saying. 'You're not buying from just anyone, you know.' She said this as though it were true: and I was sad and surprised to hear her. They had gathered and collected all these bits and pieces, these dogs and pictures and coloured pots and cut-glass vases; and now they were useless and they were horrible, and they were dead.

Jacob said: 'All right, we'll look round.'

Mrs Plum shouted: 'Don't you go touching things!'

'Why should we?' He said it so reasonably that she lay quiet once more.

So we looked round, and a fearful mess it was. The cast-off ruin of a dozen life-times seemed gathered in two ground floor rooms; but above stairs there were two other rooms quite bare of furniture, and here you could see the sky through gaping holes in the thatch: sodden with rain, the floor boards were the colour of dark green mould, and when Jacob stamped on them he put his heel right through in one place and threatened as much in two or three others. Having poked into everything, opened all drawers and lifted all coverings, he went back to her and I heard him say: 'We might give you two hundred.'

I am not sure what else they said: I was overcome with a confusion of feelings at having acted so bravely and having found Mrs Plum so pitiful and sorrowful and lonely, living simply from the habit of it. Perhaps that is why I went in after Jacob and began clearing things up. I emptied the chamber pot and filled the tin with clean water from the outside pump and did my best to put a little order into that room. I took away the scraps of stinking food, and I even tidied some of her blankets;

49

while all this time she lay back and looked at us with winking yellow eyes, scarcely saying a word, with her old hands gathered like yellow claws on the coverlet; until it seemed to me that she was crying to herself, without tears, and was even frightened of the two of us. But I did not think that this could possibly be true.

In the end, days later, Ted got her agreement to sell for two hundred and forty, which Mother and Ted and Dook all thought a clever bit of work. Only Jacob said otherwise; but Ted would not listen to him. Ted still wanted to prove himself, I think, and I could see that he enjoyed flinging his money about. 'I don't want to rob an old woman like that,' he boasted: 'I don't mind if I give her a bit too much. Though mind you, Dook, I don't think I have, eh?' Dook said no, of course not, what was two hundred and forty: why it wasn't even a thousand dollars, was it?

Of course Ted took all the credit, although it was Jacob who had really beaten her down from three hundred; and Ted would otherwise have given her what she asked without so much as inspecting the cottage. But this did not prevent him from complaining bitterly at Jacob, later on, when he discovered the trick that Mrs Plum had played on us.

I am sure they would ordinarily have asked enough questions to have found out that trick; but as it was they never bothered. Ted and Jacob were so pleased to have a home at last; and Mother, having declared that Ted would never be able to produce the money when it came to the point, was so astonished when he did produce it that she never gave Mrs Plum another thought. And Mrs Plum, crafty as she was, kept the secret only too well. Within a week she had gone in the ambulance to live with Gladstone at Chudbury, and within three months she was dead. So it was too late, when we did find out, to get the money back; and Gladstone, when Ted went over to Chudbury to ask him, said that it was no affair of his, and he had no money to give back, nor wouldn't give it if he had. You might have wondered what they had from life, that family: with the old woman lying in her bed, and those two sons – Gladstone who grubbed bits of money together all his days and never seemed to notice how the years went by nor what they might be for, and Sawsbry who could never want anything better than meeting a woman in the fields and opening his trousers and waving his silly self at her and grinning like a fool. They went on living simply from the habit of it.

Not that we bothered to think about that. We were much too excited with the purchase. Before many days were out Ted and Jacob had moved their stuff from the shed on the airfield and settled into Mrs Plum's. They got to work repairing the fabric and making the place fit to live in. We all helped them to do that; and it was wonderful how much we managed. I really think that happiness began from now.

EIGHT

On one of those late winter days Mick Lissard stopped me in the road.

'No,' I said, though Mick was a friend: 'I haven't the time to talk to you.'

'Don't be soft,' Mick said: 'I've got something to tell you.'

I said he could tell me as I went along, for I was going to Jerman's dairy with a message for Mother and I couldn't hang about. But Mick was brim-full of himself: even more than usual he seemed bursting out of his clothes, his cheeks flushed as though from running too fast, his fat brown eyes shining with excitement. A very fat boy, Mick was, the fattest boy I ever saw; but fat in a country way, strong as a bull and hard to work. We had begun together in the same class at Chudbury primary; but that was nothing. Mick was as much a part of our village as Jerman's farm or Mick's father's Guernsey that grazed the Miss Titherams' orchard for ten bob a year, though they never needed the money.

'Know what?' Mick said, as we walked along: 'He's got a gun. A real one.'

'Who?'

'That new kid. Jacob.' Mick threw out a fat leg and danced on the road. 'He's got a gun, and it shoots real bullets.'

I said: 'Your brother's got a gun, hasn't he? That's nothing. Anyway, shooting's silly.'

'Not a gun like that, stupid. It's a pistol. Like cowboys have. Only it's real.'

'Plastic, I bet. You can get anything in plastic nowadays.' But I only said it for the sake of not being put down; for yesterday the Buick had arrived with Ted at the wheel, and he might just as well have come in riding on an elephant for the sensation it made. If Jacob said he had a real pistol, a pistol with bullets, then it would certainly be true. I knew it with fear and pride.

Mick was banging off imaginary pistols. He swung on me excitedly. 'Know what?'

'Go on,' I said coldly: 'and walk as if you weren't loony.'

He fell in beside me.

'Yesterday,' he said, 'some of the kids over to Chudbury was out on the airfield ragging Mr Breldon, that's Jacob's father. He's got that car, see, and they was shouting at him to know where he'd stole it.' I could see that Mick was just as much for Jacob as I was; and for the first time in my life I thought of Mick as someone with feelings of his own, and not just a fat boy who was always there, like a tree or a cow, part of our countryside; and convenient, and dull.

'What was you doing there?' I asked.

'Been over to Chudbury for cigarettes for Dad. They said come on let's see this car, and so I went with them. They didn't believe there was a car, but when they saw it they got to shouting at Mr Breldon, and I was sorry I'd told 'em.'

'Thought you was clever, I suppose.'

'They was shouting at Mr Breldon before I could stop 'em,

and then one of 'em picked up a stone and chucked it so it hit the car.'

'And you chucked another?'

'No, I didn't, then. It was Sam Rickett, and I jumped on him and got him down, seeing Mr Breldon was a friend of Poppy's, like, but the other three come at me. They sat on my head and Sam Rickett chucked some more stones. Then they all got off me and ran away.' Mick began to chuckle: 'Thought they'd get away, too.

'Well, they get away from Mr Breldon all right. *He* can't run. But Jacob must've thought it out. He'd gone round the back of 'em. So they ran on top of him.'

'One against four,' I said. Fighting always frightened me.

'No it wasn't then. I went too. But old Jake didn't worry for that. You should have seen him. He took 'em all. Hacked and hit 'em like I never saw.'

'I don't want to hear about it,' I said. But it wasn't true: I did.

'We bashed 'em proper. Then Jake made 'em go back to Mr Breldon and say they was sorry, all except Sam Rickett, he'd run away. And they said they was sorry. My, he's savage, Jake is.'

I said out of jealousy: 'I don't see where the gun comes in.'

'He showed it me. After that. Said I was his friend. He's going to be a bandit when he grows up.'

'I thought he was going off to the moon in a rocket or something?'

Mick was nettled. 'Well, he's going to do that too. He says they're going to blow up the whole ruddy world before long, anyway, so it don't matter what you do. My, he *hates* people.'

I didn't know what to say, but Mick went on: 'I'm his friend, and you can be too, Lindy, if you want.'

'Thank you for nothing,' I said: 'I can't stand boys that's always fighting. Here, you can buzz off now.'

For we had luckily reached the entrance to Jerman's dairy: otherwise I might have run away or begun to cry. I could see that they were all going to be friends with Jacob: they would all get round him and I should just fade into the background, like I always did. I should be left out all over again.

Mick said: 'What's the matter, Lin?'

'You're silly, that's all. And so's Jacob. And don't call me Lin.'

I got away from him, going up to Jerman's dairy. But the dairy smells of milk and churns were sour that day; and I wanted to cry.

Mother was scouring churns, her sleeves rolled high and a scarlet handkerchief tied over her hair and under her chin. Morton told Miss Pakeman, afterwards, that the trouble with Mother was that she did not like to work; but I know that Morton was wrong in this. Mother loved to work; but she loved the other things too. Mother never did anything by halves, nor felt anything by halves. She never let the years slip by unwanted and uncared for: she took them and shook them and worried the last possible enjoyment out of them. I sometimes think that Morton would have lived more happily if only she could have felt more strongly, and let it come out of her: Mother always felt strongly, and she always let it come out.

Scouring, she said: 'What you want, Lindy?'

I gave her my message: a pair of chickens to be plucked for the Miss Titherams' weekend. Mother was hissing quietly to herself as they say the stable men used to hiss in Jerman's stables; only Jerman's have nothing but tractors now.

I wanted to stay and watch her. It was a pleasure to see her work. Her strong round arms laboured on the churns, and beads of sweat gathered on her white temples where the black hair grew close and thick, escaping from the scarlet handkerchief. She was strong and fine and full of health; and I loved to watch her. Not stopping, she said: 'Lindy, you can go over to Ted Breldon, and ask him if he'll take me into Rolcaster tomorrow afternoon. Tell him I want to go. He can if he wants to.'

I stood there dumbly, determined not to go. I did not want to see Jacob.

Luckily for me, Jerman's Thompson interrupted us. A long lean man with a head that was somehow too small for him and a manager's smile that was somehow too big for him, Thompson liked Mother because she worked hard and gave no trouble. 'Poppy, my girl,' he shouted from the inner door of the dairy, his voice like an echo from the clanking of churns and the lowing cows, for they were not yet out to grass: 'How many you got left?'

After Mother had told him she called to me: 'Aren't you going, then?'

'In a minute.'

'You stand there a minute longer, Lindy, and I'll hit you.'

Yet I cheered up as I went along, for already the gleam of spring was over our countryside. New tips of corn were pushing emerald lines into the dull brown blurr of winter plough, for our countryside in winter seems to lose its shape and fall, as weather-broken furrows fall, into a soft shapelessness. Torn clouds over Lowton spire had silver light behind them after the morning's rain, and the hedgerows and rough grass banks along our road were scattered with a million splinters of wet, just as though a great mirror had broken into tiny pieces. Our countryside was coming alive again; and I felt like singing. And I did sing, although you would never have heard it: for I have such a small voice when I sing that nobody ever does hear it.

They were on the roof when I got to Mrs Plum's. I still thought of that cottage as Mrs Plum's although Gladstone had sent the ambulance for her a full two weeks before, and Ted and Jacob were properly established there by now. For they moved in and settled in as though they had known about that cottage for years, and meant to live in it for ever. They'd pulled out half the front hedge so as to allow parking space for the Buick; and the Buick stood there in the front garden, a great green monster that nobody could deny, waiting, as Ted explained, until their plans were ready for action.

To get this old cottage to rights they worked by day and by night, or so it seemed to me; and certainly they began on it the moment they moved in. Ted settled there as though he really belonged to our village: in fact, he was not a bit like our own people. He did not close the door on himself and his difficulties, and refuse to ask for help from neighbours for fear of not getting it; he went straight over to the *Wheelwright* and had everyone give him their advice. Mother was pleased with him for this; but Jacob took it not so well, as going against his pride.

When I came round to the other side of the Buick I found Ted puttying at window panes. 'Hallo, Lindy,' he said, and stopped to talk, pulling out his pipe and filling it: 'Going along, ain't she?'

I had never thought they could make anything of this place, its condition was so bad.

'Roof's a problem.' Ted went on, lighting his pipe: 'Lot of rain come in last night where we pulled the old thatch down. Jacob's up there now.'

He was pleased to have Mother's message. I left him comfortably smoking his pipe and leaning against the blotched plaster, while I went to look for Jacob. Here and there the plaster had fallen away, showing the laths beneath like bones in a dry dead body; I shuddered in spite of the silver sunlight coming down between white clouds, and was glad when I could look up and see Jacob perched high astride the rafters. He sat up there like a small shadow against the light.

'Lindy!' he shouted: 'Come on up an' give me a hand.'

'I can't get up,' I shouted back.

'Inside an' up the stairs. Then I'll show you.'

I went in by the back door. Inside the place was clean and bare, for we had all worked through a Saturday afternoon and Sunday: now the floorboards smelt strongly of wet dust, especially the rotting ones, but they were clean for the first time in years, and that at least was a beginning. Goodness knows how much rubbish we had burnt on Sunday night when the cleaning was finished: rags and Sunday papers and rotting lumps of mess you could never have known what they had been. Half the stair boards turned out to be rotten, and Ted had already put his foot through several more of them: none of the Plums could have gone upstairs for years but for that one great time when the old lady had thrown herself out of the window rather than be moved. I went up carefully, clinging to a rope which Ted had fixed along the staircase wall; when I reached the top it was like stepping into daylight, so much of the thatch was missing now. The rain must have come in heavily, for the floor was sodden on the landing and across the room above which Jacob sat. I went into it and saw him through the rafters, and the high white clouds above.

He called down: 'Climb out through the window, and I'll help you.'

'I'm not coming.'

'You've got to. It keeps blowing away before I can nail it.' He was trying to spread a tarpaulin over part of the stripped roof.

Well, I did get out of that window; and I did get up to the rafters. I shut my eyes at first, but then Jacob shouted: 'Don't put your foot on that gutter, it'll go if you do.' So I opened my eyes and tried not to look down. He helped me to scramble up beside him. 'You're all right,' he said, 'you can't fall.' I could ; but I knew that I was not going to.

For a while we just sat up there, clinging to the rafters with the wind in our hair; and it was wonderful so long as I remembered not to look down. It was always wonderful with Jacob so long as I remembered that: he had a way of getting himself above the ground of dull and miserable things and people, so that we seemed to look at the world as though it really could be ours.

That is how it was now: around us the red roofs glowing under cottage tree tops next to thatch, the houses of our village, were a friendly country. Its frontiers were the small trees: they reached out to woods and spinneys, elm high, until these ran and ran together into green shadows upon Manford Hill beneath the spire of Lowton church: a pleasant rolling land, rich and green and red and full of worth, that paved the arch of sky; and me and Jacob, belonging to it, sitting up between.

Up here with Jacob I was free of our village. I actually thought this: I thought, I'm free of our village. Free: is that what it really means, I wonder. It was beautiful. But Jacob would never sit still for long, unless later when I used to read to him and make him begin to read to me, and now he said: 'Hold it while I get the tacks in.' Then I had to let go with my hands and hold to the rafters with my knees, but I managed my part all right, and we got the black tarpaulin stretched between us while Jacob nailed it round until it was firmly held. Then he went down through the window; and helped me after him.

I said: 'Mick Lissard couldn't have done that.'

'Mick's all right,' Jacob said: 'Only he's fat.'

Now I felt so pleased with myself that I was ready to let Mick have his share of Jacob, if Jacob wanted that. People could do things for themselves if they'd a mind to: even I could do things for myself. I dare say it was the first time I ever saw that.

We went downstairs and Jacob made tea for the three of us. I washed up for them and Ted joked: 'Quite the little house-wife, ain't you?': which confirmed my belief that he was silly but harmless, the same as Mother said. I was thinking that I should not even mind, not now, if Mollie took a crush on Jacob: I could share him with Mollie as well as with Mick, if I had to, and even with the kids who lived halfway to Chudbury in the new council houses. I was glowing still with the happiness I had felt up there on the rafters, looking round at the world and helping Jacob; and sharing my life with him.

Jacob was saying they would need another tarpaulin.

'Scrounge it,' Ted suggested. He was thoroughly comfort-able in the old bucket-seat they had brought on the roof of the Buick, along with their other stuff: the bucket-seat, he had told us, had come from a dump near Enfield. It made a fine armchair, far better than anything of ours. Now he lounged in this seat and smoked his pipe, shirt collar open and sleeves rolled up, and looked like a man come home from the sea. His lined face was alight with good humour. You might have thought that he had done some useful work, to look at him lying in that old bucket-seat and puffing away at his pipe.

'Poppy tell me,' he went on, 'there's a lady called Mrs. Morton might have a tarpaulin. Come of having trouble with a hen house couple of year back, Poppy tell me.'

I said: 'She'll never let you have it.' Not because I really knew anything about that, of course, but because lending and borrowing between them and us were never thought of. Mother had been pulling his leg.

But Ted shot up his eyebrows, teasing me: 'Never let me have it, won't she?' he mimicked in a squeaky voice, so that I blushed for myself: 'Not if we never ask, that's sure'n certain. Always ask, Lindy, it don't cost nothing. What does the Bible say — more blessed to ask then to receive, don't it? More blessed usual, I'll grant you that.' And now he had his natural voice again, an old creaking comfortable voice that was seldom very clear; and he winked at me to make it all right again. 'So you go there and ask her, Jake. You're on good terms, they tell me.'

I was even more surprised when Jacob said: 'I'll ask her.' He got up and said to me: 'Come on, Lindy, we'll ask her.'

NINE So I went with Jacob to borrow Morton's tarpaulin; and that was also, in its way, a milestone. All I then knew of her was that she was like nobody I had ever seen; that she lived among us, doing good; and that she and Mother could never meet but that they quarrelled. I was naturally afraid of her, and kept out of her way as much as I could.

There was also a Mr Morton: he came from London every

now and then in a tall old motor car, a rather sad-looking gentleman, round and short, with a busy way of being cheerful against the grain, and a habit of wearing bottle-green waistcoats with bright brass buttons as though he wanted something gay over a sad heart. I do not think that Mr. Morton had ever come quite real to any of us: he was kind and patient and gave sixpences to several of us children at Christmas time and festivals; but none of us wanted to tease him, put water in his petrol tank, invade his garden, or torment him in any way at all. I think we believed that Morton tormented him enough.

Morton came real to us: but rather in the way that the government and that kind of thing might come real. She lived in our village as I imagine those old explorers must have lived among the savages: she came in and staked her claim and cleared the ground. She bought first one old cottage near the middle of the village, and rebuilt that; and then the next-door cottage, and rebuilt that too; and finally the third in the row, joining the first two into one and having a builder knock down the third so as to give her space for a garden. Miss Fen, who lived in that third cottage, was put to live at Chudbury in the other half of the disused school-house that my aunt Pooley lives in. Miss Fen dislikes it even more than my aunt Pooley does.

Morton took a place on our parish council. She became a governor of Chudbury primary. She was vice-president of the flower show that is held every year in one of Jerman's meadows. She spoke to Mr Harold Jerman himself, and Mr Harold spoke to her. When we had the General Election she was busier than ever, and had big posters on her gate, saying, *Vote Liberal Vote Billing*. It was just about then that she drove her car into a tree trunk fallen across the road; and was carried to hospital for a fortnight in Harry's old Morris.

I said to Jacob, while we were going to Morton's: 'Didn't know you were working for Morton?'

'Why shouldn't I?'

'Mother can't stand her.'

'Doesn't matter to me, does it?' Even for that he was angry with me: like cat and dog, Mother and Jacob were, right from the beginning.

'Anyway,' I countered, 'school's next week.'

'Oh is it,' he said violently, 'we'll see about that.'

I argued no more in case I should begin to cry; so we got inside Morton's gate without exchanging another word. This gate was new and neatly set in a close-cut privet: it was painted with two notices, one of which said *Beware of the Dog* while the other said *Private*. There was no dog, but that was nothing, for Morton's was the most private place I have ever been in (I have never been inside the Miss Titherams' gate, which is probably even more private). You felt this privateness like a breath of cold air as you went through that gate: it was worse than the barking of a dog.

We walked along the garden path between emerald moss and standard roses, and knocked on Morton's beamed front door, and waited. It was too late for turning back. Then Morton came up behind us and said: 'Children, I see.' We might as well have been giraffes.

'If you want to tell me something you will have to wait,' she went on: 'and please don't move off the path. Just stand quite still where you are.'

She must have been pruning roses, for she carried a pair of pruning scissors; although I should have thought it rather late for pruning roses. I think that pruning was the main thing, for Morton, about a garden. 'You can wait,' she said again, 'I'm cutting things back.' She was very good at cutting things back. Later on, when I came to know her better, I was thoroughly ashamed at myself for having thought these things about her; but I still believe that they were true.

We waited; and I could see that even Jacob was a little over-awed, for Morton was in one of her special and most private moods. The more private she became, so far as I could ever tell, the more strangely she got herself up. Today her trousers were

61

black and exceedingly tight all the way down to her ankles, where they showed red socks and embroidered slippers peeping from goloshes; but her jacket was exceedingly loose all the way up, and made of bright blue cloth. She wore long ear-rings of golden chain that almost touched her shoulders, and her face was a dull rich red except where the light danced in her rimless spectacles. It was not every day that you could see a sight like this in our village: the younger Miss Titheram does it to please the older Miss Titheram, her cousin, but they do it behind closed doors and you can never see it nor the other things they do, or the village says they do. The good thing about Morton was that she did it for us all: she walked up and down the village road like that, for exercise, and nodded to us as she passed or waved her silver-topped walking-stick.

This was the only point that Mother would concede in her favour. 'She's got a nerve,' Mother said, 'with a face like that.'

'Now,' she said at last, clipping the pruning scissors together and turning towards us; 'tell me what it is.'

Jacob was beginning when she went on: 'How nice of you to come to see me, Jacob. But I don't want you today. I want you tomorrow. Tomorrow morning at nine o'clock sharp, please. But what are you doing with poor little Lindy?'

Jacob said he wasn't doing anything with me.

Morton smiled. 'What a funny thing to say, Jacob.'

'Excuse me, miss,' Jacob said: 'but Pa says you got a tarpaulin we can have.'

'A tarpaulin? How very surprising. Now I wonder how your father could know I had a tarpaulin?'

Jacob nodded to me: 'Her Ma told us.' And he said it just as though he had already had a thousand interviews with her. 'It's in the back of your garage. Under a pile of stuff.'

Morton raised her eyebrows, which were black and sharp as though put on with paint. 'You're not the sort of boy who comes asking for things, I hope? That's called scrounging, you know. You'll never come to any good if you scrounge.'

Jacob took no notice of this. He said: 'It's an old one. There's a hole in it. You don't need it, do you?'

'So you are scrounging, then?'

'No.'

Morton put down the pruning scissors on the window ledge near the front door, took off her gardening gloves, and put them down as well. 'And I see your father has a car, too. I'm glad he's so well off. I'm sure he's much better off than I am. And yet you come asking for *my* tarpaulin?'

'Yes.'

'Well, don't be frightened. You people nowadays expect to be given things, it's what we've taught you, so we can't complain.' I thought Jacob might be angry because she said that he could be frightened; but he just stood there dumbly, with his fists clenched behind his back, rather as though he was talking to a public monument. Morton was saying: 'You won't always be given things, you know. We shan't always be able to make life easy for you. You'll have to fight for yourself one of these days. As we have all had to. No good being a little softie in this world, you know. Not even in the Welfare State.'

'No,' said Jacob.

'Well, come along then,' she went on; 'It's better you asked for it than stole it.' She led the way to the garage, and her black trousers were so tight that you could see the line of knickers underneath, and I wondered if this was what Mr. Morton liked when he came home to rest, at weekends, after his tiring work in London. You can never tell with people, though he looked too comfortable a man. My aunt Pooley who sometimes worked for them had told me that they had wanted a baby the year before, but it went wrong and now they could never have one. When I thought of this I tried to think of Morton doing what Mother did; but that was impossible. My aunt Pooley, who hates nobody, also said that Morton had cried a lot the year before; but that seemed impossible too. I was still a very silly child.

After Jacob had pulled out the tarpaulin from the back of the garage Morton agreed that he should have it in return for a morning's work. 'I don't want to get you into bad ways,' she said. 'You people can't always be given things.'

This put her into a good humour. She asked me how I was doing at school. I said that it was holidays now; we should begin again next week.

'Well, look at me, child. Always look people in the face. No more missing the bus, I hope?'

I said no, there wouldn't be.

'Because I shall take steps if there is. You tell your mother not to be a silly woman. She must make sure you get to school regularly. We don't pay all these taxes to have the money wasted.'

I said I would tell Mother.

'And you had such good reports before you started getting into silly ways, didn't you?'

'Sometimes,' I said.

'You're turning into a clever little girl. Mr. Prother has told me. You can grow up to be a useful citizen if you want.'

'Yes,' I said.

'And while we're on the subject, how is your mother?'

'She's working at Jerman's.'

'Working? But that is splendid. Tell her that I hope she keeps it up. I shall speak to Mr. Harold about her.' She took up the pruning scissors again and put on her gloves. 'I wish I could work in a dairy.' And then she told us how she was always cooped up with a typewriter except when she escaped to her garden; but I scarcely listened, for I had heard it all a dozen times before. Morton never tired of explaining that she was a writer, and what a terrible life it was, so hard to bear. We always noticed that Mr Morton, whenever he was present while Morton was telling us of this, looked like a man with his cross to bear; but he would smile and seem cheerful for all that, and open his jacket over his bottlegreen waistcoat with its winking buttons, and slap his chest like a man who wants to tell you what a good life he has.

Morton called after us: 'Tell your mother, Lindy, that I'm keeping my eye on you.'

Jacob asked: 'Why does she say that?'

I said miserably: 'You know why.'

'None of her business, is it?'

But I could not bear talking of it. The last time Morton had been at our place, making a fuss over my not going to school regularly (which Morton said was a shame, seeing what a bright child I was turning into and had such good reports: and which Mother said didn't matter, she could not always be up in time to send me off), Mother had called Morton an interfering bitch and Morton had called Mother a tart and threatened her with the police. I did not want to think of it.

'She says if educated people don't set an example we'll never learn.'

'Learn what?'

'I don't know.' I didn't, anyway.

But Jacob said confidently: 'She's all right.'

I suppose he said it because he already hated Mother: but I was wretched at his saying it, for it made a difference between us. When we came to our gate I left him and went upstairs to my room and cried for a long time against a dollie that I had.

TEN BUT it wasn't a time for crying, and I soon got over that. And indeed I was happy nearly every day, so many new and interesting things were going on. Even Mother noticed the change in me, and said I might be growing up at last. With Jacob I was doing things I should never have done before, climbing and carrying and running; and the other children, who copied Jacob more and more, noticed this and began counting me as one of themselves; and I suddenly had a place in our village.

Ted and Jacob changed the cottage too. They changed it out of all recognition, and that seemed another miracle.

No sooner had they moved in than Ted's money was all spent. Mother said she was glad of it. 'You were getting me worried, Ted, to know where it was coming from.' We all felt that, I think, even Ted: there was something unnatural about Ted's having money.

It was after the money ran out that the real miracle began, for it is no miracle to change things with money. Then it was that Ted set out to *organize* the things they needed: a word, he told us, that they'd had in the war when I was born. Jacob also knew how to organize things. In fact it was not long before I began to organize things myself. All of us children were set to work at organizing things. For days we organized; and it is wonderful to think how well we did it. That cottage was like a lean sow bought for breeding: it sucked in nourishment. It ate up everything. It needed more and more.

First of all they stopped the weather getting in. 'First aid to the wounded,' Ted called that. Then they began to rebuild. 'Never had a real house before,' Ted explained to Mother, who was laughing at him for the big ideas he had. 'But I like this place, Poppy, and it's ours, see. It's ours.' That was something he often liked to say. 'Know what,' he shouted across the hedge one day: 'It's like I'm captain of a fleet of ships. There's me 'n Jacob like we was ships steered out of bad weather an' coming into calm water 'n a good harbour, eh? Time for a rest 'n refit. I could do with a spot of easy, you know.' And it was nice to see him in his motor-car seat, smoking his pipe, like an old sailor battered from the seas, grey-haired, tired, taken suddenly with fits of being afraid and then as quickly cheering up again.

'You know,' he said to Mother, 'it's like remembering how many times I've nearly been run over.'

'Run in, you mean,' Mother said.

But Ted replied gravely: 'Don't mock at me, Poppy. We're going to get things organized proper, this time.'

She was always mocking at him. She warmed and chilled to him by turns. She could seldom let him be, just to sit and smoke and enjoy the cottage that was his: she must be teasing him with hints drawn out of the past, hints that she never explained and that Ted seemed unhappy to remember. 'That's all over, Poppy,' he said once. 'You let sleepin dogs lie. They've nothing on me now. An' if I don't start creatin, but just lie quiet and make a quiet livin, why, they'll let me. That's all forgotten.'

'You're getting old,' Mother said.

To that Ted only shook his head, which with him was a sign of agreement, and puffed away at his pipe and remarked after a time: 'We'll get the car working in a week or so. Soon's the house is in order. Then you'll see, Poppy – we'll have a nice little bit of a business, you 'n me Dook there.'

Mother replied sharply: 'We'll see about that. You've left the difficult part to me, haven't you?'

'It's easy, Poppy my love,' he protested: 'We don't need dozens of 'em, just three or four like, eager to get their chance at a bit of fun 'n brightness. There's a fellow up at Enfield who'll give us a lift. We'll go 'n talk to him, see.' They sent me out of the room at this point; but I thought that Mother was looking pleased enough.

Meanwhile, we organized. What this could really mean grew large and wonderful as the days rolled by, but was fully demonstrated only when we had the planks from Mr Harold: after that I understood that practically anything would be possible. None of us, previously, would have thought of going to Mr Harold for so much as a blade of grass: not because Mr Harold was mean or thoughtless – he was reckoned a good farmer and a decent landlord – but because there ran a well understood distance between him and the village with Thompson, his manager, established in between. We should have asked Thompson.

But when Mick Lissard said that Jerman's was taking down a thatched barn and putting up a corrugated iron one in its place,

Ted laid by his pipe at once and said to Jacob: 'Off we go, my boy. That's us.'

They discussed it as though the planks were already theirs.

'How many we need?'

Jacob said: 'Fifteen, if they're good an' long.'

Mother said it might be better if she instead of Ted were to ask Thompson. But Ted declared that it was useless to go to Thompson: he should go straight to Mr Harold himself.

He went next day, and returned triumphant. Mr Harold had not only had him into the breakfast room: he had given Ted all the old planks he needed on condition that Jacob should wash down Mrs Harold's Humber once a week for six months. What was more, he had actually instructed Thompson, and that in Ted's presence, to deliver the planks in one of Jerman's trucks. Even Mother was astonished.

The planks arrived that afternoon in a truck driven by Tom Lissard, Mick's elder brother who was usually on tractors; and they were long creosoted planks still in good condition, as anything of Mr Harold's was bound to be, considering the careful way his place was always managed and the money he put down.

Jacob took it all as a matter of course. He was mad about motor-cars anyway; and the washing was to be done on Sunday mornings early, which he said he shouldn't mind at all, because it would not interfere with the rest of the day. Besides, Mr Harold had a Jaguar, and he'd never had the chance, he said, of getting his nose inside the bonnet of a Jag.

We organized all manner of stuff after that. We organized two large panes of glass from greenhouse frames that Ted happened to find in one of Jerman's outhouses. We organized a supply of putty from the back of Winthrop's at Chudbury while Ted was buying nails in the front. We organized a brass knocker from a dump near Lowton, and a comfortable bench to sit on in the garden from goodness knows where; Ted brought it home on top of the Buick. We organized Tom Lissard into ploughing up the back garden, because Tom happened to be ploughing the field alongside; and we organized a scythe from Mr Morton, without telling Morton, when he was down from London at the weekend and poking with a little hoe at Morton's garden. I think he would have liked to come too, along with his scythe, for Morton's garden was in apple-pie order, she had a man over from Chudbury twice a week; only Morton would have disapproved. He took us round the back and handed us the scythe himself and warned us to be careful, scythes were so dangerous. He had soft blue eyes and a deep red face, and was never anything but gentle when he talked to us or, so far as I know, to anyone else.

'I suppose you can use it? Trouble is, you see, that I can't. So I can't show you.' And he laughed in a sudden way, like a man who's glad of a chance to laugh at all.

'Harry does.'

'Oh, Harry? Yes, of course Harry does.'

For we had also organized Harry in spite of there being Dook still with us; and on that particular Saturday Harry came from Chudbury and took the front garden, weeds and all, right down to the level of the earth and went off to the *Wheelwright* with Ted, afterwards, for pints of beer.

I should never have thought it possible, but in the end we organized Mother as well: she gave in one evening, quite of her own, and promised to scrub the house from top to bottom.

'That's nice of you, Poppy,' Ted said; but I could see that he doubted if she meant it. So could Mother, for she laughed in his face, and went on: 'I'll give you a break for once, Ted. I'll do it. But on one condition.'

There was some part of Ted that seemed always looking to be hit: he blinked at Mother when she said this, and screwed up his eyes and gave her a poor little smile. Beside him she was wild and savage, so that he never seemed sure whether she would bite him or kiss him; but now she only pulled back her splendid black hair until I thought it must hurt her, and explained: 'I'll do it on condition you get Mrs Steppins to help as well.'

Now this was very like Mother, setting people deliberately at odds, just for the fun of it: for the fact was that Mrs Steppins never came to our place and never spoke to us if she could help it. Mrs. Steppins really belonged to our village but she wanted to forget it. She considered herself a cut above the rest of us because her husband, a Rolcaster Steppins and not a Chudbury Steppins, had risen to be chief mechanic at Jerman's, and was responsible for all the machinery there. Mrs Steppins herself was set on rising level with Mrs Thompson, or at any rate on being on friendly terms with Mrs Thompson; and lately she had sent their little boy, who was not allowed to play with the rest of us, to a private school in Lowton where Mrs Thompson sent her own little boy.

All of us but Ted and Jacob knew this very well. We also knew that Steppins had come hanging round Mother when Mrs Steppins was absent on a visit to her parents the winter before. Then it had been that Harry had objected for the first time that we could remember, perhaps because he thought that he deserved to have Mother to himself in wintertime, since he couldn't in summer, or perhaps because he did not feel the same way about Steppins, who was local, as he did about Dook, who was not. Mother had taken Harry's side when Steppins continued slipping round to us on Saturdays, uninvited; and it had ended in a fight. Harry and Steppins bashed each other good and hard one night; but Harry won so easily that he had to carry off Steppins in a wheelbarrow and put him to bed. And then, to cap it all, Mother told Mrs Steppins on the first opportunity that she should keep her husband to herself; whereupon Mrs Steppins complained to Mrs Thompson and asked for Mother to be sacked. Mrs Steppins was a foolish woman, you can see, and believed everything that Steppins told her; which was little enough, by all account, and that little generally wrong.

So that when Mother made it a condition that Mrs Steppins should also help, and Ted innocently agreed to ask her, we naturally expected trouble. We went with him to Mrs Steppins's,

Jacob and Mick and Mollie and I; but we did not go in. We listened behind the front door. Mrs Steppins was very polite, she was always very polite: she told Ted that she was surprised, exceedingly surprised, that he could ask her to cross the same doorstep as a person like Poppy Wellin. She would be happy to help him set things to rights on condition that Mrs Wellin should not help as well: she would be very happy to do that, she said, hadn't she heard how Mr Harold had given Mr Breldon those planks? If Mr Harold could help Mr Breldon, then she was sure that she could too. And so on and so on.

Ted came out, looking rather puzzled; only not for long. I saw then that he was neither so slow nor easy to fool as he occasionally appeared. He went straight back to Mother and told her what had happened; but a little more than that too.

'I told her, Poppy,' he explained, 'that you was a lady I had the deepest respect for. If she wouldn't work with you, then she wouldn't work at all, I told her. Not for me, I said. I'd rather scrub every livin plank myself, I said.'

To me, at any rate, it sounded rather thin; but that was because I knew there was not a word of truth in it – he'd thanked Mrs Steppins very much for her kind offer and said it was very good of her. I thought Mother was bound to see through it. But there are things you can never know about people, even though you may live with them for years.

Mother looked surprisingly confused and said quietly: 'Well, Ted, I really don't know.' She was even blushing a little. 'It's a long time since anyone in this place took my part.' She gave him an awkward glance that was almost shy. 'I must say I'd forgotten what it was like.' People can be lonelier than you think.

It was plain sailing after that: right through the scrubbing and the cleaning and the beating of mats and the washing of crockery, such as there was (for we never had time to finish organizing the crockery), with Mother working away and saying not a word but to sound pleased and happy at the way things were. She

71

went through all that work like a beautiful machine. I never saw her so tamed and calm, not even with Dook: she really loved good work. Ted could not admire her enough: I don't think he had ever seen a woman work as hard as Mother could when her mind was set to it. So long as she could work she was happy: but when she couldn't work then she had to have the other kind of life, and there was no stopping her.

Jacob kept out of the way during the cleaning and the scrubbing: I knew that he did not trust her. As for me, I neither trusted nor distrusted her. For me she was like the weather or the way life is: there is no sense in liking or disliking it, you have to bear with it and try to manage.

After the cleaning there was little more left to do. 'Next Saturday,' Ted announced, 'we'll celebrate, eh? Harry'll come over, won't he? An' Dook. We got to have Dook.' His eyes moved like turning mirrors. 'Must have our Trans-Atlantic partner, eh, Poppy?'

Mother agreed to that. She was in the mood to agree to anything. She was standing on the threshold of clean slate while Ted sat in his motor-car seat on the weed stubble near the window, and looking so strong and handsome that even Jacob seemed to notice her. She had just scrubbed the big slate threshold slab, and stood there now with her fine white feet bare on the dark grey stone, and her strong legs planted wide. Ted got up and went over to her and gave her a little kiss on the cheek. It should have been a moment of pleasure and comfort; and yet I remember it bitterly, and for no reason that I can explain, as a first true glimpse of the strife and struggle that lay ahead. There was a recklessness in Mother's face and in the strong vigour of her body, as she stood astride the dark stone slab, that seemed altogether at odds with this quiet occupation of building a home.

Ted was saying contentedly: 'It's a deal, Poppy, is it?'

'It's a deal, Ted.'

I remember she was wearing a bright yellow blouse and had

72

tied a cornflower blue scarf about her hair, and somehow or other we were standing in a half circle, looking at her as she stood astride the threshold, as though from now onwards it would be she, and not Ted, who would order all our lives. I glanced at Jacob and saw that he had also understood this or something like this: he looked pretty much upset. I was beginning to feel miserable for him when a klaxon honked loudly and Dook's long motor-car drew up beside the gate.

Dook pushed through the gate and came trotting towards us. He was delighted with himself; he was nearly always delighted with himself. I never knew anyone so often and so regularly pleased as Dook was. 'Say!' he was calling: 'Got some news for you.' He made straight for Mother and caught her in his arms and whirled her round and round. I think that is what Mother liked so much about the Americans: it is what I rather liked myself. They were always so violent and so excited. You felt they might take off for Tennessee or one of those places at almost any time; and you might just as easily go with them, and no one able to say a word against it. The weight of the village on top of us seemed to lift quite away with Dook in the house: it was like being giddily released for a lovelier fate, or like being born again, if you can see what I mean.

Ted was lighting his pipe, as happy as ever. 'We've finished the job, Dook. Like a new pin, eh?' He waved his pipe vaguely at the cottage.

Dook said it was a lovely job, a real lovely job. He liked to make people happy with themselves. There was never anything mean about Dook.

He was saying when they came out again: 'Well, now you let me tell you something. It's fixed, Poppy.'

Mother had her crooked little smile of pleasure. 'Go on, tell us,' she said.

'The boys want you to drive 'em over Wednesdays and Saturdays. Parties of four. Ten bucks each.'

Ted screwed up his eyes, so that he might have been smiling

or he might not. He asked: 'Ten dollars means forty a night, does it?'

'That's what I said.'

Mother asked: 'What's forty dollars?'

Ted replied: 'Fourteen quid. Bit more.'

Mother said: 'I think it's all right.'

'It's got to be,' Dook said. 'I told 'em it was.' He grinned. 'Tips are extra, of course.'

'Oh well,' Ted agreed, 'if tips are extra.'

I wanted to ask Jacob what all this could mean; but he had disappeared. It would be no good asking the others.

'Hi handsome,' Dook was calling to me, 'come and give your uncle a nice big kiss.'

So I did that instead. He was kind to everyone; and perhaps he was not much to blame, really, for the things that he helped to make happen. I don't suppose he would ever have thought of doing these things at home. And when things afterwards went wrong he was genuinely sorry; only of course it was too late then.

But that, in any case, was a time of happiness for me. We had finished the cottage and I felt a new kind of life was beginning for me as well as for the others. I shut my bedroom door every night now, and that old black trunk had lost its power to turn me sick and sad with fear. Even my hair seemed easier to manage; and I also knew that I was growing up at last.

Our rebuilding of the cottage had made quite a stir, what with Mr Harold's giving the planks and Ted's holding forth on progress in the bar of the *Wheelwright*. All this had given him a place in our village, and people came to see what we had done, and passed complimentary remarks that set us fairly glowing with satisfaction. Even the story that the Buick was stolen property ceased going the rounds. Even the elder Miss Titheram, whom nobody had seen walking in the village for a long time, came in a tweed coat and skirt with brightly polished brogues, to 'inspect progress', as she put it, and congratulate Mr Breldon.

74

It turned out then that Jacob was working for the elder Miss Titheram as well as for Morton: by this time, I think, he was working for practically all that sort of people in our village. It seems to me, looking back, that I went about singing.

Then school began. For me, of course; and that was nothing, because I loved school. But it began for Jacob too.

PART TWO

ONE

You might think that children always dislike going to school; but that is not true. School for me was rest and peace and consolation: I liked school and school liked me. I liked getting away from home, away from Mother. I liked the bus with its high yellow sides that collected children, and our lot too, from all the farms and hamlets round Chudbury and drove along the country roads to Chudbury school and returned us home in the afternoon. I have never understood who could have paid for and provided this bus nor why it came so punctually, and never missed, with a cheerful driver called Fred who always welcomed us: he and his bus came out of a world that seemed otherwise without connection with us, and I took it for another miracle.

There were, as a matter of fact, two buses. There was a big yellow one for most of us; and another little blue one, scarcely more than a baker's van, for the two or three from our parts who had won the scholarship and gone up to Rolcaster Grammar. My friend Mollie was the only one from our village: some of the children, after that, used to shout names at her and throw mud when it was wet.

Those who did not win the scholarship – all but one or two of us, in fact – stayed on at Chudbury Primary until they went out to work. I do not know if other schools are like ours: but Chudbury Primary also had a senior department. They called it, for this reason, an 'unreorganized school'; it means that if you do not get the scholarship you stay on there until you are fifteen, but at fourteen you move into another classroom (or another part of the same classroom), and do the same work over again until you are allowed to leave. I could never understand the point of this, and used to think they should have asked Ted to 'reorganize' it for them – and either send the seniors to a proper school or let them leave and earn some money as soon as they were fourteen.

You take the scholarship exam when you are eleven. It is not a proper exam, of course, because everyone knows beforehand who is going to win it and who is not. Years before I took it I knew that I was not going to win it; and of course I didn't. Never more than one child in a year had ever passed that exam from our school: or ever could pass it, according to Mr Prother, because there were no more places at Rolcaster Grammar than would allow for one child a year from our place. For my year it was a snotty boy called Barnes who passed it: just like my friend Mollie, the year before, this boy had always been at the top of the A-stream. The rest of us in A-stream were supposed to stand a good chance of getting the scholarship; but those in B-stream took the exam only because they had to take it – they hadn't any chance of going to Rolcaster; while those in C-stream, the duds and loonies, scarcely bothered to take it at all.

Mother never cared whether I won the scholarship or not: I am not sure she as much as noticed that I was supposed to try for it. The only time she appeared a little proud of me was when Mr Prother put me up into the A-stream, when I was eight or nine, I can't remember which, and said to her: 'Very bright child you've got there, Mrs Wellin. We'll get her to Rolcaster if her health can stand it.' She was pleased when he said this: I knew it from the sudden little frown she had whenever anyone unexpected said an agreeable thing to her; but she was embarrassed too, and answered Mr Prother by asking him whether this meant that she would have to keep me in idleness for the rest of her life? But I knew, even then, what was really in her mind: she simply disbelieved that the world of rules and regulations, the world of Mr Prother and Rolcaster Grammar and respectability, would ever bring her any good. We lived next door to that world but not inside it: no matter what we did we should never get inside it. Mother thought that, and I thought it too. My friend Mollie would go to Rolcaster and have a life of being wanted by people: I should not go to Rolcaster and I should not be wanted by people. It seemed quite understandable to me then.

That was perhaps a reason why I clung so hard to Jacob, then and later: he belonged with us, outside the fence, but he didn't care. In that way he was stronger even than Mother was, for Mother really did care now and then, and care very much, although she hated showing it. I have sometimes thought it was this greater strength of Jacob's that Mother hated most in him.

When Jacob came I had another reason for not minding that I had missed the scholarship; for Jacob, although he was past fourteen then, had never so much as tried for it. But in any case I didn't believe that I was clever: it was simply that reading and writing and multiplication came easy to me, and I enjoyed the Bible stories and I knew better than anyone else the Christian names of the Royal Family; which is more difficult than you might think, they have so many and rare ones too.

School began within a few days of our finishing the main work on Ted's cottage. I saw that Jacob was very much against school. I should not have given this a moment's thought if Jacob's being against school had seemed the same kind of grumble that you'd get from Mick Lissard or almost any of the boys. But it was not that kind of grumble. He seemed upset; and possibly even scared. Not that I saw it so clearly at the time, for I was much younger then, and had yet to go through all these things; and could scarcely think straight about Jacob, in any case, for loving him so much. I simply knew that he was afraid of going to school.

Miss Pakeman likes me to say that I was sorry for him, but that is untrue; he was too strong and wild for anyone, least of all for me, to be over him enough to feel sorry for him. But I was hurt for him as well as for myself; and perhaps, at first, I was secretly ashamed for him too. Later on, when everything

81

was settled for better or for worse, I soon stopped feeling any shame for him: I only felt proud of him then, and loved him the more. Even if we could never belong to everyone else, he made it seem that we belonged to ourselves: and for me, so long as I live, the place that he built in the woods for us to live in will stand for safety and happiness despite all the sorrow that it brought. He took me beyond Vixen's Wood, one Sunday morning, and showed it to me. But that was after school began.

TWO I GOT up early on the day that school began because I thought that I would go and make Jacob's breakfast for him: his father never did unless it was late in the morning. You might think it would have been easier to have had him over to our place; but there was no chance of that. Even if I could have persuaded him to come, Mother would have thrown him out. For the closer the friendship between Mother and Ted, the more that she and Jacob seemed to grate on one another's nerves.

Before seven o'clock I had dressed and washed more carefully than usual, and tied a pink ribbon into my frizzy hair: then I went downstairs and took a drink of milk out of our pail, and walked over to their cottage. I thought he would still be in bed, but he was sitting downstairs, working on a model boat that he was carving from a lump of wood, so I knew at once that he was not going to play truant on this first day, as he had threatened. I also knew that he had expected me, and was glad that I had come.

Although I could not see how badly he was feeling, for he kept his head down over the work he was doing, and his long fair hair needed cutting as it almost always did, I asked him cheerfully if he would like an egg.

He said he didn't mind; but he said it as though he hated me as well. There would be no sense in talking to him in that mood; but I tried. I loved him too much not to try.

'Why don't you want to go to school?'

He sliced away at that lump of wood as though wanting to murder it. 'Who said I don't?'

'But you don't, do you?'

He glanced at me with hard and furious eyes.

I said quickly: 'I'm not mocking you.'

He jabbed the knife into the wood and I could see that he was really struggling with himself. I was a bit frightened, and went into the kitchen to make breakfast.

Never mind, I thought while I was cooking breakfast, he'll be up with me among the As. He knew nothing of the Bible, it was true, and I had been upset to find that he seemed never to have heard of the Royal Family, but those are things you can easily catch up with. 'It's children with some *go* in them that I like,' Mr Prother used to say; and Jacob had all the go in the world. We'd have months of school together; maybe even years. We'd sit together, learn together, escape from the village together. I could have sung for joy, cooking breakfast that morning. I even thought I might begin teaching him the Royal names. That would give him a bit of a start; and Jacob's being a strong boy, surely good at games, would do the rest. Mr Prother loved any boy who could play football well; and I was sure that Jacob could, although when I asked him he denied it.

I called through the kitchen door to him, repeating the names. He actually said them after me; and then I was scared myself. But I made him say them over and over; and he did.

When I carried in his breakfast he had put away his knife and the piece of wood, and was sitting with his hands clasped round his knees and his head a little bent. 'You got tummy wobbles?' I asked. He did not even swear at me for that.

After breakfast we went out into the crisp morning that was still rimed with frost, and started along the road toward Jerman's corner where the buses wait. That morning we must have been a little late, for most of the others were already there. I looked up at Jacob, but he would not return my look. His face was fixed hard like someone expecting to be licked; and the colour of it seemed almost grey in that grey morning light.

It was strange to feel that he was scared and I was not; for the first time in my life, then, I understood vaguely how everything would be. I saw the end, in a way that I cannot explain, even before I knew the beginning. It made me sad, but it also made me brave.

I reached out and took his hand. He let me hold it until we came quite close to Jerman's corner and the other children. Then the high yellow bus swept towards us round the further bend, halted and reversed and waited while the children climbed in; and Jacob and I ran quickly down the road.

THREE
If he went to school on that first day it was only, as he admitted to me afterwards, because of me. But it could not last.

'He's going into the Bs,' Mick Lissard shouted in the break. 'Prother's just told us.' Mick was delighted, because he was in the Bs, and so Jacob would be with him and not with me. They put him with the Bs; and we scarcely saw each other except at playtimes, and not much then.

That was nothing to what followed. One day in the second week, just as we As were doing history and some of the older Cs, who had to share our classroom but for a thin partition, were having Activity and making so much noise you could barely hear yourself speak, the classroom door opened and Mr Prother, who occasionally teaches the top Bs in another room, came in with Jacob.

Everyone stopped talking. Everyone looked at Mr Prother and at Jacob. He went over to Miss Warren, who was teaching us and also supervising some of the Cs, for old Miss Christopher, who helps with the Cs – she doesn't try to teach them, of course, they're too stupid, it wouldn't be any good – was ill that day.

Mr Prother began whispering to Miss Warren while Jacob stood there by himself and would look at none of us. At first I thought they had changed their minds about him and would put him where he surely belonged, among the As; but I soon learned better. For Miss Warren called him over and took him down the classroom to the partition, and beyond it to the half room where those Cs were having Activity. Mr Prother walked out just then, so I went after Miss Warren and peered through the door in the partition. Others followed me: I could not stop them. There was no shame in a boy of Jacob's size being among the Bs; but to be among those older Cs was a terrible comedown, especially for anyone as touchy as he was. I watched Miss Warren telling those Cs to go to their places so that she could find one for Jacob; and I saw her put him next to a Chudbury boy who was just not normal – we had two or three like that, they were weak in the head and Mr Prother often complained that they ought to be in a special school. They could not read or write, and they just held all the others back. Now they put Jacob among that lot. His face was dead white and he sat down clumsily as though he did not know what he was doing. Please don't misunderstand me: it is not that we children cared about As and Bs and Cs. But the loonies were a different matter. To be pushed down among the loonies was enough to make you the laughing stock of everyone else. For the loonies were everyone's game; only when they happened to be strong and tough (and often they are, that's a funny thing about them) could any of them hope to be left alone. From now on Jacob would have to fight his way against the rest: he'd always be the funny one, the loony one, and he would be always alone. I thought he was like a cornered animal, sitting next to that slobbering loony from Chudbury; but suddenly he looked up and hunched his shoulders, and it seemed to me that he was scared no longer. I could not understand the reason for that.

But the reason why they pushed him down among the loonies was soon enough known: although he was going on for fifteen, he could not read even the simplest book.

The trouble began without delay. That morning, at break, some of the Bs began trying him out, just to see what fun they could have; Jacob hit one of them so hard they had to send the boy home. Mr Prother came running out when it happened, and seeing that the boy was smaller than Jacob but not knowing that there had been half a dozen of them, he caught hold of Jacob and accused him of playing the bully. Mr Prother was very keen about fair play; and I am sure he meant well. Only he could not possibly have known, for the most part, who was in the right and who was in the wrong.

'Did you hit this boy?'

Jacob said yes. He stared firmly in front of him, where the rest of us were gathered, but not as though he could see us.

Mr Prother still held him by the shoulder of his jacket. 'Well, he's smaller than you. Why did you hit him?'

'I wanted to hit him.'

'Is that sufficient reason?'

Jacob said nothing, and Mr Prother tried again. 'Well, look here, you can't go round just hitting people when you feel inclined. It's bullying. It's cowardly.' Mr Prother was angry by now: his face was flushed and his voice trembled. Jacob could do that to people quicker than anyone I know, except perhaps Mother: just by sheer mulishness he could make people see red even when they knew they had much better see nothing of the kind.

He shook Jacob's shoulder, and the rotten stuff of Jacob's coat tore a little. This made Mr Prother angrier still. He began shouting: 'Hit someone your own size next time, won't you? Hit a big boy like yourself. Good heavens, hit me if you like.' He let go of Jacob and stood away from him; and I screamed for I saw what would happen. Jacob came suddenly to life and sprang at Mr Prother.

It was really a fight, and I don't know if Mr Prother would have stopped it so easily but for several boys who caught Jacob's arms. They were teased for doing that afterwards, yet everyone was glad of it at the time. It was not so much sympathy for Mr Prother that made them do it, I think, as that they were frightened of what might otherwise happen. We were all frightened. They dragged Jacob off Mr Prother and got him down on the asphalt of the playground and held him there.

Mr Prother behaved well. He straightened his clothes and told them to release Jacob at once and went into his house with him without saying a word. It seems that Mr Prother talked to him for a long time; but Jacob would never tell me what was said. When they came out again they looked like enemies still; and Mr Prother had a worried frown as he shouted to us all: 'Now that's enough rough-housing for today. Forget the whole thing. So far as I'm concerned, it's already forgotten.'

They left Jacob alone for a while. Nobody but me would speak to him; or perhaps even dared to speak to him. In the second week two or three of the bigger boys started chasing him again; then the fighting began all over again, and it went on for days, sometimes with Jacob winning and sometimes not. Yet none of them would fight him single-handed; and gradually they tired of it. They simply left him to himself.

Miss Warren tried to get Mr Prother to bring Jacob back among the elder Bs. I overheard her telling him that Jacob's influence was ruining what little discipline remained among the most backward of the children. 'I really think,' she said, 'that he would quieten down if you took him back.'

But Mr Prother would not have it. 'He can't read. He can't write. He hasn't the remotest idea of multiplying six by six, let alone twelve by twelve. And he seems utterly incapable of learning.'

'He is a difficult case, I admit that.'

Mr Prother said in a tired voice: 'No, I won't have it. We can just about cope with the normal ones. The abnormal ones shouldn't be here at all. It's a problem *I* can't solve.'

I could not blame Mr Prother, but it still seemed desperately unfair. I knew why Jacob could not remember anything he was told to learn: I knew it from his face and his hands and everything about him. He simply lacked the confidence.

Yet if Mr Prother could not solve the problem, Jacob could. From about the third week he began to slip school altogether. At first only now and then: but gradually, as the winter continued, more and more until most of a week might pass without his so much as putting in an appearance. Mr Prother must have known this: I suppose he felt that on the whole it would be kindest to ignore it. I am sure he meant it for the best.

FOUR   WE had broken up for Christmas before Jacob would show me where he spent his days. He showed me on a rimy winter's evening with darkness like a tousled mist upon the woods, cold as the weather and frightening, so that even the cawing of the rooks in Jerman's elms was a noise of anger. He made me promise not to tell, and we started down the road to Morton's cottage. For a moment I thought despairingly that it was at Morton's that he spent his days.

Mother had said this once, though not in front of him; and I had understood why. She wanted to tease me by suggesting that there was something wrong between Jacob and Morton, but she also wanted to score a point against Morton. For once, though, I was glad of Mother's spitefulness, for it was true that Morton had taken a liking for Jacob, and I was jealous of that. When Mr Prother, at the beginning of Jacob's refusing to go to school, had come to ask Ted what might be done about it, and

Ted hummed and hawed and obviously hadn't the least idea, it happened that Morton had given him a lift back to Chudbury. Later on I had overheard him saying to Miss Warren: 'Well, that's the most you can say, but maybe it's enough. He's out of harm's way if he's working for her. He's better there than here.'

Our shoes crackled on the road. I summoned up courage and asked him: 'What's she been doing for you?'

He gave me a quick glancing look, his eyes gleaming: 'She's crackers, seems to me. Talks and talks, I dunno what it is she's saying most of the time. Read me a story once, too.'

'Oh, a story?'

He stopped to slide on a boggy length of road that was now fast frozen. 'Well,' he shouted, 'it's about a man who reckons there's people, a kind of people, up there in space.'

I was scornful. 'Old as anything, that is.'

'Wasn't the same, Lindy. This man reckons there's these people up there, and they're watchin us, they're watchin and waitin to come down here and show us how to get on better. They go around in flyin saucers and they can read your thoughts even though you can't see 'em.'

'What d'you mean,' I said, '*even* though you can't see 'em? You can't ever see 'em. They're not there to see.'

He had finished sliding now and we were walking together along the road. He said: 'I dunno. Says in this story these people up there – I forgotten what she calls 'em – aren't going to let them make a war here.'

'Who's going to make a war?'

'I dunno *who*, but someone is. What this man reckons, anyway. Why do you think they got these planes an' bombs an' stuff otherwise?'

'That's silly,' I said crossly, 'they always have those things. Doesn't mean there's going to be a war. Ted says the last one was enough for him. And you haven't answered my question.'

'What question?'

'About Morton.'

He shrugged. 'She's all right, only she's crackers.' It was all he would say, and perhaps it was all that he thought.

'Looks like we're going there now,' I said nervously.

'No we're not then.' In fact we had turned off the road beside the gravel path that led to Morton's cottage, but instead of entering her gate we kept on toward the woods beyond. Within fifty yards or so this path had dwindled to an overgrown track, and soon the track itself was swallowed in grass and nettles, for nobody would come this way. It led only to thickets round the airfield they no longer used. I feared being stung by the nettles, and hung back a little, but Jacob had thought of that. He could be more thoughtful, when the mood took him, than anyone else I ever knew. He showed me how to go safely round a great lolling bed of nettles to a bushy thorn tree: beyond the tree, though you could not see it from the track behind, he had trampled a regular pathway through the frozen undergrowth. He said confidently: 'They think I'm working for her all the time I'm here. That's why I come this way.'

He looked at me with glowing eyes when I praised him for the pathway through the undergrowth. Even now I can see him standing there, waiting for me with glowing eyes while I shook a stone from my shoe. He was wearing an old jacket of Ted's, patched and ragged, and trousers that were also too big for him so that he'd had to tie them higher with a length of string about the waist. He needed, as usual, a haircut: I'd badgered him about that, but Ted would never give him the money. Yet none of this dragged him down nor made him seem ridiculous: he never so much as noticed it, but wore those rags just as he went about in our village – as though they had really no connection with him but by chance.

This is what made him so different from Mother, although in other ways they were alarmingly the same, for both were very strong and sometimes very cruel: he wasn't always trying to get away from himself, as Mother was. On the contrary, I think he was trying to get *at* himself and to build a new life that would be really his own. Where Mother had to have other people to build for her, Jacob needed only himself – and me as well, later on – in order to start building for himself. And if he did go the wrong way about this, then it was mainly for the reason that nobody wanted to help him, or knew how to help him: except me, of course, and when it came to the pinch I failed him.

The narrow pathway he had trampled, hidden among bushes, led away to a belt of woods beyond the airfield. For a moment or two I thought of Robin Hood and Sherwood Forest; but it was cold and real, here, and not in the least like that.

We walked through purple twilight. Even the twilight seemed a friendly darkness now, although it was desperately cold: we walked from one wide band of colour into the next, through purple and blue and grey, towards the clear night sky. Possibly this is what happiness also means: walking at night through a cold wood, and trembling with a joy that is not yet really born.

We came out of the woods into a wide flat stretch of winter wheat, and clogged our shoes with half-frozen earth until we struck the edge of the old runway, where we kicked them free again. Even that desolation of wrinkled tarmac, reaching towards the darkness like a river of dirty ice, did not frighten me; although it was a ruinous and sorry place in the ordinary run of things. On either side of it there were long stretches of ploughland where the winter wheat was growing, though now in the darkness I could barely see it, and bordering these rivers of ice and plough there were the woods behind us and the woods in front. A long disused cottage made a hump of darkness nearby; Jacob skirted this, crossed the second of the runways, and went straight on through the opposite stretch of wheat. After a time we plunged into the woods again, and now it was almost too dark to see where we were going.

I called despairingly that he should wait for me.

His voice came muffled over his shoulder. 'It's just here.'

I bumped against him in the darkness. 'There,' I heard him

say contentedly, but I could see nothing. Between us and the sky a tree spread twisted boughs. Then I felt him move from me and called out after him.

'Just step in front of you. There's a way behind the bush.'

I got past somehow or other, scratching my legs and arms, and his hand caught me and pulled me forward. A faint rift of light seemed far overhead. Then he struck a light and I saw that we were standing inside the trunk of that tall tree. But beyond this, and leading out of it, there was a rough shed of planks and boughs, a sort of thatched hut that you would never have guessed was there. I called out in admiration. 'It's very clever.'

'You haven't seen it yet.'

The yellow wick of a paraffin lamp glowed from his fingers. I stepped over the bole of the tree trunk, slipped through the broad crack on the other side, and joined him in this hut that he had built. He had really done a great deal of work. 'Now you can see, Lindy,' he was saying: 'There's two beds and a cupboard full of plates and spoons and things. And boxes you can sit on.'

I said stupidly, I was so cold: 'What's it for?'

'It's for living in.'

I shuddered. 'I wouldn't want to live here.'

'Nobody asked you to.'

But he had; and the fact that he had was stronger than the fact that I was shivering with cold. 'It's a lovely place,' I cried, angry with myself.

He began to show me all that he had built and brought here so as to make a place for living in. He had certainly organized a great many things: on either side of the hut there was a narrow bed made of sawn-off planks with blankets folded neatly across them, and between these a cupboard made to fit across the end. I opened the cupboard and saw there was pretty well two of everything; and every pair was a proof that he had really made it for the two of us. I said that it was super, really super; and then we sat on the bed and I wished that he would give me a kiss.

92

'We could live here,' he said, 'I've got it waterproofed.' He had a queer little smile, but he did not kiss me.

'Easy to live here,' I agreed.

He got up excitedly and went over to the door and showed me how it could be shut against the bole of the tree, making it entirely snug and private. Like this, I thought, he was hating nobody and wanting to be rid of nobody: like this we could sail through the world.

'It's a secret.'

'I'll whisper it into a grave,' I teased him: 'over at the church, and then I won't want to tell anyone.'

'It's got a name. I invented it.'

I managed not to ask.

He looked at me sharply: 'I call it Engamore.'

It struck me as a funny name. 'But what does it mean?'

I should not have laughed. He said over his shoulder: 'It's just a name.'

'The Wood of Engamore,' I was saying out loud, 'it's a nice name.'

In the little glimmer of the paraffin lamp I could see no more than the outline of his face, hard and anxious, giving nothing away. This was the moment that I had to choose for bursting into tears: I cursed myself, and cried. I wailed in sheer despair at life's ever coming right for us.

But he sat beside me and stroked my hair. I remember that his voice was shy and rough, not boyish any longer; and even in despair I was somehow glad for us.

FIVE

IF Mother could have left well alone she might have spared us all the misery that followed; and spared herself too. But the devil was in her so far as Jacob was concerned: she could never seem to forego a chance of baiting him. He took it pretty well for the most part, avoiding her whenever he could, sitting quietly under her taunting provocation when he could not; but this stubborn silence only made her worse with him. She seemed bent on goading him beyond the point where his silence would break down: she seemed longing for a fight. Perhaps the secret of her hating him so much lay simply in his refusing to submit: Mother had never run into anyone like that before, not in our village nor, I think, anywhere else.

This everlasting quarrel was for months the only sadness in my life. Otherwise there were good times when I could forget even about this, for Mother and Ted had their business by now, and were often away. They went away in the evenings; but for all that Mother stayed on at Jerman's dairy, and often enough came home with good overtime as well as her regular money. There was more cash in the house that year than I had ever thought possible. Altogether we lived in a high old way: Ted had entirely refurnished the sitting-room of the cottage, and put in a new fireplace because the old timber one had smoked. This is where he sat in off-days while winter was turning into spring and the days were growing longer, and the trees coming into bud and the country coming alive again; sometimes, before that feast of warm coals, I would sit with him too. The chairs were new and warm and comfortable, and they stood before that smart bricked fireplace on a bright red rug. 'Makes you look like a million dollars,' Dook had said in his friendly way. I liked him all the more for saying it.

Another winter ended. There is always a morning, late in wintertime, when you know that spring is on the way: out in our country this would be a morning when the cold sharp light of winter had softly melted, during the night, into a long low mist. Sometimes, then, you could barely see as far as the turn in the road: at other times, although you might not see the fields, you would be able to see above the mist as far as Lowton spire. This was a warm and friendly mist, not like the bitter fogs of

94

November. Everyone knew that it promised a change of season; and everyone was cheerful for that. Townspeople notice only the putting on and the putting back of clocks, I've found: but for country people the signs of change are days of big importance, and they talk about them as though no one could be sure, otherwise, that the seasons would change at all.

Early one Saturday we had our first misty promise of spring. It sent Mother whistling to Jerman's, as we thought; and it sent Jacob to the woods, or, as they thought, to Morton's. Ted came down late while I was clearing up Jacob's breakfast things, and hummed a little tune and said he shouldn't be surprised if he wasn't out in the garden again before long. I was well pleased with myself that morning, what with one thing and another, and told him that he should sit down in front of the fire, which I had already lit, and I would bring him some breakfast.

'Two eggs or three?' I called from the kitchen.

'Ah, make it three, Lindy. Eat drink and be merry. That's the ticket, eh?'

When I took in his breakfast he was tucked comfortably into the best armchair and concentrating on the agreeable job of paring his nails. 'You're looking smart,' I said. He was wearing a new tweed suit of thick material chequered in huge red and yellow squares, a saffron coloured tie with a horse-shoe and hunting whip embroidered on it in red, and a white soft shirt; his shoes were of light brown suede with pointed toes, and were covered with a decoration of holes and triangles. He seemed thoroughly comfortable. 'No good looking shabby in my trade,' he said.

'What is your trade, Ted?'

'Business,' he said with a wink, 'just business, Lindy. Just what makes the world go round, eh?'

'Well, it seems to suit you,' I arranged his breakfast things on a low table beside him.

'Of course it suits me.' He chuckled contentedly. 'Come on a bit, haven't we, since them days on the airfield?'

But he still had this odd trick of ending everything he said with a question, as though trying you out, as though careful to say everything in such a way that he could always unsay it again afterwards, if he wanted. He talked as though he nudged and elbowed you towards an idea, gently, deviously, always half afraid lest you might jump back on him and bite him for it. It was part of all that great uncertainty in Ted which made him so difficult to pin down: you could never quite know where he was, perhaps because he never knew it himself. He was simply not made to stand misfortune: faced with that he would float away and speak of something else, or disappear.

The better his business went the smarter and tidier he appeared. 'I've got to take care of my appearance,' he had explained to Mother; 'You know what it is with them boys, Poppy, they like a man to do himself well. They pay for appearances, see. They know what they're after. That's America for you.' He loved to ruminate about America. 'We'll get over there just as soon's the business will stand it,' he had long since announced: 'You 'n me, Poppy, we'll get over there and pick up the latest ideas, eh? We'll go over on the *Queen Mary*, won't we? Just to take a look, Poppy, you 'n me, 'n brush up our ideas, like.'

Mother has said: 'I'll believe it when it happens.' But she smiled too, the crooked little smile she had when she was really pleased. She liked Ted in these expensive and expansive moods.

'Productivity,' he announced, 'that's the ticket, eh?'

Mother said with a quick laugh: 'Those girls can't produce more'n they've got.'

'Oh, those girls,' Ted replied scornfully: 'those girls ain't nothing. That's just for now. *That* won't last. We got to get busy, Poppy. We got to exploit success, see?'

This was his mood while winter gave way to spring: it seemed to me that the whole of our countryside was in the same mood of change and growth. It was also our mood on this particular morning when Mother followed Jacob to the woods, 'just to see', as she shouted at us afterwards, 'what the hell he does with himself there.' For she already knew, it came out, that he did not spend his time at Morton's.

At midday Ted and I were still enjoying the warmth and comfort of his sitting-room. After Ted had breakfasted I cleared away and washed up and came back with a book that I was reading. I found him smoking his pipe just as I had left him.

'No business this morning?'

He took his new expensive pipe out of his mouth and smoothed his hand over his chin and remarked in a peaceful drowsy way that you had to think, in business, if you wanted to survive and prosper. 'Now I'm considering one or two things,' he explained: 'I'm considering them carefully, see.' He put up his feet on the little table that stood to one side of the new brick fireplace, and closed his eyes. I went back to my book.

After a while I knew that he was staring at me and, looking up, caught him off his guard. There was almost a feeling of pain in the way he was staring at me.

'Anything wrong, Ted?'

He shook his head and said after a while: 'You're a queer kid, ain't you?'

I knew that I was, and hated knowing it; only this time, I saw, he had said it not to hurt me but for some other reason of his own. He went on: 'You ought to be a poor miserable little sod, and yet you ain't. You ought to be Christ knows how miserable, but there you sits in front in the fire, purring like a kitten, and readin a book.'

'Why shouldn't I, then?'

'I dunno,' he muttered, suddenly gloomy; and then irritably, changing his mood: 'Well, go on, get on with it 'n don't bother me. I'm thinking, see. I don't want to be bothered.'

'I wasn't bothering you.'

He would only grunt in reply; and sat with the pipe smoke about his face, gazing into the fire.

Perhaps half an hour after this, when I was still quite cheerful in spite of Ted's discontent, and getting into a good part of my book, we heard Mother's footsteps on the path. She sounded in a hurry. I wondered why she should have come back from Jerman's before her usual time until I remembered her having said something about not working late today: but before I had time to think this out she had flung open the door and burst in on us.

Ted shouted at her: 'What's the matter, Poppy? What's happened?'

Her face was smeared with blood: her hair was wildly out of order: her blouse was torn and twisted as though she'd dragged herself through thorn and brambles. Even then I couldn't help thinking, flushed and breathless though she was, that she had the strength of all of us put together. I felt weak, and my heart began to flutter. I wanted to run away.

There was never any running away from Mother. She ignored me, though, and said to him in a voice that trembled with anger: 'It's me or him, see?'

'Now, look here, Poppy,' Ted began, but she overwhelmed him. She stood with her arms folded, the door behind her still open and the cold air searing in, and said with a false and pent-up carefulness that Ted could choose – it was she or Jacob, one or the other, not both.

By this time, though, he had come to know her better. He made no move. 'Go on,' he said, 'tell us about it. What's he done now?'

I admired him for that. It was the first time he had ever seemed likely to stand up to her; and it took her by surprise. He rounded on me and shouted: 'Here you, go 'n make y'r Mother a cup of tea, sittin there like that.' This was sensible of him, for I am sure it made Mother feel a little better. I went into the kitchen but I left the door ajar.

He got her to tell him, little by little. I cannot tell it in her own words; and so it seems flat, now that I am writing down what I remember. But the truth is that the telling of the story was a kind of battle, a battle of wits, with Mother giving way in gusts of angry talk: and the feeling between them so hot and close that I thought I should be sick with excitement, out in the kitchen though I was.

She had taken the road to Jerman's in the usual way, but had noticed Jacob walking ahead of her beside the hedge near Morton's place. 'He's always going off by himself, isn't he? Well, where's he go? What's his right to sneak off like that in our village?' So she had followed him carefully in case she was seen, and noted how he disappeared behind the brambles at the end of Morton's track. Mother knew those woods of old, but she had seldom or never walked in them for years: now she followed him to the hut he had built. She saw him dodge round the blackthorn tree and into the trunk of the elm, and went in after him. 'Well, he's got himself a place there, a place to live in. He can bloody well go and live in it.'

'Now, come on, Poppy,' Ted coaxed her.

She had called out to him. He had turned round and jumped on her. They had fought each other in the darkness of the tree. In the end she had 'got him off of her' and stumbled out and come on home: and just look at the state she was in, and Ted could choose, and on and on and on, so that I could scarcely bear to listen.

'All right, I'll beat him for it, won't I?' It was as near to a promise that Ted would ever come.

She screamed at him then. I couldn't hear what she was saying for the fear and pain inside me. I had to grip the kitchen table while my breath came in tearing gulps, and I was far past weeping. There was a sharpness in my belly as though someone had kicked me there. A wetness seemed flowing down my body. Of course it was only the excitement; but the excitement was more than I could bear.

Then I heard Ted slamming the kitchen door and after a while, to my astonishment, I thought I heard them getting down together. I suppose that was the excitement too.

But it seemed a cruel and terrible thing, just then; and I ran out of the house. I ran past Morton's and through the woods to the place he had built for us; and there I found him sitting on the bole of the elm beside the blackthorn tree.

He watched me coming, and when I was quite near he said: 'All right. I didn't ask her to come. I'll shoot her next time.'

He had his pistol in his hand. He was cleaning it with a rag.

SIX — AFTER a while I asked him whether he was coming home now. He made no reply to that but finishing cleaning the gun, spun the chamber that holds the bullets, clicked the trigger several times, and went back into the hut. I climbed in after him and found him sitting beside the door: he had the gun pointing straight at me.

'Don't', I cried, 'you'll hurt somebody one of these days.' I felt tired and disappointed: the hut no longer seemed a magical enchanting place, but a miserable game for boys.

He grunted something or other, went into the hut, and reappeared without the gun.

'Someone'll find it. You're supposed to have a license.'

He answered bitterly, his blue eyes flickering: 'No, they won't. And she won't come here again. She'll have more sense.' He understood as little of Mother as she of him.

I saw that he was deliberately hanging back: he wanted to come with me but could not quite summon up the confidence for it. Now I felt almost motherly, tired and motherly; and the feeling was new and strange, but not unpleasant. I coaxed him: 'I'll go in first and see what it's like.'

We walked slowly through the wood and across the fields of wheat that were little more than a gentle emerald varnish on the dull brown plough; and the tiredness I felt gave way to pleasure. There is nothing so beautiful as our gentle woods and fields when the spring approaches. They are like a promise of happiness

100

that is bound to come true. But then I am easily satisfied: Miss Pakeman says it is the saving of me. 'You've got high survival-value,' she says, 'you don't have to begin all over again, every time. You just keep on going.' It is what I have always thought of my aunt Pooley who lives in half the schoolhouse at Chudbury, Miss Fen having the other half: she has had to put up with every sort of misery, but you would never really know it. Mother used to say it was only because she was slow in the head.

That day it was Dook who made it up to everyone, and let us go on living as though nothing much had happened. When Jacob and I came up the road from Morton's turning we heard music coming from Ted's cottage. I thought at first that Ted must have the television on, but it was too early in the day for musicals; and then, as we came closer, I saw Dook's car outside the gate and heard Dook's voice singing to the strum of a guitar.

'You can wait a bit,' I said to Jacob in the garden, and left him there.

In Ted's sitting room you might have thought that nobody in a lifetime had ever said a cross word. Ted was still in his armchair while Mother perched on the arm beside him now, and they were drinking champagne with Mother holding a silver-papered bottle in one hand and a glass in the other. Dook was guying an act in the middle of the floor, the chairs a little pushed aside; and over by the window, throbbing with the rhythm that he made, there sat a negro airman I had never seen before. Ted waved a happy hand at me, so I shut the door and sat down on the little fireside table.

Dook finished his act in fine style, pranced round the floor, and ended with a big theatrical bow to Mother. Then the negro airman began playing a straight quickstep and Mother danced with Dook. She was still in bare feet, without stockings; so Dook and his friend must have come quite unexpectedly; but there was nothing to show that she remembered any unpleasantness.

I slipped out at once and got Jacob inside and up the stairs to his bedroom. 'Stay here a bit,' I whispered. 'It's going to be all right.'

The negro airman had stopped playing when I came back into the sitting-room, and was mopping his brow with a white handkerchief while Mother poured a glass of champagne for him. He stood up and thanked her when she gave it to him. He was the most dignified man I have ever seen, that negro airman: he might have been playing hymns from the serious and solemn look on his face. I stared at him a good deal, for you don't see a negro much our way. What surprised me most of all was that he did not seem to know he was a negro.

'Cool cat, aren't you?' Mother said, trying him out.

He smiled at that, but not as though he especially liked it. 'Oh thank you, ma'am,' he said. I was more surprised than ever.

Mother thought that too funny for words, being called ma'am, and burst out laughing. The negro airman looked upset. 'Have I said anything, Dook?' he asked.

Dook said: 'Sam, you ain't said nothing. Time you did.'

'Oh I never talk much,' Sam explained. He sat down on the window sill again and looked out of the window as though he were dreadfully bored: perhaps he was, or perhaps he was only offended.

Suddenly Dook noticed me. 'Hi handsome,' he called across, and spread out his arms. I leaped into them and gave him a kiss. I whispered: 'Is it all right?'

'Sure,' he whispered back, 'sure it's all right. Nothing to worry about.'

Then he took me by the hand and led me over to the negro airman.

'Corporal Samuel Tucker,' he bawled in that voice of his: 'I want to have you know the sweetest child in all this county, Miss Lindy Wellin. Here, shake a paw.'

The negro airman stood up again and we shook hands. There was a cold papery feel about his fingers and I could not like it, although I tried. 'Glad to know you,' he said as though I were quite grown up. Then he asked Dook: 'She her daughter?'

'Sure thing.'

'Congratulate you, ma'am,' said the negro airman.

Whether it was that he played the guitar so well at one moment, and behaved with all the dignity of the Reverend William Williams at the next, or the solemn dignity that went with his long body and long fingers and long sad face, that negro airman fairly put a spell on Mother. She suddenly turned ladylike, something you would rarely see her do unless it was for making fun of Mrs Thompson or Mrs Steppins. At first I thought she was making fun of herself: she poured out another drink for the negro airman and took it over to him, not at all in the wild flying way she usually had, but with prim shoulders and small steps; and when she gave it to him her voice would have been a gift to Mrs Steppins, if only Mrs Steppins could have heard.

Ted must have thought the same thing as me; for he bellowed into a sudden laugh. Mother turned round slowly and looked him up and down as though she had never seen him before. 'Anything the matter with you, Ted Breldon?'

Ted's grin stayed on his lips, but without any pleasure: he cleared his throat, frowned, coughed again, and shook his head. 'Sorry, Poppy, can't think what got into me.' And for the rest of that afternoon he said no other word except to offer drinks.

Mother straightened her hair and tucked in her blouse and smiled in a dreadfully polite way at Corporal Tucker; but the only person upon whom this had no strange effect was Corporal Tucker himself. He said in his long hollow voice: 'That's a pretty daughter, ma'am.'

I was a little readier for what happened next because from time to time, in the company of strangers, Mother would occasionally pretend that there was nobody in the world she cared for nor loved except me. I say she pretended; thinking back on

103

it, though, I am not quite sure about that. Perhaps there were times when she really imagined herself into that kind of feeling for me. Once on a bus at Rolcaster an old gentleman had spoken politely to her about having such a pretty little daughter, and given me sixpence to spend on sweets. She had taken me straight from the bus stop and bought me a new frock, and for the whole of that afternoon had pestered me with asking whether I should like this or that impossible thing, such as living at the seaside or going up to London for the circus, as though we ever should. I could not bring myself to believe a word of it whenever she treated me like that; and in the end she saw that I disbelieved her, and such occasions generally ended in a row.

This kind of feeling came over her again with the negro airman. She called me across to her and put her arm round me and nestled me to her. 'She's all right, aren't you, Lindy?'

'Sure thing,' said Corporal Tucker.

'You bet she is,' said Dook. Only Ted was silent.

'She's all I've got in the world, you know,' Mother went on; and although she spoke in this ladylike voice she was putting on I daresay that she really believed it. 'I wouldn't lose her for anything.'

'Guess you wouldn't,' said Corporal Tucker. 'Motherhood's a beautiful thing, everyone knows that I should think.'

'Sure thing,' said Dook, helping himself to another glass of champagne and sitting down beside Ted.

Mother was still delighted with herself. 'Lindy dear, your frock's a disgrace. Go on over and change it.'

I went and changed it. I put on my new cotton frock that was only two summers old and came in again; and the sitting-room was quiet and peaceful. And peaceful it remained for all the afternoon until Dook and Sam had to go back to the Base again. We all went out with them to say goodbye. It was almost like belonging to a proper family.

Even Jacob came down and joined us. When she saw him Mother said, just as though nothing much had occurred between them: 'Well, there you are. Don't you go and be a silly boy again.' And that was how we came through it for this time.

I can still remember how we stood outside the garden hedge, waving goodbye to Dook and Sam, and then turned in one by one at the gate and walked up the old flagstone path among the flowers and weeds we had always known; but soon enough it was like a dream, a long sad dream like that negro airman's face.

SEVEN YET the truth of that time, I really believe, is that I was not in the least unhappy but for such times when everything went wrong. Even when I was sorry for myself I suppose you could have called me happy in a contradictory way: I was miserable, then, because I knew by now what it was like to be happy. I was growing up: I was changing within myself; and that was a consolation too. Every single day could start a new life, or so it seemed.

Our days went quietly enough. Ted was making good money from the tarts beyond Rolcaster; and for Mother, apart from the money, he was really just right, since he let her go entirely her own way and treated her more as a sister than anything else. He was growing fat and comfortable, too, and quite different in appearance from when he had first come to us. He paid attention to his clothes. He shaved after breakfast. He pared his nails. He seemed altogether more solid: there were moments when he seemed entirely real. He slept a great deal during the day and all of the night as well, unless for the nights when he was called away for what he liked to call his business conferences. He drove the taxi back and forth whenever the men wanted him; but that was seldom for more than their regular trips between Chudbury and Rolcaster.

All this suited Ted down to the ground; and he never tired of saying so. 'You don't need to work so hard,' he would suggest to Mother now and then; but Mother never took any notice of that. She went on working at the dairy, and even Harry was back in favour. Apart from rows between her and Jacob – and we grew, in time, even to ignore these, for you can't have everything in life, and it would have seemed unnatural not to have had *something* the matter with us – we were almost as other families were. So that whenever good things came our way we made the most of them: we talked of that negro airman's coming to see us, and his dandy manners and his glittering guitar, for weeks on end, although we never saw him again because he flew off back to America.

A fear persisted that Mr Prother might lose patience and report Jacob for staying away, just as he had reported me, several terms back, for repeatedly missing the bus. But Mr Prother was a sensible and kindly man. I expect that is why he came to see Morton about Jacob instead of sending in a report to the authorities. Being a governor of the school, Morton would have a say in the matter. 'If I report the boy,' Mr Prother explained to her, 'they'll have to take it up, and then there'll be trouble for him – and trouble for the school as well. That won't make it any better for the lad. He's going on for fifteen. He'll be leaving anyway before long. So don't you feel I could just let him be?'

Morton herself told us this. You might think it unlikely that she should: I would have thought so myself but for the fact that by this time it had got to the point with her, more or less, where Jacob could do no wrong. I tried to feel glad about this: but not with much success.

He was potting plants for her when she told us, or rather when she told him; for I was sitting to one side in the shadow of the garage, and she failed to notice me at first.

'I told him I thought it was perfectly right. I told him we make a great mistake if we think we can pour all of you into the same convenient mould. So you needn't worry about that, Jacob.'

Jacob said he didn't mind. He seldom said any more to her.

She would talk to him for hours, rambling on about this or that, mostly far above our heads; and never seemed to require an answer. Yet we were comfortable together. I was seeing her in a new light these days. I was even growing out of my jealousy of her place in Jacob's estimation.

She said: 'Well, you're pleased with me, aren't you?'

He gave her one of his rare welcoming smiles.

I said: 'You wouldn't let *me* stay away.'

She peered at me through the opened doors of the garage: the light was behind her, so that the shape of her seemed stranger than ever, her legs like thin black props and a jacket she was wearing, of stiff embroidered material, sticking out like wings. No: I was certainly not jealous of her. I almost dared to be sorry for her.

'Of course I wouldn't,' she said a little crossly, for at that time she had not yet quite come to like me, perhaps because the memory of Mother's treatment of her was too painful. 'And of course I shan't. Yours is a different case, You can be a bright little girl, if you want, and now you're growing into a young woman it's important to have you regularly at school.' And she was off again about the taxes. 'You're the kind we are paying for, you know.'

'You're paying for him, too,' I said mutinously.

'Well, well,' Morton returned, 'I suppose that you, my child, are the spirit of the times. The angry young woman of to-morrow, I shouldn't be surprised. But now you can listen to me for a moment while Jacob is finishing his work.'

She drew up a garden chair for herself. Mr Morton, who was at home for the weekend, came up just then and leant against the garage door, listening. I always felt, with him, that he was firmly on my side: as a matter of fact, though, I think he was on everybody's side. He could not bear disliking people. 'I was just trying to explain, darling,' Morton said, 'why it is that we can't afford to let the State mow us down without a word of protest.'

He laughed at that. 'My dear, it's the other way round – we can't afford not to.'

I was never sure whether she liked his jokes: they were not very funny. 'Oh, that's absurd. It's old-fashioned. My mother thought the servants were all the same because they looked the same. Nowadays, of course, your precious politicians have turned us all into servants, and you still want to treat everyone as though they were just the same as everyone else. But they're not. This child is bookish. That one isn't.'

'Very convenient,' said Mr Morton patiently. 'Pots a nice plant too.' He was the most patient man I have seen. He never interfered. He behaved towards Jacob and me as though we were as old as he was. Once he had asked Jacob what he did with the money that he earned. 'Keep it,' Jacob had said. Mr Morton wanted to know why he kept it: he never managed, he said, to keep any himself. 'Because I'm going to America,' Jacob had explained. I must say it was the first I heard of it; but Mr Morton took it quite as a matter of course, and said: 'Oh, do you think it's any different there?' And when Jacob said yes, of course it was different, he nodded carefully and agreed that it might be so. It was just his patient way of saying it was not.

'Convenient or not,' Morton continued, 'it doesn't suit your precious politicians. They want everyone to be a useful producer – that's the new phrase, I believe. A useful producer. Like ants. That's why we have to resist. And I shall continue to resist for as long as I am able. They'll defeat me in the end, I know, but for as long as I am able I shall do my best to dish their game.'

'You'll find it rather expensive, I'm afraid.'

'They can't take any more from us, can they? We're bled white as it is. But I'm not going to have this boy pestered with lessons he can't understand. They'll turn him into an ant over my dead body.'

'I don't think we ought to let it come to that, my dear.'

'Well, I have told Prother that he can't expect to turn out

children like parts from a machine. There's such a thing as individuality, thank goodness, left, and I am not going to give way. Jacob's talent lies in quiet practical work. It's against the spirit of the age, but I can't help that. I don't like the spirit of the age. If all your precious friends had their way we should go from the cradle to the grave without a single thought of our own. No wonder everything's so broken down. No wonder everyone's so lonely.'

I said: 'Ants aren't lonely.'

Mr Morton had a good laugh over this, but Morton was rather cross with me. 'They're the loneliest creatures in existence. They're the supreme Welfare State.'

'But they don't pay taxes,' Mr Morton said, still chuckling.

'Which is just what we are coming to. Soon enough they'll have taken everything. We'll be the slaves of the State. Oh, I know we can't win. But at least we can resist. In our feeble way we can resist, and I mean to. That is why I moved from London.'

'Of course,' agreed Mr Morton. He was still in his London clothes.

'I'm helping Jacob to become a useful citizen, not a useful producer. I'm protecting him from this ant State you admire so much. He may not have much book knowledge, but he'll be a good craftsman. A true gardener. An individual.'

Mr Morton gave us a slow wondering glance. 'Ah, do you think so?' he murmured.

I put in: 'He's going to be a jet pilot.'

Morton said rubbish to that: for a bright little girl I could be sometimes very stupid. Mr Morton looked solemn and Jacob, as usual, said nothing. He trusted nobody, except perhaps me, and he gave nothing away.

After that he went to school no more than once a week or so. Then he would sit quietly at the back, among the loonies, and say nothing and quarrel with nobody. Even Miss Warren seemed taken in.

THE Easter holidays brought wet and sorry weather.
EIGHT   February mists were still with us. They lingered on
beyond their season, clinging to fields and hedges
in a milky vapour that the springtime sun could barely penetrate. There were days that April when we could not see across
the road, and even Dook, who drove his motor-car along our
country lanes as though piloting a liner on the wide free ocean,
gave up coming for a time. Mother had Harry to mind her
whenever she needed company: for Ted was as often asleep as
awake, yawning in his chair no sooner than breakfast was done.
Jacob and I were left more than ever to ourselves. Sometimes
we went out through Vixen's Wood to the hut he had built;
but seldom at this time, for Jacob would not trust the beaten
tracks we made in the sodden undergrowth, for fear that others
might find the way; and often we sat upstairs in his bedroom
while I read space adventures to him.

Now and then, on days of thickest fog, we went for long
exhausting walks. I should rather have stayed at home; but
these milk-white days when the world was hidden, and our
village was hidden, drew him out along the secret roads where
he could walk unseen, and be sure that no one watched or
worried him. Although it is not so very far from London or
from Cambridge, our countryside has always the feel of distance
in it: as when I was very young and used to see, from my window
over Jerman's orchard, the spire of Lowton church far off
beneath the clouds and think it the gate of Heaven. In smiling
weather such as we had that summer, later on, you could lie on
your back in the tufted grass and watch the sailing clouds as
though lifted among them, and almost feel the distant earth
spin and murmur there beneath. You could wander in our
woods and meet never a soul all day. You could fancy yourself

alone in the world, and think that the rest of the world, for the time being, had lost the way to find us. You could feel wonderfully happy in that solitude.

But when the February mists were down, swallowing everything beyond ten yards of your feet, this feeling of lostness and loneliness became for me an evil magic. Then it would be fruitless to remember that the summer would be following after, ripe and clear and public: then for a while our countryside would be wrapped in death, and not even the noise of aeroplanes seemed to penetrate its milky silence. I used to think, then, that the rest of the world, going about its business, would never again recover us; and perhaps in this there was something more than imagination. The world beyond our countryside went by on the main road, miles and miles away: it missed us altogether. Roads came into our countryside, but they were small winding roads that came from nowhere in particular and went away again to nowhere in particular, built for a kind of England that must have died out long before, so that Jerman's combine could get along them only by clipping the hedges on either side, and Mr. Morton's tall old motor-car, driving to and fro between the village and the distant railway station, looked as though sailing along the bare ground like a barge on Broxted canal. They were country roads, I know; but the life had somehow gone out of our countryside. 'It's dead, isn't it? Had it, eh?' Ted remarked one evening while he stood at the window and gloomed into the mist: and I shuddered and huddled nearer the fire, for there was a kind of truth in what he said.

But Jacob liked such days. He appeared to feel safer when the mists were down. Then he walked boldly along the road through Chudbury like he owned it, and beyond Chudbury into the tight streets of Lowton that was altogether enemy land or the outskirts of Danesfield and Duckfield, with me dragging at his heels, cold and wet and miserable but not letting him go alone. Once we traipsed as far as Thaxted, half across the county it seemed to me, and saw the grey spire of Thaxted Minster beyond a vale of mist as we tramped down the long hill that comes from Saffron Walden. I can remember how tired I was that day, half running to keep up with him through cold blind miles: I thought he was like a thin wolf, grey and hard, invading our countryside because it was hungry from a lean winter. He went along the road in quick long steps, dancing away out of sight whenever people came towards us through the mist, seldom answering if I begged him not to go so fast, unmindful of the cold and wet, his jacket open, his shirt unbuttoned; but then at last, when he turned for me and waited for me or gave me his jacket to wear, he would make everything right again with a gleaming confidence as though the world lay at our feet, and he would be its master.

If we talked, we talked of getting right away from here. That was his theme. 'We'll get away from here, Lindy, we'll get right away.'

We stood on the brink of Thaxted vale and the spire of Thaxted church rose from the mist like the standard-bearer of this dream.

'Where shall we go?' But I knew what he would say: I wanted only that he should say it again and again.

He shook back his head. 'I dunno. There's places.' That was also part of the game we played: to discover the possibilities, each time, as though they were new.

'There's America.'

'No, not America. Ted's going to America if he can. Ted and Poppy – he'll take her. She'll make him take her.'

'That's what they both say.'

'We won't go there.'

I said: 'Then we could stay here, couldn't we?'

But he smiled with the quick confidence that he sometimes had, at moments when he felt himself entirely trusted, and shook his head. 'You can't do anything here.' And that was something else that seemed entirely clear to us, something so clear that it needed no discussion or dispute: our places here were firm and fixed, immovable, and nothing could ever change them. We had to escape: we simply had to escape.

Going home through the mist with hunger eating into us, he talked on about his plans, not easily (for he never managed to talk easily) but eagerly and firmly so that I loved to hear him. This was the day he told me that he had saved seventeen pounds: when I praised him for it he exclaimed scornfully that it would not be nearly enough – we should need much more than that. He said we, and not I, for it had somehow grown between us that we should go there together, wherever it was, and make a life that would be ours to share. We should go to the other end of the earth, as far away as possible, to Australia or one of those places: we should go there in a ship and we should meet the people who lived there and they would be glad that we had come, and listen to what we wanted and help us to get it.

I forgot that I was tired and hungry. I forgot about our troubles. I saw him while he talked of the plans he made as somebody among other people, not better nor worse but the same, having a place among them, belonging to them: yes, belonging to them – that is what I really saw. That he and I should make it so that we belonged to people, and they to us. And just then, as it happened, this vision of escaping and belonging was linked with a chance encounter which came to mean a great deal to me, later on, although I do not quite know why. I think of it as one of the moments in my life with a sense and meaning that are absolutely good.

Walking home from Thaxted, we emerged from the mist over a long hill-top where the sun broke through in chill beams that were none the less a joy to see. We spread his jacket on the crisp cold grass and sat for a while, huddled together, our arms embraced, looking into the pale sun. Nothing passed us but for a motor-car. But this motor-car stopped after it had passed us, and backed to where we sat: an old polite woman put her head out of the driver's window and inquired if we were all right? We said that we were, and she drove on into the mist below, where Thaxted lay concealed; as she went she gave us a friendly smile, and I waved to her and Jacob remarked with quiet satisfaction, just as though it were a simple thing for him to say, that it was decent of her to stop and ask us. I can still remember her friendliness as though it were yesterday: she had white hair and a cheerful face, pink and white as though nipped by the wind; and she wore a small mauve hat. I also remember having thought that Australia would be full of such people who would help us if we wanted, or else drive on with a friendly uncomplaining smile.

That encounter had an effect on both of us. We talked of it on the way home. And it appeared certain to me then that I knew the way we should go, and it would be a good way: that after all there would be nothing strong enough to stop or hinder us: that we two should find our way across the world into a life that could be ours. Just then I was certain that I understood him: out of his anger and distrust there came an ordinary person who would live an ordinary life. For weeks after that, even when he was barricaded behind a blind perversity, I told myself that I need only be patient and I should find him again. I thought then that I could see an ordinary life for us, somewhere beyond the mist, but ahead of us and nowhere else so that we were surely going towards it; and I trembled with a fearful gratitude as they say the Prophets trembled when they saw a vision. It wasn't a vision: it was only a loving happiness, but perhaps there is no difference.

NINE   AFTER Easter the mists were driven out by good weather. This good weather was to stay with us all through the summer – a golden summer as we knew it later on, a summer in hundreds: even now, before it had properly begun, old Jeffreys, who is our oldest man, was known to have prophesied a drought. He prophesied it to Mr Morton in the pub one day: I heard him myself.

Children are not supposed to go into pubs. In our village though, so long as Mrs Chamfrey was upstairs in bed, there was no objection. Mrs Chamfrey's son Oliver, who keeps the pub on his mother's behalf and is under his mother's thumb in spite of his years, was too easy-going to worry about it; and Miss Edith, who had come to our village many years ago in order to marry Oliver but had never managed it, knew better than to offer an opinion. I used to be sorry for Miss Edith: or I should have been but for her continually expecting me to be sorry for her. Mrs Chamfrey treated her as though she was in service: Oliver, so far as he noticed her at all, treated her as a relative to whom he was showing a kindness: and Miss Edith, doing all the housework and getting no pay, seemed never to have quite abandoned hope of Oliver, although, from as far back as I can remember, everyone else had. She was the only woman in our village with whom Mother never quarrelled: she was too ground down and sorry for herself.

She and Mrs Chamfrey, that is: not even Mother would have thought of quarrelling with Mrs Chamfrey. Being over ninety and confined to her bed upstairs, Mrs Chamfrey was not much seen by our village; but she was certainly felt. On the two or three occasions when I myself was summoned to her presence I was thoroughly astonished by the brilliance of her small grey eyes in a face as crisp as old paper, and the sharpness of her questions. She had wanted to know what Ted was doing, and had even gone so far as to summon Ted as well: he returned from her with indignant disapproval, shook his head repeatedly, and said he thanked his stars for not being born a countryman. 'Asked me how much I'd paid for the cottage, and where I'd got the money.' He blew out his cheeks with disgust. 'Told me I was stupid to buy the cottage. You hear that, Poppy? Said the council 'ud never let us stay. You'll have to get out, she says, you should've asked me first. Poppy – you hear that, eh?'

'She generally knows what she's talking about.'

He had his back to the fire and his hands under his jacket tail.

'Should've asked her, eh?' he was grumbling to himself. 'I never heard the like. We paid for the place, didn't we? There's a law, isn't there? Thank Christ there's a law.'

'Going a bit far there, aren't you, Ted?'

But he was much too upset to answer back. He stood swaying in front of the fire for an hour and more, grumbling to himself, like an old barnyard cock that's been chased and ruffled and made to look foolish by a neighbour's dog.

Whether it was the finding out or the remembering that was more of a surprise in Mrs Chamfrey I do not know: there was little or nothing in our village that she failed to discover and remember, sooner or later, partly from questioning Oliver and Miss Edith, partly from calling up people to stand at the end of her bed and answer questions, and partly, as I used to think, by magic. Partly, I expect, from habit too: like most of our old people she had lived here all her life, had served at Chudbury Grange in ancient times when aristocracy had lived there – it's the American service club now – and, according to Miss Warren, had more history in her bones than all the books about East Anglia that ever were written. Miss Warren had interviewed her on the subject and discovered, as she let us know, that Mrs Chamfrey's grandfather must have heard, when a little boy, the news of the Battle of Waterloo. Personally I should not have been surprised if Mrs Chamfrey had heard that piece of news herself. She was immeasurably old, and she remembered everything.

I once asked old Jeffreys if he had ever heard tell of the Battle of Waterloo, and he hadn't because the only war for him was the war against the Boers. Those old wars are nothing nowadays, I know; but all the same they are the wars that matter to our village. The war against the Boers was the war that mattered to Oliver, as well, for although his guardsman's whiskers belonged to the Great War, he hadn't wanted to go to that one but to the Boer War. He'd had to go to that one, because everyone had had to go: just as to the one they had when I was born. But people in our village do not talk of those Great Wars. Everyone, it seems, has to have a war in their life; and I have discovered that it is always the war that happened when they were young. In Chudbury there is a monument with a long list of names on one side, and a short list on the other; and it stands there as if it scarcely belonged to the place, although the names on both sides are all of men from Chudbury and round about.

One reason for this may be that our village is an ancient village. It was here when William the Conqueror came: Miss Warren has looked it up in the Domesday Book. Yet for a good many years now it has somehow stopped living. The old people are still there, of course; but they are like ghosts among the bright new cottages that the Miss Titherams and Mr Thornton and Morton and the rest have bought and painted and polished up. Even when Mr Morton was down for the week-end and wore his green waistcoat with brass buttons and a new cloth cap and sat in the bar of the *Wheelwright*, and did his best to make conversation, he could seldom succeed. He succeeded, as a matter of fact, once that spring – I remember it because we had just returned from a day at the seaside. I happened to be standing in the bar of the *Wheelwright* because Dook wanted some beer for Ted, and had asked me to go across and fetch it. Then it had been that old Jeffreys gave his opinion on the weather, and cracked his ancient joke, which we had all heard a hundred times before but which never failed to make him chuckle, about its all being the fault of the atom bomb.

For splendid hours that day we had been at the seaside, Jacob and I, with Dook in Dook's motor-car, and two of Dook's friends from the Base and two girls they had. Such a lovely day: full of jokes and candyfloss and Dook's cheerful liking of every-one and wanting everyone to be as cheerful as he was. Not that he always succeeded in that, but this was scarcely his fault: he could never get hold of our ways, and consequently people misunderstood him. Dook's idea of cheerfulness was noise: noise and going fast. Not going anywhere in particular: but just *going*. He and we and his friends drove into Frinton that day as though we really were the first to hear the news of the Battle of Water-loo, and had a duty to tell it further: with Dook's friends sitting on top of the back seat, for Dook's car was a convertible and very big, and a girl called Mary and another called Suzy sitting beside them and acting as though they were Americans too, instead of holiday tarts from London which is what they really were, and the big klaxon honking, and Dook driving his motor-car as if piloting a liner on the wide free ocean: honking, scream-ing, whooping, laughing, we drove into Frinton. Into Clacton, yes, you might have got away with it in Clacton: but Frinton is a classy place without the benefit, so far as I know, of a single soda fountain; and we made a bad impression. I was the only one who noticed it, for Jacob never expected to make anything but a bad impression, and Dook and his friends had no eye for that kind of thing. As for Mary and Suzy, they sat on the back seat and screamed and let their skirts fly up over their knickers, and treated Frinton as though it stank of old fish. They made a bad impression too.

Dook brought the two of us back again about six in the evening and blew into the cottage and banged off a paper bag in Ted's ear. Ted woke up without any pleasure; but as soon as he saw that it was Dook who had done it, and not Jacob or I, he stopped snarling and switched on his false professional grin – by this time he'd got very good at doing that – and began shouting in the odd way we all seemed to shout whenever Dook was around. Dook always shouted: all those fellows at the Base always shouted: they could not seem to hear each other in a small voice. I never minded this because it was their natural way, however peculiar, but with Ted it was just one more false-ness on top of all the other falsenesses that I had learnt to recognize by now.

Within a second or two they were bawling at each other and slapping each other on the back and trumpeting with laughter.

'Hi, Ted, want some beer? *Old man*, eh?'

Ted roared: 'We got plenty beer, Dook.'

'No you ain't,' Dook roared back: 'you ain't got a darn thing. Waitin on me to come 'n buy you some, wasn't you? *Old man*.' Dook never tired of laughing at the way the English spoke English, and liked to make a wild imitation of it with a funny voice and accent. He never stopped teasing Ted, either, for all the money that Ted extracted from his friends and himself; but he never spent any the less for that, so far as I could see, and nor did they.

He called to me: 'Hi handsome, hop across and get some beer for the *old man*, will you?' He tossed me two half-crowns. Ted shouted: 'That's it, Lindy. Go and get some beer, will you?'

Not that Dook was taken in by Ted: in my opinion, he was never really taken in. He simply thought that you could have anything you wanted so long as you could pay for it, and that *if* you could pay for it then you ought to have anything you wanted. He was a kindly man; only he was not at home.

Over at the *Wheelwright*, after that shouting match, it was like the peace that passeth all understanding in the prayer-book. An old brown silence seemed to varnish the room and the people in it. Old Jeffreys sat along the bench against the wall with a labourer from Jerman's, William Batt by name, next to him: they had their elbows and their glasses of beer on the long table that Oliver keeps in front of the bench, and looked like men who have lost the power of speech without much expectation of ever finding it again. Mr Morton was sitting cross-legged in a wheelback armchair near the fireplace, his jacket open over his green waistcoat and its winking brass buttons, and was extremely glad to see me. I knew that well enough because he started up and smiled and said hallo Lindy and then sat down again, and smiled again, and tried to look exceedingly at home.

Oliver was just bringing him a pint of beer.

'Thank you, Oliver,' Mr Morton said.

'Turning warm, sir, isn't it?'

'Yes yes, I suppose it is. Hardly notice it in London, you know.'

Oliver regarded Mr Morton as though he had just been given a piece of bad news. Then he shook his head with sympathy and tut-tutted and looked awfully sad. 'Nasty in London, I shouldn't wonder?'

'Oh well, you know what it is,' agreed Mr Morton. Then he suddenly cleared his throat and leant forward and said in a loud deliberate voice: 'What's the summer going to be like, Mr Jeffreys?'

Old Jeffreys can hear as well as you or I, of course; but he doesn't let on that he can, he can't afford to, he'd never have peace from Mrs Jeffreys if he did. She is even older than he is – older than Mrs Chamfrey, they say – and no longer in her proper mind: she babbles and shouts at him, so that he has grown a way of seeming altogether deaf. He even has to make the bed for her.

Mr Morton repeated, raising his voice: 'I say, Mr Jeffreys. The summer. Rain or fine?'

'I reckon she'll be a good 'un,' old Jeffreys said, turning his head away and looking slyly down at Mr Morton's shoes. He never looks at you if he can help it: that is another of his ways.

After that there was a long silence again.

Oliver said: 'Ah well, turning warm, isn't it?'

It was really very nice of Oliver: he knew that Mr Morton wanted to have a pleasant gentleman-farmer's kind of conversation – the kind that Mr Harold has whenever he meets our village people – and he also knew that Mr Morton would scarcely manage it.

'Yes,' Mr Morton said bravely, 'I suppose it is.'

But old Jeffreys did speak again. He looked away slyly and said: 'She'll be a drought.'

Mr Morton received it as important news. Even Oliver was taken by surprise. 'A drought, Mr Jeffreys?'

'I reckon she will,' old Jeffreys said.

'Oh I don't know. Now why should you expect that?'

But then there was another long silence.

Oliver said after a while: 'Yes, it's really turning warm though.'

They stopped and started several times like this; and the reason I stood there and said nothing was simply that I wanted to see whether Mr Morton would really manage it, for once, and have the kind of conversation that he wanted, the kind that Mr Harold has.

He tried hard. 'What do you say, William, a drought, eh?'

William looked sarcastically at Oliver and then at me. But he shook his head. 'Can't never be sure, can you?'

Oliver hopped from one foot to the other in troubled agitation. He noticed me at last and called sharply: 'What you want, Lindy?'

He went off for Ted's beer, to the tap at the end of his passage, like a man who is glad to have something to do. Mr Morton pulled out his tobacco pouch and his country pipe – a large black one with a fat bowl – and filled it carefully, politely offering tobacco to William and to old Jeffreys, who refused it; and all that eased things for a while.

It was when Oliver came back with two jugs of beer for Ted that old Jeffreys brought himself to pronounce his regular joke. 'Ah,' he said suddenly, 'it be that bomb, I shouldn't wonder.'

I left them with Mr Morton leaning eagerly forward in the silence. If it was not quite the conversation that Mr Harold might have had, strolling up the road on a Saturday afternoon, it was after all a close thing. I was glad for Mr Morton's sake; only he did not seem in the least amused.

TEN WHEN I returned to them with the beer they had given over shouting and were gazing at the telly. I said here you are, and put down the beer where Dook could reach it; but Dook put out his arm and gave me a little hug and whispered: 'Look at this, Lindy. It's interesting.' So I watched the telly with them instead of going upstairs to find Jacob. A conjuror was doing tricks. Old tricks mostly, they were; but the conjuror had a line of patter that made us laugh. He kept shooting up a hand from his stiff white shirt-cuff and taking money out of the air. First he would point into the air and say: 'The Wise Man says, there's nothing there.' Then he would shoot up his hand and catch a bright half-crown. Showing that to you he would say: 'But the Fool says, yes there is.' 'Folly Pays' was the name of his act, the announcer told us afterwards: 'Folly Pays, or a Fantasy on Illusion and Reality.'

'Nice kid, that announcer,' Dook remarked sadly.

Ted grumbled that it was all a lot of crap, he'd seen tricks like that since ever he was a nipper, better tricks too, *and* you could see 'em for sixpence in the stalls. Something had switched him into a bad mood. 'Besides,' he added sourly, 'you got to work for it. There's nothing pays but hard grind.'

'I dunno so much about that,' said Dook, adding something that made Ted snort contemptuously.

Then Dook decided it was time for him to be gone: it was one of his duty nights.

'Thanks for a lovely day, Dook. Thank you ever so much.'

He gave me a friendly hug. 'Don't mention it, handsome. Folly Pays, don't it?' I saw him to the gate and waved goodbye.

Ted had switched off the telly and was staring vacantly at nothing in particular when I returned. After a while he rose from his chair and got himself over to the fireplace and leant his back against the wall above the new bricks and just stood there, staring at me now. I took little notice of that, for I never minded Ted, and went over to switch the telly on again. They were only giving the news so I switched it off. I tried to read a book. But it was no good: I couldn't ignore Ted's sudden misery, it sagged on him like a suit of old clothes. There is a moment, now and then, when happiness fades so clearly that you can almost see it go. I had to ask him what the matter was.

122

He shrugged. 'Tired, I suppose.'

'But you've been sleeping all day, haven't you?'

'Have I?'

He was staring at me with moist eyes, brown and sorrowful, like a beaten dog. He pulled a hand out of his trousers pocket and began fidgeting with his flies with slow fat fingers: I actually thought for a moment that he wanted to unbutton and show himself like Sawsbry did; but his hand wandered away to the mug of beer on the table. He took a long swig and put his hand back into his trousers pocket and crossed one leg in front of the other and stared at me again. Suddenly he appeared to have lost all confidence: he was like the Ted we had first got to know, the Ted who came miserably and whiningly from the airfield and begged for Mother's help.

'Them Americans,' he began in a small soft voice, 'they make me tired.'

'Dook's nice,' I said indignantly, 'we've had a smashing day.'

'Ah, make me tired, they do. What's it cost 'em? All piss 'n wind. Here one day 'n gone the next. Times I hate' em. Hate 'em like poison.'

'Well, where would you be without them?'

'Ah, damn sight better off, I shouldn't wonder.'

'That's not true, Ted.'

But I couldn't see what he was after. His eyes were creased in a silly soft smile that concealed what he meant, whatever it was, and his lips sagged open as though he were a little short of breath.

'You been to Clacton, eh? Any girls with 'em?'

I spoke of Mary and Suzy.

He nodded slowly: 'What'd I say? Promise you one thing and do the other, don't they?'

'You got out of bed the wrong side.'

He half turned and spat into the fireplace. There was a grin on his face now, but a grin that seemed to have come round several corners. 'You want to know what's wrong with me?'

I began to be worried. He saw that and enjoyed it.

123

'You asked me, didn't you? Well, I'll tell you, seein' as you asked me. It's finished, if you want to know. If you really want to know.'

Suddenly he looked at me squarely: he came round all those corners and fetched up right in front of me for once. And now it was certainly the old Ted of the airfield, broken down and penniless and glad of small favours, just as though we had built up nothing here in our village, just as though he'd soon be moving somewhere else and would have to begin all over again. Now he was back again at fidgeting with his fly buttons; and his grin became a silly weak smile, a whining smile, like a tame dog that's hungry and sniffs round a rubbish dump for something to eat, for anything to eat. I did not mind his fidgeting, for I knew that he meant nothing by it, or nothing that he would really want to do: but I did mind the rest of him, the sagging misery that hung upon him. He was looking at me now as though expecting words that would make a difference, and give him back a little courage.

'I don't know what you mean, Ted. What's finished?'

He only clicked his tongue with sudden impatience, reached again for the mug of beer and took another swig, and said: 'Oh I dunno. Nothing really.' Whatever he had meant to say he changed his mind, yawned, and relapsed into his armchair again. Mother came in just then, back from work at the dairy, and for once in a way I was relieved to see her. 'Ted's got depressed,' I told her. But Mother would never tolerate that kind of mood in Ted nor in anyone else: besides, she had come in from the evening air, fresh from work and glowing with the energy she had, and Ted's mood seemed small and unimportant now. 'Oh him,' she called from the kitchen: 'he'll recover.' And it did pass off soon enough – perhaps because Ted's warnings were never more than exceedingly obscure, or perhaps because Ted himself seemed never more than half present with us. That was the condition, I think, of his managing to get through life at all.

Mother was pleased to hear of our day at the seaside. She was always easy and relaxed after a hard day's work and was often glad to see me then. 'Well, that's nice,' she said when I had finished: 'But they weren't too pleased over at Jerman's. You'd better tell him to ask them, next time he takes a day off. They'll dock it off his pay in any case.'

We had expected that; I told her that Jacob was not yet used to going regularly to work, he'd begun only a few weeks before.

'Just because. You tell him he'd better be regular till they've got used to him. No good me telling him, is there?' And she smiled at me and ruffled my hair. 'Anyway,' she went on easily, 'he's got plenty of money, hasn't he? Works hard and doesn't spend a penny. What does he do with it all, Lindy? Doesn't seem to spend it on you.'

I was so pleased with her mood that I almost told her he was saving it for fares to Australia, but just then Ted's voice came through the door: 'I reckon I'd like to know that too. What's he do with the money he earns?'

'You'd better ask him yourself.'

Ted was cross and irritated now, or as much as he ever dared with Mother about. 'That boy's getting beyond me, Poppy. Never could get much out of him, but now it's like drawing blood out of a stone to get him to tell you the half of what he's up to. Hey, you,' he called to me suspiciously, 'he ever tell you anything?'

'No, he doesn't,' I lied.

'I used to be pals with that boy,' he went on, whining a little with the misery he didn't dare let out, 'shared everything, we did. But now he won't hardly speak to me.'

'Don't come grumbling to me about him,' Mother said briskly, 'you know what I think.' But she was still much too pleased with the stir and bustle of the dairy to want a row over Jacob, just now, or over anyone else.

Ted went on: 'He's got another think coming. I'm workin day 'n night, and there's him, earnin money an' you'd never know it. I'll charge him rent.'

'He's only been earning a couple of weeks.'

'That's enough out of you, Lindy. And when he does get to talkin he talks a lot of flamin nonsense. Was tryin to tell me the other day that they're goin to use that old airfield again, they're goin to store bombs 'n stuff there, they're goin to have another war. I ask Dook, 'n Dook says it's all a joke. And there's another for you.'

Mother asked mildly: 'What's up with Dook, then?'

'You 'n your Dook,' he went on bitterly. 'Seems to me I'm the sucker. Everyone laughin 'n jokin 'n havin a rare old time. An' me workin 'n worryin, eh? Well, I ain't going to do it, see.' And he actually slammed the kitchen door behind him.

Mother had washed her face and neck and arms in the sink. Now she was drying herself vigorously and feeling all the benefit of that. She said with a laugh: 'Old Ted's fair got the creeps, hasn't he?'

But for all her easy-going friendliness it occurred to me at the time, as I went upstairs to find Jacob and ask what he would like for supper, that we had all of us turned some kind of corner. And when I come to think about it afterwards, and try to set it down as it really was, I believe that this was after all the crossing of a boundary in our lives. Not that I saw it so clearly at the time: I felt the change only as a worry that I could not really grasp. Perhaps there was never any choosing one way or the other: perhaps from the very first we were drawn on and on in such a way that there could never be any getting out of it. I have tried to explain this to Miss Pakeman; but Miss Pakeman says there is no such thing as fate.

ELEVEN YET our day at the seaside, almost the first that year, had been one of our good days. It began well and it ended well; although there was a time, soon after we had got to Frinton, when I thought we might as well go home, we were so miserable. It began well with our roaring honking hurry into Frinton, but after that there seemed nothing to do but walk along the sea front; and you soon get tired of that. Also, there was Al on our hands. Al was a newcomer: unlike Dook and his friend Butch we scarcely knew Al at this time. He had come from America only a few weeks earlier, it seemed; and he was finding it difficult to settle down. The reason for this, according to Dook, was that he missed his home town. Butch said that Al was miserable because he was just naturally born that way. Al said that England didn't suit him: which was easily understood, I thought, because there were times when it didn't suit us either.

Whatever the reason, there was no comfort in Al. Even his crew-cut and the gold bracelet he wore on his wrist failed to give him a cheerful air: there was no getting away from it, he was exceedingly miserable. He was tall and lean, which seemed to make his misery sharper: his arms and legs made strange outward-jutting movements as he walked, agreeing with his discontent; and his grey close-shaven profile, although it was young and handsome, was also cold and disappointed. He was hard to please, but more out of habit than anything else; and even Mary, who was fairly in fits about him, was beginning to be critical. This made him unhappier still. There is nothing worse than being asked what the matter is, when practically everything is the matter: and I could see Al's point of view in this. When he took it out on himself by complaining against Frinton I was quite ready to sympathize with him.

'This place,' he said, 'ain't real.'

I could see what he meant by that, even if I couldn't explain it properly. I tried. 'It's very respectable,' I said.

'Respectable,' Al said, 'what's that?' He had a sawing note in his voice which stood, I think, for all the wrongs that were being done to him.

'Well,' I explained, 'it's people of the better sort that come here. Classy people. Rich people.'

We were leaning in a row against the railings on the front, just where the main road comes up from the railway crossing, opposite the shopping street. We were chewing gum.

Then Butch had to interfere. Butch was altogether different from Al, for he was plump and short and practically incapable of noticing the wrongs that were being done to him, if any; or of minding them even if he did notice. There was an india-rubberiness about Butch that made him rather more than human; and, possibly, rather less too. If Butch ever struck a hard patch in his life he would simply bounce away from it. You couldn't dislike Butch; but then you couldn't exactly like him either. He teased Al continually; and Al took it all as though it were serious. Hard patches in his life hurt Al. Being in England was one of them.

Butch hooted: 'Hey, Al, see what she means!' An ancient motor-car, high and open and as old as the hills, had chugged out of the shopping street. A very respectable lady was driving it. She wore a tweed jacket and a large red hat. Beside her there was a very respectable gentleman with a rather stout face and a funny peaked cap on his head. 'See that model, Al. That's real respectable. That's rich. Yip-peee!' He made a loud noise that was something between a raspberry and a whistle and waved a fat friendly hand at the lady and gentleman in the car, who were upset by this.

'You're making a bad impression,' I said.

Al said sarcastically: 'She says you're making a bad impression, Butch.'

Butch exploded happily: 'Why, that's awful. Am I really making a bad impression?'

'Yes, you are,' I said.

Suzy and Mary took their side at once, or rather they took Butch's side, for Al could scarcely be said to have one – he was taking it out on himself so badly, just then, that he was against everyone and everything – and I had only Dook to support me. Dook was always the peacemaker. He was older than the others, but he was also more sensible. He put his hand gently on my shoulder and gave it a friendly squeeze. 'Okay, fellows: let's get out of here.' Nobody could quarrel with Dook, not seriously: he was a comfortable American. Whenever he smiled he looked funny, and what was more he wanted to look funny, so that you had to smile with him; and his ears flapped out from his fat round face, thick little ears the colour of good cheese, and made him funnier still. He came from somewhere far over in America where they have a lot of pig farms; and I think he must have loved those pigs, for there were times when he looked a little bit like one himself. I was very fond of Dook.

'There's a fun fair at Clacton,' he said.

Al asked: 'That rich and respectable too?' He was still taking it out on himself, and it was hard to know what best to do for him. His feelings were hurt. He looked frostily at Frinton sea front as though it pained him.

'No, that ain't respectable,' Butch said cheerfully, making it worse: 'That's just a dump, fellow. Kinda place for you and me, ain't it, Lindy?'

My feelings were also hurt. 'Well,' I said primly, 'I suppose so.'

Mary squeaked they should take no notice of me. 'Still wetting your drawers, aren't you, love?'

Suzy thought that was very funny, of course, but I said it was vulgar. They were really not much older than I for all their dolled-up faces and their purple eyes and their urchin hair cuts. They had thin white arms, hollow and thin and London-white; and when their skirts flew up, and their skirts were always flying up, I saw they had thin white legs as well; but they cuddled up to Butch and Al, after we had climbed back into Dook's car, like women of Mother's age. Only Mother never cuddled up to men, that I know of: she had them cuddling up to her, if that was what they wanted, or what she wanted, and I think this is why Dook liked her so much. He really liked Mother: nothing that happened later on will make me think otherwise. I wish Mother could have married him and got away from Ted and gone off to America: sometimes I had good dreams of that, and even dreams of me and Jacob visiting them there. I don't suppose, in fact, that Mother would ever have married anyone. If she had, though, Dook would have been the man for her: in the end he would have tamed her with his quiet determined ways, and kept her tamed. He was the only man she ever knew, I think, who could have done it.

I sat close to Jacob in the car, while we were going over to Clacton, and held his hand. I put my skirt hem over our hands so that he should not feel shy. Nobody else took any notice of him: whenever he wanted he had a way of seeming not to be there at all. But I wasn't fooled by that; I knew that he was listening to it all and drawing conclusions.

Al kept on, nagging at himself, about Frinton's being respectable, while Dook tried to make it up to him. 'You don't get it, fellow. It ain't like home. People over here don't love each other like they do at home.' He gave me a careful understanding wink.

'No I don't get it,' Al kept on saying in his sad empty voice. 'She says it's rich. Rich – you could buy this dump without noticin the hole in your pocket. '

'It ain't for sale,' Butch teased. 'Not yet anyway.'

'I just don't get it.'

'Another time,' said Butch, 'another time.' He was really enjoying himself. He held Suzy squashed up close to him and kept his hand inside her blouse. He liked to tickle her and make her giggle. I thought she was a silly girl, for she giggled anyway. When he put his hand up her skirt she giggled even more and slapped him and let him do it again. But once I caught her looking at me seriously. You're scared, I thought, you're new to it.

Al was nagging away: 'What's respectable about it, then?'

'They don't like noise,' I tried to explain.

I felt his empty grey eyes boring into me, and I was sorry for him but a little scared too. Unlike Butch he took no interest in sex that I could see: he just had Mary trying to cuddle up to him out of sheer habit. He was not enjoying himself. 'Noise? Why that old flivver was making more noise than a P.39, wasn't it?'

'Human noise,' I said.

'Aw shut up,' Mary said. 'Don't take no notice of her, Al.' But Al was not really taking notice of any of us. 'It's a dump if you ask me,' he said indignantly, so that you knew he was suffering badly from the bad things that were being done to him, and began biting the nail of his right hand thumb. Mary pulled his hand down from his face, for it was really no fun for her; but he shook it free and put it back again.

Dook said easily: 'Sure it's a dump, Al, that's why we're taking you over to Clacton, isn't it, Lindy?'

'People of the better sort, my ass,' Al complained: 'Want a bomb under 'em, that's what they want. Wake 'em up a bit.'

Butch looked up for a moment. 'Can't drop bombs on dear old England, Al. Got to save 'em all for You Know Who.'

Jacob spoke suddenly: 'Who for?'

'Hi silent, did you actually say something? Here, Al, this boy can speak. You didn't know that, Al, did you? You didn't know this boy could speak?'

'Stop teasing, Butch,' I said.

'Teasing? Who's teasing? I ain't never been more serious. That right, Al? We're *serious* guys.'

Al was muttering, but more to himself than to us: 'Put a bomb under 'em. Wake 'em up a bit. Respectable, my ass respectable.' You could tell that he was suffering from the pain of all those wrongs: he would never otherwise have talked about bombs. Dook never did; and nor did Butch.

Jacob said: 'Who for? Who you savin those bombs for?'

'No one,' I said, squeezing his hand: 'They're only joking.' But he ignored that.

'Oh I dunno,' said Butch, working away inside Suzy's blouse: 'Old Whiskers over there, haven't you heard? We're goin to blow Old Whiskers off the face of the earth. Ain't we, Al? Just you 'n me, any time now. Make the earth a bit more respectable.'

Suzy squeaked: 'Don't, Butch, you'll bust my bra.'

'No I won't then. Never bust a bra in a long working life.'

Jacob asked again: 'When you going to do that?' I squeezed his hand again to make him stop, but no answering squeeze came back. He really wanted to know.

Suzy let out a long little scream, 'Oh Butch, you've bust it then.'

'No I haven't.'

'Yes you have.'

Butch looked inside and said as though he really were surprised: 'Now look at that, will you. There's bad workmanship for you. Can't think what England's coming to. Never you mind, honey, we'll buy you another one.' He grinned happily at us, making fun of himself. 'Wait a minute, though, did that boy actually speak again? He did? Al, did you hear that? Al, you tell him. You're the politician.' He gave us all a broad wink. 'He's in the know, Al is. Soon's he gets back there to the United States they'll be on to him on the phone and they'll say, Al we want you. The President wants you. He wants to know your opinion, Al, he's at your service. Any time you can spare for the President, Al, they'll say, just you come on right over 'n put the old man wise.'

Al said in his grey empty voice: 'We'll do it when we damn well please. Next month if we want to.'

Dook was laughing: 'He means it, Jacob. He'll do it, you'll see.'

'Sure, we'll do it. We got the stuff, haven't we?'

Then we noticed that Suzy was weeping. Butch had already noticed it, and was trying to comfort her because he had torn her bra and was promising to buy her half a dozen new ones if she wanted. 'All in different colours, honey. Black 'n green 'n blue 'n white and what the hell you want.' But Suzy went on quietly weeping. She went on weeping all the way to Clacton;

but Al went on talking too, and between the one and the other we were suddenly very miserable.

'We got the stuff, haven't we?' Al was keeping on: 'Well, what we waitin for? How much longer we got to sit around this goddam dump?' He was really suffering.

Suzy wept and snivelled. 'Don't you cry, honey,' Butch was comforting her, 'we'll buy a storefull of 'em. We'll put them dinky little tits into the classiest bras they got. You won't know yourself. You'll dream you stopped the traffic an' God knows what else.'

Al's voice came boring through just the same: 'We got the stuff in store, haven't we? We got men trained to fly 'em over 'n drop 'em, haven't we?'

Nobody wanted to listen to him. 'You won't know yourself, honest you won't,' Butch was saying: 'You'll think you're one of them stars. We'll buy fur ones for 'em if we got to. Real mink fur. Keep 'em warm in wintertime.'

Dook was laughing to himself but nobody else seemed to think there was anything to laugh about. Mary was getting no change out of Al, and looking daggers at me. 'It's all your fault,' she snapped.

I said: 'You wouldn't dare, Al. Those others have got bombs too.'

Al snorted: 'They can't reach America with 'em, can they?'

Even Butch had forgotten to tease him. 'Just like them stars, honey. We'll put 'em into mink if we got to. We'll put 'em into silk 'n satin. Christ, we'll have 'em framed an' make 'em into a national monument.' But the tears were running fast down Suzy's face, and rouge and eye-black were running after them.

Nothing seemed capable of stopping Al. 'We'll drop 'em over there just when we want, see. Get it over with.' His voice seemed further and further away, and colder and sadder than ever. 'Goddam dump,' he was arguing with himself: 'goddam dump.'

133

Dook was still laughing. 'Mink and bombs,' he said to me 'You think they go together, Lindy?'

Then we were in Clacton at last, driving along the front to the far end where they have the fun fair. I should think it is the best fun fair in the world, although Dook once told me that the fairs in America are bigger and better still. They have shies and competitions and slides, at Clacton, and every sort of slot machine and dodgems and miniature cars you can drive yourself. We went on the dodgems. There was nobody else about, for the season had only just begun, almost the day before I think: so we had those dodgems to ourselves. Jacob and I shared one. We drove into the others and crashed and bumped around and had a fine old time. After that we went off and drank coffee or ginger beer. Suzy had stopped crying and Al had stopped being upset.

Al even took me for a ride in one of the cars you can drive yourself. He drove it seriously as though it were a proper car. I said I was sorry for being rude. Al said not to mind. 'Not your fault, is it? You was born here, wasn't you? Guess we've all got to be born somewhere. Some's luckier than others, that's all.'

He told me that he came from California where the sun always shone and the sky was always blue and you could have the best kind of life in the world, the best kind of life that anyone could have anywhere. He grew happy while he talked of California.

Towards five o'clock Dook said that he had to be getting back. The other two were off duty that evening, so we left the four of them at Clacton. I looked carefully at Suzy when we said goodbye; but I couldn't tell if she was still frightened.

In the car going home – but more for Jacob's sake than mine – I asked Dook: 'Al didn't mean all that about the bombs, did he?'

Dook only grunted in reply to that, but when I pressed him he broke out at last: 'Al – what does he know?' Suddenly he began shouting: 'What do I know? What does anybody know?' Then he cackled into a laughter that was somehow not funny and said more quietly: 'It's all a great big mystery, Lindy, that's what it is. You just don't want to worry your heads about it. There's people taking care of that.' He winked at me. 'Important people too.' I couldn't get another word out of him.

Soon after six we had arrived home and Dook came in with us and banged off a paper bag in Ted's sleeping ear. I felt warm and safe with all the fun of Clacton and the seaside.

PART THREE

ONE

WHEN I come as far as this, remembering what befell us all and trying to set it down, I begin to lose heart. 'Can't you see it a little more clearly?' Pakeman has complained: 'Can't you tell it better?'

She says this to encourage me, for by now she knows quite well that I can't. 'You're rambled on,' she said last night, reading over what I have written, 'but you've scarcely given a picture of the village. Try and get outside yourself a little more, Lindy.'

I know what she means. The other day I read a long article that she herself has written about what happened in our village – she doesn't give the names, of course, so that you could not recognize the people or the places unless you were in the know – and it is true that she has understood it all quite differently from me.

Words for her seem to be real things. For me, at any rate, this considering and remembering has to go into words that do not seem real. I was happy with Jacob – but the word is nothing to what I really felt: and in any case I was happy with him less for anything we had than for what it was obscurely promised that we should have. When I think of myself with him, I think of a promise that seemed to breathe for us in the fluttering leaves of our wood: the promise of a world for us that lay somewhere in the still summer distance beyond the calling of the rooks in Jerman's elms. And when I think of myself without him I think of the sawdust smell of what is dead and rotted: I think of the black trunk on top of the wardrobe in my old room and the lid coming open and the lumps of horror falling dead upon me. Then there is nothing, for me, that ought to be considered and remembered: there is only the slamming shut of day after day.

Then I cannot bear to remember: I wail and beat my head against the wall.

Pakeman looks back calmly into the past. She does not understand, when I tell her, why I have to shut the doors and keep them shut. She keeps on telling me that it will help me if I make myself open them, which is why I have to write everything down: that the pain of remembering will disappear once I have thought things out, that the remembering is like a medicine to cure me with. She says that I am sorry for myself, but that is not true. It is simply that I loved myself only while Jacob loved me.

What she has written about our village is much longer than what I have written. She took notes for weeks on end; but even without the notes she could have described our village. She considers and remembers as though nothing stood in the way. She looks back patiently and widely. But it is not like that for me: I can look back only through small chinks of memory. I cannot push wide the doors no matter how much I try: or when I do contrive to push them quickly open they snap shut again like the badger traps which Thompson used to set in Vixen's Wood, and Jacob and I would regularly spring. That is when I wail and beat my head; and Pakeman, if she is with me, gets hold of me and lays me on the bed.

I bang myself less than I used to: because, she says, the medicine is working, the medicine of remembering what happened. 'You'll survive,' she keeps saying to me, 'you'd survive anything. It's a pure case of natural selection.' She has blonde hair and spectacles and a friendly smile. She doesn't smile at me very often; but when she does I think she really means it. 'The human species,' she had also said, 'would have passed out long ago if it weren't for specimens like you, Lindy.' Which is funny enough when you remember that Mother only had me by mistake.

You have to wonder about people whom you like, and I have wondered about Pakeman. Once, when she was trying to explain to me why Mother had to get down so much with men, the question came rushing out of me faster than I could stop it, and then she blushed and seemed not a day older than her twenty-eight (for that is something she doesn't in the least mind telling), and remarked that that was her own affair, wasn't it? She is plump and nice to look at; and when she smiles it is with all of herself, her lips and eyes and voice and thoughts: yet there is also something hard and difficult in her smile. People ought to like her very much; only she does not quite seem to want them to.

There is a Dr Warden who comes regularly, and I believe that Pakeman is particularly happy when she can be here at the same time; although I am not sure if she would admit this even to herself. Dr Warden is a thin young man who is extremely clever: he is always laughing at little jokes of his own that nobody else can see. Pakeman can't see them either, or I don't think she can: but in spite of that she does not find him tiresome. He has to take an interest in my case, and occasionally they discuss it in front of me.

'Amazing village, after all,' Dr Warden said the other day.

'Well, it was rather, you know.' There is sometimes a little flush in her cheeks when she is talking to Dr Warden, and this makes her prettier still; but Dr Warden thinks far too much of himself even to notice it. 'Pagan, really.'

'Yes, and that Polly Garter – what's her name – Polly Wellin –'

'Poppy,' she corrected him.

'Yes, yes, the central female figure.' He has gold rimmed pince-nez and he can never quite forget how superior he really is. Sometimes I have felt inclined to tell him that anyone could be superior with all the advantages that he has had; but I think it would hurt Pakeman's feelings if I did.

'Extraordinary woman, eh?'

'Oh, you have to see it in pagan terms. You have to see it in terms of a – well, a fertility cult, really.' They can rattle on for hours about my case, and it does seem to bring them a little closer together. 'There's no other word, really, for those orgiastic furies. And that woman – I've never seen anyone like it. The most gloriously female being I have ever set eyes on.'

141

Dr Warden laughed gently, 'Really, now, really?' he said.

He likes hearing her talk of Mother and of Ted and of the rest of that side in our lives; only he is not so pleased when she gets on to Morton and Miss Titheram and Mr Thornton. She really lets herself go about them; but I can see that he doesn't like it. I am trying to summon up courage to tell her about this.

'I tried to make it clear to her,' Pakeman was saying, 'that there are no bad children, only bad parents. Consequently, no bad individuals, only bad societies. But she wouldn't agree, you know?'

He coughed and looked severe. 'No, I suppose not.' You could see that he didn't agree himself.

This is where she ought to have stopped; but she had it in too much for Morton. 'Safe non-conformity – that's their ticket, you know,' she went on, 'Careful mockery of the established order – for that's a guarantee of non-involvement. Yes, but even greater care to keep the mockery subdued. Because revolt, you see, is quite beyond their limp capacity.'

He was arranging himself to seem bored and impatient; but Pakeman really wanted to tell him what she thought about Morton. She rushed on: 'They'll preside at garden parties or judge the vegetables at Harvest Thanksgiving: put them in front of a genuine social problem, and they'll run a mile. Individualism – that's what they'll fling at you. But it's just another word for despair.'

'Ah, would you say that?' he said, and yawned.

'And their houses, you should see them – they give you all the answers. Humble-pretentious, luxury-poor, with little lawns and little pergolas, yapping dogs and a horror of children. Mrs Morton, now. She'd preside over the governor's board of the local primary school – but she'd practically go and hang herself before she'd have sent a child of her own to it. Oh, she was absolutely astonished when she learned where I was educated.'

'Was she, now?' But in my opinion he didn't believe her in the least. She ought to have seen that: I was embarrassed by her not being able to.

'But our primary, I told her, didn't have earth closets when I was a kid. We had a decent board of governors. They bothered. Of course, it wasn't in the country.'

He was now looking exceedingly bored. But he cheered up when Pakeman returned to Mother again. '*She* believed in something anyway. It wasn't much, but it was something. She was about as far from elegant despair as you can imagine.'

'An English pagan goddess,' he suggested with a silly giggle.

'Oh, but yes – that's really what she was – making the lightning flash. And yet herself a product of the storm, you know.'

'Aphrodite and Medusa, perhaps?'

But he could not put her off. 'Oh yes,' she cried, 'something like that. They had an old parson there, it's true – fifteen stone-cold rooms, you know the sort of thing, and a stipend smaller than a farm labourer's – but *he* couldn't do anything. He pushed around three parishes on a bicycle in summer, but in winter he just sat at home and froze. They carried on without him. They went back to the holly and the mistletoe, All that, you know.'

She assailed him with words. 'You know, I really think – a sort of collective madness. A modern hysteria. Catharsis – a longing for catharsis. Such as our world knows how to assuage only in war.'

He took off his pince-nez and fiddled with them. He was trying to seem interested.

She hurried on. 'Yes, that's it, really. And here in that village she – this woman, this extraordinary woman – she erected the Maypole of her pagan cult. She conducted the only kind of war she knew.'

She was really very pretty now, and I think that even he noticed it.

'And there, too, in the midst of it,' she was saying, 'these two children. Could we have saved them? Oh, it's an interesting question. But quite hypothetical. We simply don't have the means. Nor the will either, come to that. They were left to themselves. They pursued their chosen path.'

She has said and written a great deal more about us; and I wish that telling it to Dr Warden would help her with him. But the trouble is that he doesn't really admire her: he doesn't really think she is good enough for him.

And in any case, as you can tell, she has seen it all quite differently from me. It is sometimes hard to recognize what she saw. Yet it is true that we did pursue our chosen path. Only it was not we who chose it.

TWO

SOMEWHERE near the beginning of that path lay the fact that Mother took a mighty pride in her work and was jealous of a rival, any rival. 'They're trying to get rid of me,' she would say from time to time: and 'they', in her opinion, could be almost anyone from Morton to Mr Harold himself. With a trail of bitter feelings left behind her she could still want people to love and cherish her; and when they didn't she was desperately hurt. 'I don't give a so-and-so,' she would go off, blasting and swearing: 'they can take me as I am, or they needn't take me at all. *I* don't care.' But she cared very much.

One day late that Spring, Mother heard from Thompson that he was taking on another dairy hand: one of the Steppins girls from Chudbury, a big girl just out of school. 'She'll be under you, Poppy, of course,' said Thompson: 'you need a bit of extra help, times, don't you?' But he did not fool us with that: we knew that he was taking on Shirley because his wife wished to do her friend Mrs Steppins, Shirley's mother, a kindness. Mrs Thompson was a good farmer's wife, but she liked to play mistress of the manor now and then. I saw Mother give Thompson one of her measuring looks, slow and hard. She said it would be all right with her; but that did not fool us either.

Of course I knew Shirley Steppins, and tried to comfort

Mother on the way home. 'She's a good worker. She'll help you with the churns.'

Mother replied gaily: 'Got a lot to learn, haven't you, Lindy?'

And in this she was right: for no sooner had Mrs Thompson persuaded Thompson to take on Shirley as Mother's assistant than Mrs Steppins spread it around the village that Shirley's reputation would suffer from being put to work under Mother. I had it from Mick Lissard whose sister went with another of the Steppins girls.

I protested: 'But they knew she'd have to be under Mother, didn't they?'

Mick could never keep a secret from me. 'They don't like Poppy,' he explained, 'they're going to take her down a bit. They're going to get her out of the dairy.' I said it was a shame.

'It's the Americans, Lin.'

'What's wrong with them?'

'Always round your place.'

'Why shouldn't they be? They don't do any harm.'

But Mick lost courage. 'I ain't going to say any more, Lin.' And I could not make him, either; although I tried. I wasn't very good at trying: but then you wouldn't normally have had to be, not with Mick, only on this occasion I could not wring another word from him.

When it reached Thompson's ears he declared it was a deal of nonsense, and if they didn't want Shirley to work under Mother then they should never have asked him to employ her in the first place. He said that he wasn't going to risk losing his best worker by taking her out of the dairy: he wouldn't shift Mother, and if Shirley couldn't be under Mother then she could go and work for someone else. To do him justice, he would listen to no argument about this. Mick told me that Mrs Thompson had even gone to the length of provoking a proper flaming row with him; but I do not actually believe this.

Having failed with Thompson they did the next best thing, from their way of looking at it, and got Shirley to leave Jerman's and try for work in Rolcaster. Now you might imagine that Mother would have welcomed this, for although it again gave her more to do it also left her quite to herself, which was what she most liked. But that was not the way she took it. I was present in the dairy when Thompson told her. 'Don't mind, do you, Poppy?' he added: 'Nothing but a lot of trouble, that girl.' He stood nearby while Mother worked, his tiny head cocked forward a little on his tall thin shoulders, his long arms flapping uselessly beside him. I could see that he was afraid of Mother's tongue, but still more of his wife's.

Mother made no answer at first. She was milking, for the electric milker had broken down the day before, and the cows were having to be worked by hand. This is hard work even when it is irregular: and Mother, who had not milked regularly for months, even for years, because Mr Harold was always one for putting in machinery and had had electric milkers ever since I could remember, was fairly sweating with the effort. Her scarlet headscarf struck a bright patch against the cow's black flank; I remember this well because a shaft of daylight from the cowshed windows made it sharp and brilliant. Thompson might not have seen how tired she was: perhaps he only saw that brilliant scarf and the stubborn shift of Mother's arms and shoulders as she milked.

She went on milking. I was quite close to her, close enough to see better than Thompson the taut set of her neck and shoulders and the ripple in her arms while her hands thrust up and down beneath the cow's belly. But perhaps Thompson could guess all that: perhaps he could guess, from where he hovered near the cooling-room door, how beautifully she worked, and tirelessly, and well. Now that I look back on those days I think that one truth about Mother was that she loved to make her body work as it was meant: she loved her own strength and all the things that she could do with it, whether it was working or dancing or milking a cow or getting down with a man. And for these things she could do so well – for all these things, in my opinion – she liked to be approved and praised. You might call it her weakness.

Thompson wandered in from the cooling-room door, hesitating, and stood beside her for a while. He coughed and began to say something, changed his mind and shut up again. Then he went away and leant carefully against one of the cowshed posts: he always did things carefully. He stood there for a bit, looking at Mother with his tongue curling out and licking his thin lips, and snivelled once or twice; and these snivels were another echoing noise behind the pissing of the cow's milk into the pail and the occasional shuffling in straw or rattling of headchains or shifting of hoofs that go hollowly with cows in a milking shed. Then he said carefully, staring hard at her: 'You're a fool to mind, Poppy. You're worth the lot of 'em.' He was suddenly a little short of breath.

But Mother was too upset to notice that, or, if she did notice it, to care as she might otherwise have done. She simply pulled her head from the cow's glossy flank, out of that dazzling shaft of light, and looked across at Thompson leaning there, and said nothing. Now I could plainly see the weariness in her face, and how beads of sweat had dimpled her neck and made channels through downy dust that lay upon her white skin, and ran beneath her blouse. Before Thompson had come into the shed she had unbuttoned the top of her blouse and tucked it back, beneath her milking coat, so that it might have seemed to anyone coming in as though she had nothing on beneath. Thompson was staring at her white skin; but she paid no attention. I think she had altogether forgotten about having unbuttoned her blouse: she was never one to imagine she needed that kind of aid to attraction. She drew her bare forearm over her brows, let her hands go limp on her knees, and said at last that she was fair sick of this place, if he really wanted to know. When she said this I grew frightened, and began shivering; for she looked scared and wretched and beaten, and I had never seen her like that before. I suppose it was another of the moments when

147

children grow up. I almost pitied her then: it meant, I suppose that I almost loved her.

Thompson said in his thin high-pitched voice: 'Don't you be a fool, Poppy.' He was staring at her carefully: his tongue made little regular circling movements round his lips.

Mother replied sharply: 'Work for two, is that it?'

'You done it before, didn't you?' But he added quickly: 'I wouldn't mind asking Mr Harold for some more money. Sets a lot of store by you, Mr Harold.' Thompson had his share of craftiness too: he couldn't have survived as Jerman's manager otherwise, for Mr Harold was a tetchy man for all his generosity.

Mother was staring down at her hands. Perhaps after all she was only resting.

'Mr Harold knows you're a worker, Poppy. Don't you be a fool, now, and do anything silly.'

But Mother said slowly, and almost as though surprised at herself: 'Don't know as I want more money.' Her shoulders seemed to curve in and sag with weariness; it struck me horribly that she might even be in tears. When she looked up again I saw that it was only the sweat in her eyes. Thompson was pleading with her: 'Now don't you be a fool, Poppy, don't you be a fool.'

Mother was silent again, so he levered himself away from the post and came round to the other side of the cow she was half-way through milking, and stood looking down at her. He stared hard at her. She might have seen him staring at her, but she seemed not to care.

Thompson went on coaxing her, pleading with her, and all this in a strangely womanish way in spite of his staring eyes and agitation. After a while she put back her head and returned his look.

'You're worth the lot of 'em, Poppy,' he was saying: 'There ain't one to touch you.'

She let him look at her: at her white throat and her white bosom where the milking coat had fallen open; but as though he were a doctor, and not a man like all the other men. I sat as still as a mouse. I felt that I ought not to see her like this, exposed in misery and defeat, almost like a child.

'They'd don't want me here, do they?'

Thompson's eyes were narrow points of eagerness. 'You don't want to worry, Poppy. Who cares if they do or don't?'

She would not let it go. 'It's my place as much as theirs, isn't it?'

'Of course it is, Poppy.' You might have thought the pressure of his eyes would have bored into her body; but I do not think she as much as noticed he was looking at her.

'They don't want me here,' she repeated.

He was somehow holding himself back. 'There's others,' he let out carefully: 'there's others as do.'

He must have known her better than I thought. But she clung to that beaten mood. 'I'd like to see 'em work this dairy, for all their big talk.'

'They couldn't do it, Poppy. You know that, my love.' But he said it with affection. He said it as though he really liked and wanted her for her own sake.

Mother saw him as he was, then, or let herself see it, and put up her hands to her coat and buttoned it across in front: suddenly, jumping from one mood into the next, she smiled and said almost gaily: 'Well, you see about a rise, Tommy, and I'll think about it.' I got up in a hurry to fetch another pail, now that her mood had changed; and when I came back from the cooling room she was calling something to him that made him laugh and preen: now he looked as pleased with himself as he could ever be, and started for the milkshed door as though he noticed for the first time that I was there too. Mother thrust her hands beneath the cow's belly and butted her head gently into the cow's flank. The cow looked round, swished its tail and was motionless again. Milk began hitting into the pail.

Thompson went striding out of the shed, shouting as though he had made his fortune: 'It's all right, Poppy. I won't let you down.'

After him Mother called: 'You'd better not.' And then she actually began whistling. I was relieved, but all the same I did not quite believe it, and found myself creeping behind her on tiptoe until I could catch a glimpse of her face. When she saw what I was doing she looked at me a little sharply, but changed her mind and smiled with all the confidence she usually had. After that she worked on as though she had only just begun, and took no notice of me for at least half an hour.

I sat waiting. Soon she had nearly finished. Then we heard Thompson come stumping into the cooling-room again; and Mother, who was well on with the work, looked pleased to have him there. She pointed to the filled pail: 'Get in with this one, Lindy, will you?' As she pushed the hair from her black brows, I saw that her face was glistening and her brown eyes were alight with the swing and effort of working quickly: by now she was in one of her best moods. Thompson stalked past me as I hobbled into the cooling-room with the heavy swirling pail of milk: he had his head cocked up, his funny little pinhead, and cried cheerfully: 'Good for you, Poppy. Won't know the difference, the boss won't. Might's well do without that old milking machine altogether, what with you about.'

'No you bloody well don't,' Mother said: 'or else you pay me double.'

He cackled with enjoyment. From the cooling-room door I could see them half-way down the narrow corridor between the backsides of the cows, Thompson again leaning his long body on one of the posts, and Mother sitting with her head thrown up as she looked at him through dusty sunlight. Thompson was delighted with himself: I had never seen the like, for usually he was a careful man who said the least that could be said, and that without any pleasure. He was laughing now as though quite unaccustomed to it: the noise of it came in sharp hiccups down the corridor between the cows, hiccups that jerked back the sharp chin on his gristly neck. As I returned with the empty pail I saw Mother's eyes gleaming with the glee of mischief that she had, now and then, when Dook or one of the others was around: she was not so much looking at Thompson as looking, it appeared to me, wonderfully through him. I was taken by surprise, for Thompson was a lean unhandsome man, not a bit the sort of man to take Mother's fancy, I should have thought, who liked men best when they were round and strong and full of jokes and laughter.

She was saying to him: 'Hey, Tommy, it's *me* that's getting this rise, isn't it?' At that he fairly bent with the effort of bringing up his hiccups: they sounded so painful that I wondered if he were laughing or taken with a fit. 'That's a good one, Poppy, that's a good one,' he hiccuped. His big flapping hands slapped floppily on his knees.

He cackled away for a time, until I came down the corridor with the pail when he stopped as suddenly as he had begun, shouted that he was going over the counting house to see if he could find Mr Harold, and said that Mother should send me to tell him when the last cow was milked.

Mother was not really laughing, but I could see that she was ready to be pleased with herself again. As I walked by with the pail she called to me in a suddenly soft voice that my hair ribbon was undone, and I had better come to her and let her re-tie it for me. It was the first time for weeks that she had spoken to me with this particular voice, a voice that warmed me whenever I heard it but also sent a tremor of warning down my spine. I waited patiently while she re-tied it, and I thanked her as well as I could.

Suddenly I felt her arms embracing me. 'Come on, Lindy,' she was whispering with her lips in my hair: 'Say something nice to me, won't you? We're doing all right.'

I was so much overcome, and perhaps so much excited with the warm clasp of her arms about me, that I could think of nothing to say. I was quite thrown out, and for want of words caught clumsily at her hand and kissed its firm brown skin.

Mother was still laughing, but she pushed me away roughly:

'Funny little fish, aren't you? Can't even kiss me properly.' Yet in spite of her disappointment she was trying to like me, then; and afterwards, remembering that, it seemed to make the consequences sadder still.

THREE I TOOK another pail, one of the last, into the cooling room, and had scarcely emptied it when I was surprised to see Mrs Thompson coming through the other door, not from the milking shed but from the yard. At first she appeared not to notice me in the dimmed light of the cooling room. But that was a day of black bad luck.

My feeling uncomfortable with Mrs Thompson came in the ordinary way, I suppose, from the fact that she was really two sorts of people. She was a kindly woman who was always ready to do a good deed quietly if she got the chance, an excellent farmer's wife who was everybody's friend, and even Mother's friend from time to time, just so long as no one questioned her position. Mostly, of course, no one would have thought of questioning her position, because being Thompson's wife she was certainly placed in a higher position than the rest of us, and it was only natural that Mrs Thompson should have valued this. She had a right to our respect.

There were times, though – and this was certainly one of them – when she came out in a different way: beyond her own doorstep, as it were, and dressed for going to Rolcaster she was what a number of people could not stand at any price – what my aunt Pooley called an old ewe dressed up lamb-fashion. Then she was as touchy as a cow in season, for people laughed at her, and she naturally hated that. Mother was just as naturally one of those who laughed the most.

Mrs Thompson stood finely dressed at the cooling room door,

blinking until she properly saw me. 'You're Mrs Wellin's girl, aren't you?' she said then: 'Is Mr Thompson about?' Yet I had time to be sorry for her tight blue dress and her awkward new shoes and the weary glitter of suspicion behind her silver-rimmed glasses.

'He's up at the counting house, Mrs Thompson.'

'You're a little girl for staring, aren't you?' she said angrily: 'What are you doing here, anyway?'

But just then Mother shouted for me. I went back to answer her. When I returned from the milking shed with another full pail, I saw that Mrs Thompson had taken a few steps into the cooling room and that Mrs Steppins, Shirley's mother, had joined her. Mrs Steppins shook her head and muttered to Mrs Thompson as I came in.

I said: 'I'm carrying milk for Mother, Mrs Thompson.' We had really worked hard that morning.

I put the pail down. I had to put it down in front of them because they were standing between me and the cooling chamber and they would not move: they looked down into the pail as though wanting to be sure that it carried milk and not water. Mrs Steppins said: 'Laura, I'm surprised to see it that dirty. I thought you was extra particular about dirt an' that.'

So it was really Mrs Steppins's fault, as you can see; for Mrs Thompson, in the usual run of things, was far too good a farmer's wife to have interfered over the farmer's head. Only it happened by misfortune that Mrs Thompson was dressed for going out; and going out with Mrs Steppins, furthermore, who was not quite up to her position. This was agreeable to Mrs Thompson as well as to Mrs Steppins, for she liked doing good to people; and going out with Mrs Steppins who was beneath her position did good to Mrs Steppins. But even I could tell, as we stood in front of that pail, that Mrs Thompson could not possibly have Mrs Steppins finding dirt in Jerman's milk, and pretending to be surprised and critical and no longer being done good to: she had to set that right.

'Mr Thompson *is* very particular,' she said, 'we've never had dirt in our milk that I know of.'

I explained: 'The machine's broken. And there isn't any dirt.'

'Nobody asked your opinion, Lindy,' Mrs Steppins said.

Mrs Thompson was peering at the milk. 'Well, I don't see any dirt in it, Mildred.'

'Don't you, Laura? Well, it's no business of mine, I'm sure.' She liked to copy Mrs Thompson's manner of speaking.

'Well, I'm sure if there is any dirt –' Mrs Thompson had bent over the pail until I feared that her glasses might fall into it. 'I must say I don't see any dirt, Mildred.'

'I'm sorry, dear,' Mrs Steppins replied, allowing herself a superior voice that she would never have used in the ordinary way: 'There is some, though.' She pointed with a mauve-gloved finger. The three of us stared into the milk; and it was true. A fragment of dried cowdung floated there. I should never have believed it.

I said quickly that it was my fault, and looked at Mrs Steppins as crossly as I was able; but that did not the slightest good. For she was really the same kind as Mother, only not properly built for it: fair and plump, with wide blue eyes and a pouting red mouth, she somehow carried her body about with her as though it were an everlasting worry, like a mother with a misbehaving child. This worry that she carried in her body seemed to nag at her so that she had to nag at other people, to relieve herself: mostly she nagged at her daughter Shirley. Lately she had taken to nagging Shirley for trying to look grown-up, although it was hardly Shirley's fault for developing a figure that made the fellows in Rolcaster turn and whistle. Mrs Steppins might have wanted to go Mother's way of independence, but I suppose the years slipped by until it was too late for that, and perhaps she regretted it: but in any case she failed of Mother's terrible determination and of Mother's body too, so she had to go the other way, the way of bettering herself. But this worried her as well: between the one thing and the other, Mrs Steppins was a mass of worry. People laughed at her for putting on airs; and that upset her. Mother laughed at her for not succeeding with men; and perhaps this upset her a good deal more.

I thought vainly of a way of keeping them apart: vainly, for Mother chose this moment to come in. But that is no way of putting it. She swayed in like a princess, slowly and taking her time, relaxing from her work, not looking where she went, not caring either. The warmth and speed of all that morning's toil was alight in rosy splendour on her cheeks and arms and neck: her long black hair glowed fine and glossy, and all her skin had the dew-rough firmness of a healthy peach, smooth and good to see. Even without shoes, for she had kicked them off on the step of the cooling room door, her ankles were slim and long. It was never any wonder that men loved her so much: looking at her now, I almost loved her myself.

She made them both seem pale and tired beside her. To my mind she made them both seem old and sad as well, with their flesh not clean and fine upon them but sorry and sagging; for as she came in – thinking herself alone with me – she threw back her head and mopped the sweat from her throat and neck, pushed back her milking coat and dabbed between her bosom so that the blouse slipped away and showed one naked breast that was round and white and wonderfully firm. I heard Mrs Steppins, who was just behind me, utter a small sighing noise; and then Mother looked up and saw them and burst into a laugh.

'Lord bless me, Mrs Thompson,' she said, pulling her coat together, 'you goin up to see the Queen or summat?'

They could only stare at her. I felt myself starting to tremble. But Mother was still warm and glowing; and pleased with herself, ready to be friends with them.

'Sorry for showin myself in front of ladies,' she went on gaily. 'Didn't know anyone was here but Lindy.'

Mrs Steppins giggled nervously, 'So long's you don't show yourself in front of gentlemen.'

'Oh, I shouldn't mind doing that now.'

She meant it for a joke, of course: she was pleased with herself. But Mrs Steppins took it seriously. She giggled and said: 'Well, I'm just as glad my husband don't work here.'

I saw that Mother was uncertain how to answer. In the end she said airily: 'I'll bet you are, Mildred.'

'There's no need to be rude.'

'Was I rude?' She burst out laughing again. They must have felt how soft and faded they were beside her: I don't see how they could have helped feeling it. 'Sorry, we've had a proper morning of it.' I was suddenly angry with them for teasing her when she had worked so hard.

I suppose Mrs Thompson had to say something, what with being dressed up for going to Rolcaster and having Mrs Steppins with her. She pointed to the pail where the scrap of cowdung floated. 'We don't like dirt in our milk, Mrs Wellin.'

Mother seemed dreadfully cast down. I wanted to shout at them for making her miserable. 'Sorry,' she said at last, 'machine's broken.'

It ought to have gone off quietly, even so; for Mrs Thompson was a sensible woman who understood the toil of milking by hand. Only now there was Mrs Steppins with her mass of worry; and there was also this thing of being made to seem soft and sorry just as she was dressed up for going to Rolcaster.

Mrs Steppins said: 'Makes me shudder, dirt in the milk an' that.'

Mother was never one for staying cast down. She always hit back. She said: 'You come and work these bloody cows yourself, then.'

Mrs Steppins pretended not to hear this but turned to Mrs Thompson, who looked boiling hot with the tightness of her dress even though the cooling room was cold, and said they should hurry now or they would miss their bus.

Mother stooped down and pulled at one of the cooling chamber doors. It always opened stiffly, but now she swung it back with a vicious click so that it caught Mrs Steppins on the soft part of her thigh. Mrs Steppins squawked and went hopping on one leg, rubbing the hurt place with her mauve-gloved hand. I had to laugh; and that made matters worse.

'Mind yourself,' Mother said rudely, pushed Mrs Steppins aside and seized the pail that I had carried in, the pail with the cowdung floating in it.

Mrs Thompson called sharply: 'There's dirt in that, Mrs Wellin.'

But Mother now was in a fine rage. 'You keep out of my way when I'm working,' she snapped. Her milking coat had come unbuttoned again and she had forgotten to button her blouse.

Mrs Steppins said: 'You always go half naked here, Poppy?'

'It's more than you'd dare to, with a shape like yours.' I was trembling worse than ever: I was really worried now. They should have known better than to go provoking Mother who could never stop herself from answering back. Besides, it was terribly unjust.

'At any rate I wouldn't show myself to every pair of trousers in the place,' said Mrs Steppins; and now they were back at their old quarrel. I ran across to Mrs Thompson and caught her hand; and the two of us stood there, hand in hand, while Mother and Mrs Steppins went for each other.

'They wouldn't care if you did.'

They stood there with a hot and sudden hatred that you could feel inside your own body: Mother with her chest sticking out as though challenging Mrs Steppins to show as much, Mrs Steppins with her hands clutched nervously in front of her, a pale and frightened look on her face.

'You're a proper bitch, aren't you, Poppy?'

Mother said nothing.

'What they give you for doin it, eh?'

Mother still said nothing. But she did not button up her coat. She stood there with her white arms hanging loosely and her hands a little clenched. I thought she was going to hit Mrs Steppins.

I began stuttering to Mrs Thompson that she should stop them; and Mrs Thompson evidently thought so too, for she called out to them that that was enough, and Mildred had better come along, there was the bus to catch.

Mrs Steppins seemed not to hear this. 'Well, go on, then, cover yourself up. It's nothing to me.'

Mother could be very vulgar when she wanted. She poked a hand suddenly at Mrs Steppins's soft flesh. 'Isn't it?' she said. 'Seems it ought to be.' Mrs Steppins slapped her face. Mother slapped her back.

I must have screamed, for someone cuffed me, probably Mrs Thompson; and then a man's voice, Thompson's voice, was shouting at us. He came running in, tripping on his long thin legs, and rushed up to them and somehow got between them. He was shouting at his wife: 'Laura, how many times I tell you –' And suddenly they were all quiet.

In that quietness Mrs Thompson's voice was heard softly, apologetically, admitting herself in the wrong for interfering but not liking the admission: 'There was dirt in the milk.'

'Well, I shouldn't wonder as there was dirt in the milk, seeing she had to milk 'em all by hand.' He was properly enraged with them, or he made himself seem to be. Yet even though he had a right to be enraged, and Mrs Thompson in her decent honesty could not help admitting it, there was none the less something odd and difficult in his having the upper hand of her through defending Mother. I think we all understood that.

I was dreadfully embarrassed. Thompson swivelled his funny little head from Mrs Steppins to his wife, and then back again to Mother. 'Well, I don't know,' he said indignantly, 'Poppy done a morning's work if ever anyone did. You want to leave her alone, don't you?' Yet it was saying, just then, a little more than he should have said.

For the trouble was that he could not take his eyes from Mother, and Mother had forgotten to do up her coat again. She stood there in forgetfulness, looking up at him with the puzzled frown of surprise that overcame her whenever anyone unexpectedly defended her, her white arms hanging loosely at her side and her coat lying open so that the curve of her breast and the coloured arc of its strong nipple stood out from it firmly and nakedly. And suddenly it appeared that nothing else would matter but this small simple fact: that Thompson had seen her naked breast and that Mrs Thompson knew that he had seen it, and that this put Mother hopelessly and finally in the wrong.

Mrs Steppins said slyly: 'You want to cover yourself up, Poppy.'

Mother realized it then, and savagely pulled the coat across her chest and throat; but not before the damage was done and duly registered.

We heard Mrs Thompson say chokingly: 'I don't look for that kind of behaviour here.'

'What's that, Laura?' But already he had lost the upper hand of her: already he was guilty, and she knew it.

Mother, in all innocence, finished it off herself. She said to him quietly, sincerely, without a trace of anger: 'They don't want me here, Tommy, I told you that.' She said it without guile, as resting on a confidence she had in him; and somehow this nakedness was even more provoking than the nakedness of her breast had been.

Mrs Thompson broke in sharply: 'Tommy is it? Tommy, did you say? Who's Tommy, then?'

He should have stood up to her, but he could not bring himself to that. 'You're acting stupid,' he said sulkily.

He wilted while she glared her accusation. They must have known each other very well, and perhaps they had long since grown tired of what they knew. I don't know: you can never really tell. People suddenly uncover themselves: but what you see, even then, may be only half the truth – may even be the lesser half. They had lived together for a long time.

Mother's clear hard voice rang out: 'Tommy! You can see it's like I said, they don't want me here.' Even now, I think, she was innocent of wanting to hurt them; she was only defending herself, she was only longing for him to defend her too.

'Like she said?' Mrs Thompson began to let her anger loose. She could do that now: she had a reason to be angry, or she thought she had. 'I'd be glad to know what that means "Like she said".'

He tried again. 'Laura, you stop being silly, will you?' Even now, retreating though he was, he could not quite allow himself to abandon Mother: he was a fair man, whatever his lusting after her, and he knew how well she had worked that day.

Mrs Steppins had walked across to Mrs Thompson: now they were standing together, looking over at Thompson and at Mother with accusing anger. It was easy for them now.

Mrs Steppins called out: 'Laura, you'd better come on. They want to be alone, seems like.'

Thompson fumbled with words: to no avail, for what Mrs Steppins said seemed undeniably the fact. And Mother, cost her what it might, could not resist this triumph of being defended. She smiled up at Thompson, looming and hovering above her, and appeared beside their dowdiness more beautiful than ever, slim and strong and marvellously graceful in spite of her milking coat and her soiled bare feet. Her brown eyes were mild and trusting as she looked up at him, her mouth was soft and true: the whole sweetness of youth seemed to inhabit her. He loomed and hovered and could not drag himself away.

'How long,' demanded Mrs Thompson at last, clutching the words from her anger and confusion, 'how long has it been like this?'

He shook his head hopelessly. 'Don't you be stupid, Laura,' he repeated, 'don't you be stupid.'

But Mother ignored that. She nodded up at him, wretchedly hovering, and gave him another sweet smile and said something quietly to him that the rest of us could not overhear. Then she turned slowly on her heel, the milk coat swinging at her bare legs, and went to fetch her shoes at the cowshed door. Having put them on, she went on through the door without another word. I could only run out after her, knowing that she thought she had won, knowing that she had not. I remember that moment, even now, with a breathless terror.

For this was how we began the next part of our lives. Two or three days later, to Mother's amazement, Thompson wretchedly gave her a week's money, some penitential words, and the sack.

I HAD walked over to Chudbury for groceries.
FOUR 'There's young Mick Lissard was looking for you,' Mrs Hampton said.

'What's he want?'

'Didn't say. Come on his bicycle.'

He was waiting for me outside Chudbury village where the road forks for the bigger one to Saffron Walden and the smaller one to Rolcaster. It is a favourite place for waiting and meeting, especially in the summer, with a comfortable wooden bench large enough for two that is placed on the grass verge beneath high beech trees, and commemorates the Coronation: that is why, they say, the Council always has to repair it. Mick was sitting on the back of this bench and kicking through one of the seat laths. It is quite true that the Council always does repair it.

'You looking for me?'

'They sacked Poppy.'

'Who did?'

'Thompson done it.'

'Did it,' I corrected him. I can remember correcting him.

'Give her a week's money and told her Mr Harold wouldn't let her stay.'

'That's not true,' I said: 'I'll bet Mr Harold never knew a word of it.'

Mick had given up kicking through the lath: he looked

terribly disappointed. 'Ain't you surprised, Lindy? I come over case you didn't know.'

'Thank you, Mick. No I didn't know.'

'But you ain't surprised?'

'Of course I'm surprised.'

'You don't *seem* like it.'

I sat down by him and got out my handkerchief and blew my nose. A year ago or not much less I might have burst out crying: but now I felt not in the least like doing that, and I remember even thinking what a good thing it was that I had grown up at last. But I was glad to sit down because my legs had started to tremble. I asked him where Mother was.

'Well, I dunno where she *is*. I only know she got the sack and everyone's talking of it.'

'I expect they say she deserved it, don't they?'

He fidgeted beside me on the back of the seat, and began kicking at the lath again. I watched him: somehow it grew important to us both that he should kick it through. 'That's what Jacob says.'

'Does he? Jacob?' But I had known it all beforehand, or as good as known it: not only this, that Mother was in trouble and Jacob would never in the least admit to understanding why nor want to help to make the trouble less, but would do whatever he could to make it more: but also, numbly, distantly, many other things. There are such moments when you can almost see the past and the present and the future as being one and the same, just as if no time but now existed: and you are standing outside of everything and looking in, seeing it all at once.

Sitting there then with Mick it seemed to me that my life must always be like this: that there would be nothing, in the end, to be sung for nor wept for, but only the *need* to go on living. That surviving, if you like, is the true glory: surviving as yourself, as what you ought to be and to become, no matter what the world may do to you or try to do to you. And when I look back on all this time, then and later, it is not the trials

162

that came upon us nor this fact of Mother's being sacked that I remember, but the long dark curve in the road that goes into Chudbury beneath the solemn beech trees – the road a little wet with the morning's rain and the trees above us filling out with summer leaves, and me sitting beside Mick Lissard on that bench as though everything had happened already, and nothing in the world could stop it.

Mick's foot went splintering through the lath; but now I did not care about that. I felt released. My legs stopped trembling. Above us the beech trees spread their cloud of fluttering leaves and above the leaves the sky was clearing for an early summer's day. It was like knowing the truth: it was like not needing any longer to be afraid. I cannot really explain it.

I said gently: 'Come on, Mick. We'll be late for dinner else.'

'Gimme the bag, Lindy.'

We walked back home together.

FIVE

TED took the news just as you would expect. That is to say, he took it with the least possible trouble to himself. He came home about seven from driving to Rolcaster, uncorked a fresh bottle of whisky, and sat by the fire while Mother told him of it. Ted had none of my worries about the past and the future: he forgot the past as soon as it was gone and he never thought about the future. I suppose he dreamed of it instead.

Of course he couldn't see what was eating into Mother: it was the sort of thing that never would have eaten into him. 'If it's rainin in Brummagem, it'll be clear in Hull,' was one of his favourite sayings: 'You've got the choice.' It was somehow evident that Ted would always have the choice, or at any rate would always take it. Trouble, for Ted, was something that worried other people because they stayed in Brummagem instead of going to Hull. Trouble and Ted might collide with each other: you couldn't imagine them being deliberately hand in hand. I suppose that was why, even at the best of times, Ted never seemed quite real. I understood Mother very well in this.

She talked bitterly while he enjoyed his whisky. The difference from Ted, of course, was that trouble and Mother not only went hand in hand, they fiercely clung to one another. This business of going to Hull it if rained in Brummagem was quite hopeless for her: she couldn't have brought herself to accept a first class ticket if you'd offered it to her. She would take the rain as an insult: as a challenge to stay where she was.

'I'm not running out of here,' she informed Ted squarely, 'so you needn't think it. No matter what they do, I'm not running out.'

Ted was not disturbed. 'No, of course you're not, Poppy. Don't have to run out, do you? Independent freeholders, aren't we?' He stood with his whisky in front of the fire, a thumb hooked into the armhole of his handsome red-and-grey check waistcoat, and held forth gravely: 'Pay our rates and taxes, don't we? Bless you, they'll be askin us to vote next time there's an election. And we'll do it, eh? We'll vote proper, just like we ought. We'll vote for the farmer's man, won't we, the farmer's man 'n property 'n that. We got the country's good at heart, bless 'em.'

But he might as well have talked to a brick wall. Mother gazed into the fire as though she had heard nothing. He went on, trying again: 'That cove Morton votes Labour, they say, and his missus votes Liberal. They don't know what's good for 'em, that's their trouble. I shouldn't think that cove Morton ever soiled hisself with a day's work, not what you'd call work. And then he goes 'n votes Labour.'

I couldn't help asking: 'What do you call work, Ted?'

He was delighted to have someone else to address, for his eyes kept shifting unhappily towards Mother: he was longing to wriggle out of listening or of having to take notice of her trouble.

'Aye, Lindy, there's a question now. Well, I'll tell you. There's all kinds of work. Now you might ask what kind of work is my work? I'll tell you.' He was beginning to enjoy himself: he loved standing in front of the fire and talking, just talking. 'My kind of work is brain work.' He tapped his old grey head. 'Working with this, see. They call it enterprise. And when you got your own business, like I got, they call it private enterprise.' He swigged the whisky down and poured another, wiped his mouth with a blue silk handkerchief and went on rather quickly, slipping a glance at Mother and slipping it away again. 'Stands to reason, don't it? You get me working day and night, don't you, seven days a week?' He stared at me with suddenly anxious eyes: there were moments when his own sayings seemed to puzzle and astonish him. Then he frowned, grinned, and relaxed again. 'That's it, Lindy, you can't get away from it. But you take any of them labourers over there in the *Wheelwright*. You take them builders what are doing up Jerman's place. And you ask yourself: are they working or are they not? And you've got the answer soon's you've asked the question. They are not working. They goes through the motions. And that's the difference, see? That's public enterprise, got it? That's what we're payin taxes for.'

He was well away now: Mother might as well have lost the power of speech. 'Now there's Poppy here. You take Poppy. Gets the sack for no fault of her own, eh? Under public enterprise what'll she do? She'll go on the dole. She'll go on the perishin dole.' He cackled with sudden laughter. 'Poppy love, you'd go on the dole, wouldn't you? Christ, I'd like to watch it, I would.' I saw Mother give him one of her slow measuring looks; he saw it too. 'Okay, Poppy, don't you get worked up. I was only tryin to say –' He could not meet her eyes; he suddenly lost his thread. 'Lindy, what was I tryin to say?'

'You said she would go on the dole.'

165

'Well, if I said that I was a perishin fool. No no, Lindy, what I was tryin to say is that she's got me to pervide for her, see?'

Mother said abruptly: 'Sit down in that chair, Ted, and stop prancing round like an old goat. You make me sick and tired.'

He did not mind that: if anything, he rather liked it. He sat down but continued: 'Stands to reason, though. We got business goin along nicely now, what with one thing 'n another. I told you there wasn't no need to go on workin, didn't I?'

She was looking up at him now as though she meant to clout him.

'What's up, eh?'

'Didn't you hear me, Ted Breldon? I said I wasn't running out, didn't I?'

'Well I dunno. Strikes me if you can't make a go of it in one place, you might's well try another. If it's rainin in Brummagem –'

'If you say that again I'll hit you. Besides, I don't care how it strikes you.'

She had her arms tightly clasped over her chest: her face was hard and brilliant: she could put fear into you when she was like this. I recognized the signs.

His confidence changed to coaxing persuasion. 'You don't have to go anywhere, Poppy, not if you don't want to. You stay here 'n take it easy 'n put your feet up. There's plenty of money comin in, isn't there?' She said nothing to that. He went on: 'All I was sayin was that we could take a little trip some-time, you 'n me. Lindy here can go 'n stay with her auntie, can't you, Lindy, over to Chudbury? Jacob's no trouble. That boy can look after hisself.'

I asked: 'Where you going, Ted?'

He lounged back again, easier now, and settled into another favourite groove. 'Go anywhere we like. Cove in Rolcaster was tellin me. You go up to London to a place they got there and you get y'rself a passport. You say, I want a passport, I'm going to take a trip. And they say, Where you want to go, Mr Breldon, sir? And you say, everywhere. Just like that. Everywhere. And they gives you this passport with it written into so's you can go everywhere. Cost you a quid.'

'That'll cost you two quid, then.'

'You're right. Poppy'll want one too. Seein as we aren't regularly hitched up, like.' He grinned at Mother. 'You only got to say the word, my love.'

'What about your other wives, Ted?'

He cackled at that and shook his head. 'You're wrong there, Lindy. Been savin myself up. All these years, for Poppy there. Haven't I, Poppy love?' In the ordinary way Mother must surely have blown up at this; now I suppose she was just too tired.

'I been askin Dook too. Lot of sense in that guy Dook. He reckons we ought to get to Miami. He says there's nowhere in the world like Miami, not for havin a good time.'

'Al doesn't think that. Al thinks it's best in California.'

Ted nodded comfortably and his greased-down hair came a little unstuck, making him more like he really was. I could never quite get used to Ted's looking smart. 'Nice boy too, Al is. But he ain't comfortable like Dook. He's a worrier, Al. He don't really enjoy hisself.' He departed on another tack. 'They're a big responsibility, them boys. There's things they understand, and there's things they don't. You got to be always explainin to 'em. Now Al don't like that, Al reckons you're laughin at him when you're only tryin to help. I tell him the other day. I say, Al, I'm helpin you, boy, I'm defendin you just like you're defendin me. Couldn't see it, though. Reckoned I was stickin him for too much money.'

'I know,' I agreed sympathetically, 'but he's nicer than Butch.'

Ted was stroking his moustaches. 'Butch is a serious boy, too. Butch is a very serious boy. I got a lot of time for Butch, Lindy. Difference is he likes it, see. Whereas Al don't.' Whenever Ted talked of his Americans he developed a bit of an American accent; and it was surprising how much nicer and easier it made him sound. In a way it made him sound more real. They don't seem to divide people off so much, in America.

Mother was pretty well relaxed by now so that Ted and I were exchanging winks of encouragement. But then Ted made a mistake: he really should have known better. He said: 'Well, at least they haven't sacked that boy, Poppy. Now that's somethin, ain't it?'

'You going to let him go on working there after this?' She fairly spat the words at him.

But the words said little or nothing of her fury. She caught herself suddenly together as though she'd been standing in the road against a gale of wind. She pelted him with her anger. Not that she said very much: Mother in her fits of rage never had to say very much, for there was so much strength in her that you could almost feel it shuddering into you. Ted would usually run for cover; but on this occasion he was perhaps too much surprised for that. He argued with her.

'Don't see what good it would do. One sackin's enough, isn't it?' But that only rubbed salt in the wound.

'I don't care what you see. If he goes on working at Jerman's after they've sacked me then it's the last I see of him, and you can make up your mind to it.'

He tried again. 'But it's no shame on you, Poppy, him goin on workin there. It's silly to say so. Got nothin to do with it.'

She snapped: 'He's living here, isn't he? He's part of our family, isn't he?' Even then, in the whirling of all that fury, the words stuck in my hearing like a lump of gristle you can't get down: it was the first time I ever remember her using the words 'our family'. I should think it was the last too.

Ted was almost indignant. 'But he's still a kid.'

'He's old enough. Going on sixteen or seventeen, isn't he?'

'I dunno if he's old enough. Dunno what you mean.'

'Old enough to be a bloody nuisance.' The words echoed, somehow or other, out of a distant past: out of my childhood, out of her's too. Now even Ted saw that it would be hopeless to argue with her: she was like a prisoner who cannot bear to see another prisoner escape. And perhaps there was something else: perhaps there was also this fact that she saw – that we both saw, just then – that Jacob's staying on at Jerman's after she had gone, turned him from a boy into a man: from someone you could kick around, if you absolutely wanted to, into someone that you couldn't. He was strong, too, and tall and muscled for his age: it was easy to mistake him for a man. Perhaps I had always thought of him as a man; but it was now, in the hush that followed Mother's shout of rage, that I completely recognized the fact. It made me look across at Mother with a new uneasiness: there was only one thing that Mother could really do to men. I shouted at her: 'You hate him, don't you?'

She glanced at me without feeling, and told me to get out. But perhaps there was a little of Mother's temper in me after all. I went on shouting at her without even knowing what I meant to say. Ted jumped to his feet, waving his arms and shouting back at me to shut up, for Christ's sake to shut up.

But I screamed at her: 'You're afraid of him, aren't you? But he's not afraid of you.'

She might have hit me in the old days. Now she sat crouched in her chair, inspecting me with cold brown eyes as if she had never seen me before. The round strong curves of her face and lips blurred in front of me. I could not see her properly. I hated her for the strength she had.

Ted was shouting: 'What's got into this child, eh? Here, wait a moment –' But I went on screaming words at her, choking up the fear and jealousy and hatred of all those years. There was a chain that bound me to her, and I was sawing through it, sawing through it so that I could be free at last to hate her and escape from her.

Somehow or other it went off. Mother never moved, never stirred to hit me or reply, but let me go on screaming while Ted clutched me to his stomach and tried to make me quiet, stuffing his handkerchief into my mouth until I bit his thumb and made him let me be. Through all that noise, somehow or other, the only importance was that Mother and I continued to inspect each other as though for the first time, and as though both of us were astonished by what we saw.

In the end there was a silence; and through that silence Jacob came, opening the door and clumping in without knowing what to expect. But the moment he saw us he must have understood that a row was in progress, for he nodded quickly and was going to turn away; but Mother said to him: 'You giving in your notice?'

He frowned, and shot me a quick look of anger. 'Why should I?'

'Never you mind why. You are.'

'Dunno what you mean.'

Ted put in: 'They've sacked Poppy, you didn't know that?' He was still holding me to his stomach. Jacob said to him: 'What you doing to Lindy?'

At this Ted let me go and said rather stupidly: 'She was rude to her mother, see.' He gathered force a bit and shouted: 'Didn't you know they'd sacked Poppy, eh?'

'Yes, they tell me.'

'Well, you're giving in your notice, see? That's what Poppy's sayin to you.'

'Am I?'

Mother thrust at him: 'Yes, you are.'

He stuck his hands into his pockets and stared at the floor. 'No I'm not.'

Ted wanted to coax him. 'It's for Poppy's sake, lad. She feels bad about them sackin her like that. We'll find you another job all right.' But in this he was wasting breath: the reasons that Mother would have for wanting Jacob to leave Jerman's were the same reasons, in reverse, that he would have for meaning to stay there. Anyone but Ted could have seen that. Mother certainly saw it: I knew she did from the slow hard way she looked at him.

'I don't want another job. Suits me over there.'

'You're leaving it, though.'

'No I'm not.'

Mother burst out: 'Then you're bloody well leaving here.'

He looked at her pretty coolly, taking his time. 'This your house, then?'

God knows how it might not have ended but that the groan of Dook's klaxon came vibrating through the walls. Mother snapped: 'Okay, we'll see.' I got away from Ted and went over and put my hand on Jacob's arm, pulling him towards the door. I moved quickly, but there was still time to catch the sneer of anger in her face. Perhaps at last she had understood the reason for my shouting at her: perhaps she understood it better than I did. I don't really know. We got out of the room and upstairs and out of sight before Dook came bounding in. We heard his warm cry of greeting and their mumbled voices in reply.

SIX MOTHER made no attempt at finding work elsewhere. She took to getting up late in the morning, dressing finely, and spending occasional days at the seaside or even in London. Little by little she turned Ted's cottage into a general home-from-home for anyone she fancied. If that had been all she did, no one could have objected very much; but Mother had other ideas in mind as well. The principal of these, as we understood when it was far too late, was to revenge herself upon the village. Ted argued with her about this, but it did no good. 'You'll ruin yourself,' he argued; and she only laughed at him. Ted gave up arguing then, apparently content to let her do as she pleased: it was from about this time, I think, that he began to fade from us.

It is easier to begin a war than to end it. We understood that, I suppose, only when Mrs Thompson came weeks later to plead with her.

Mrs Thompson succeeded in a way, perhaps, although she had to swallow her threats of going to the police or to Mr Harold, and promise to keep silent and make everyone else keep silent. 'Tell him to keep away, then,' Mother said, 'tell him to stop pestering me.' After that, true enough, he wasn't seen again at our place; but I don't know if Mrs Thompson could have minded much, inside herself, by then, except for the scandal there would otherwise have been. I suppose she reckoned that life would somehow or other go on, as it always does; and she had the children to think of.

Yet it was miserably shameful. Even now it barely seems possible: it crept into our lives and gradually grew into them and was suddenly an accepted part of them. I am not sure when he first came, whether it was soon after Mother's being sacked or weeks afterwards when the summer parties got into their stride and were a kind of free-for-all, while Jacob and I, by then, were living mostly by ourselves.

His coming frightened Ted, at least in the beginning: he said it was another step in the wrong direction. Ted had never liked transferring 'activities', as he called them, from Rolcaster to the village: only after long battles had he given in to Mother's blind determination, and even then Mother had had to agree that the girls were not to come often, and were not to stay in the village. Ted would take them back to Rolcaster after breakfast. But his arguments were weakened by its turning out that only two of the girls would agree: the others said they weren't going to mouch around a smelly village when they might be having a nice time at the seaside. I should have known which of them those two would be: they were just too silly to know any better.

But Thompson's coming upset Ted all over again. I think that Mother might have listened to him on this point; but for the fact that Thompson was extremely discreet about it, in the early days at any rate. I saw this first when I opened the door to him late one night and found him hovering there as he mumbled and grinned, with his little thin head cocked foolishly on the stalk of his neck. I ran in and shouted who it was, thinking Mother was to get her job back; and knowing what it really was only when she went to the door herself and told him to come later to her own backdoor, over the way. Yet before long he was coming often, and not always after nightfall. Ted protested; but Mother would listen to nothing that he said, neither to warning nor to threat.

'What the idea, then?' he argued sullenly.

'You'll see.'

We saw it when Mrs Thompson came. She came, by chance, on one of the days when I had left the hut in the woods, where Jacob and I were mostly living by then, in order to wash some clothes of ours. Usually I went over to my aunt Pooley's for that; but every now and then I brought the washing to Ted's cottage where there was more hot water. I opened the door to her myself.

She must have gone back a few paces after knocking. With a grey light in her face she stood a little way down the path; but I understood at once what she had come for. It sat in every line and aspect of her, dragging down the corners of her mouth, peering from her eyes, twitching in the way she held her coat together so that she was dowdy and miserable and without defence. Even her sensible strapped-over shoes looked old and foolish, her woollen stockings fouled and ugly.

I said hollowly: 'Did you want to see Mother, Mrs Thompson?'

They told, in a book I once read, of an innocent country that was invaded and occupied by an enemy, and of how the people were so ashamed they could scarcely bear to struggle for themselves. It was they who had been sensible and right and innocent; but the enemy had beaten them just the same. Mrs Thompson was like that now. More than anyone else in our countryside, she stood for life's being sensible and right and innocent; and yet it had done her no good. She stood in our pathway, old and beaten, barely able to speak.

Mother was alone when she called; and that was something to the good. For she made it clear from the start that she meant to have her full revenge. She made it as hard for Mrs Thompson as she could; and Mrs Thompson sat there and took it all, too ashamed to struggle for herself. I stayed in the room for no more than a few moments, scarcely for time enough to watch Mother's careless greeting: after that I half-closed the door and listened from the kitchen until I could not bear to listen any more.

SEVEN

YET in spite of all these things, some present and some to come, our lives seemed wonderfully to settle down again. Although I had turned fifteen I was still at school, for Mr. Prother in his kindness said that I should stay at least until the end of the summer term although he could not possibly keep me after that; and now there was nothing to worry about with Jacob, for he was working regularly at one of Jerman's tenant farms over towards Lowton, and the days slipped softly by. He used to go off every morning at half-past seven with a lunch that I had packed for him: or, if he had to leave earlier, with the knowledge that Mr Street, where he worked, would always let him eat in the kitchen at midday. He seemed to like the people and the work; and there were no complaints from them. So long as Mother had no more than a fleeting glimpse of him she was content to let him alone, and we took good care, Ted and I, to keep them apart. For a while you might almost have imagined that there was nothing out of the way about us: I was even tempted to imagine it myself.

The weather helped, for it was fine and clear and hopeful. In the fields about us there was every sign of a good harvest on the way, so that even Oliver Chamfrey grew peaceful with the sowing of wheat that he had ventured in Mrs Chamfrey's field beside the *Wheelwright*, and talked of hiring Mr Harold's combine to help him get it in, seeing how heavy it was like to be: dawn after dawn came blue and creamy-white across our long low skyline. There were calm sunlit evenings when we sat in the garden together: when even Jacob was there: when the storms and worries of all we'd gone through were altogether absent and forgotten.

I don't think Mother ever looked more fine and beautiful than in those early summer days when at last we floated easily through life. No matter how wild the parties, Mother never showed a trace of suffering from them: her flesh was as firm and white and clear as it had ever been, her hair as black and glossy, her eyes without a hint of Ted's bloodshot yellow blinking. Both Dook and Ted were good with giving her money for clothes, and now that she was idle through the day she managed to spend every penny of it. She went to London now and then, with Dook, and came back always with a new dress or a blouse or a piece of costume jewellery. But most days she would get up about twelve, make herself some breakfast, and then come out in the summer's afternoon with the ease and pleasure of a queen. There was that about Mother, too: she could wear these clothes. A tight fitting skirt never appeared foolish on her: you found yourself admiring the curves and lines of it, her muscled calves and slender ankles, her small strong feet. You were glad that her blouse strained tightly on her bosom: you enjoyed the smooth line of her neck and shoulders: you felt stronger and less ugly for her scented presence there. She did good to you with her body. That early summer – it was the summer when we first heard Rock 'n Roll – Mother got Ted and Harry to clip and cut the garden, and put down fresh turf and weed and tend it, so that we could have our battery wireless or the gramophone outside, and Mother could practise steps in her bare feet while the ash trees rustled overhead and half the village kids peered gaping through the hedge.

Our Americans often came; and they did good to us too. Whatever happened later they did good to us in those early summer days. They knew how to make Mother enjoy herself: they knew how to make her give pleasure, how to draw her out. Whoever in our village could have made this Rock 'n Roll into a country dance? They did though: they stormed up in their motor-cars and traipsed across the lawn and bawled for music: and then we had a tea party on the neat new turf behind the neat clipped hedge while the ash trees rustled over head, and Mother kicked off her shoes and danced with Dook or Butch or Al or Sam or one of the others whoever they were.

Those were the times when no other women came, and they were the best times. They were a kind of golden age. For Mother was enough for all these men: she was thoughtful to each of them, since they only looked the same, and knew their different ways and worries; and she was kind to me and ignored Jacob, so long as he kept out of her way, altogether. She appeared then to have forgotten about the sacking and the need for revenge: anyone from the village was welcome at our tea parties, although no one came, except rarely, since they took place in the afternoon and the men were at work. The women would not have come in any case, of course: though Morton once did and was persuaded – by Butch, I think – to kick off her shoes and have a go with Rock 'n Roll. Sedately, though: for even Butch seemed to recognize that there couldn't be any question of swinging Morton off her feet.

The weather was part of all this. It smiled on us without a pause. Day after day we grew into that blossoming summer until we were deep in the life and growth of it. All round us the wheat rose tall enough to sway and shadow with the breeze. The hedgerows slowly put forth their springtime thornless twigs, twisting pale lines of green along the small road to Rolcaster and across the fields until, going by them, we could walk in the scent and burr of the woods whose leafy tops, violet blue beneath the summer clouds, had long since lost their nakedness. The rolling bareness of our countryside was altogether hidden now:

along the small road to Rolcaster the woods and trees and hedgerows made our country tall with hills and mountains, and even from my bedroom window I could barely see the tip of Lowton spire above the blossom of Jerman's orchard.

Everything seemed possible. Jacob bought himself new jeans, jacket and trousers, and had his hair clipped quite short so that you could scarcely know him, and although he said as little as ever I knew that he was settling down with himself. Instead of going for endless walks we gave up tramping the countryside and spent our weekends at the hut in the woods, improving it, fitting it out, furnishing small comforts, so that you could almost say we had a proper home there now, complete with curtains for a window he had made and fat cushions for the floor that we had organized from a jumble sale at Chudbury. He had taken to smoking in his off-times now. We stocked up with cigarettes and Coca Colas and a stack of canned meat and stuff which Dook had brought over to the cottage from time to time and which we smuggled, little by little, to the hut in the woods. He was past sixteen now: tall and strong and hard. He had saved forty pounds or thereabouts: he kept the money in a watertight tobacco tin beneath a floor-board in the hut, as well as the pistol that was wrapped in a piece of oilcloth. He considered they were safer there than anywhere else. He used to add to the money, and count it up with me, every Sunday morning. Then our plans took flight and carried us regularly to the other ends of the earth.

Ted's plans also took flight. He became more comfortable and easier than ever, and very large in his ideas. He became so large in his ideas that it was often hard to see round them: he disappeared, as it were, behind them – that steady process of gentle fading which began, as I have said, at about this time. Mother let him soar and fly as much as he wished, although I think she seldom listened; she was never one for making plans – she wanted her life at once, without delay, so that she could catch and have it and enjoy it. She was having and enjoying it now: she had no use for plans.

Ted's great point was that he was getting on top of things at last. He would develop this point in different ways according to the mood and moment, but they all came down to pretty much the same thing. There was one afternoon, for instance, before the men had joined us, when Mother and Ted and I were having an early cup of tea in the garden. Ted was securely established in his bucket seat – almost the only relic from the time of re-building that still remained with us – and holding forth on the future. While Mother poured tea he got himself well away on a favourite tack – on what he called 'the prospect for this country'. It was a prospect, apparently, that underwent a good deal of change in those weeks and months of Ted's growing comfortable and easy. But the easier he grew, oddly enough, the gloomier was the picture that he painted of the prospect for this country. He unbuttoned his chequered waistcoat that afternoon and made himself thoroughly easy and crossed his feet in his new leather slippers of red morocco leather with blue decorations, resting them on the clean-cut turf which Harry had laid; and declared to us, but more especially to me, since Mother seldom bothered to listen: 'You know, the more I think about it, the more it's like I said.'

These days he was sleek and clean and close-shaven, so that even his eyes seemed almost ready for inspection. Across his waistcoat he generally wore a thin gold chain threaded through a buttonhole, from pocket to pocket; and whenever he was really in the mood for talk he would take out a new golden watch and unhook it from the chain and twirl and untwirl this chain upon a finger, gazing at it while it glittered round and round as though he expected something interesting to come of it. This is what he did now: it was the only occasion I remember when you could say that his eyes seemed really fixed and still. He twirled the chain, and watched it carefully.

Mother handed him his tea and went back to her magazine. She was a faithful reader of magazines. This afternoon she had one called *Female*: she read it folded back on itself, her legs and feet perched on a stool, the warm sun winking in the silken

178

folds of her dress. 'Go on Ted,' she muttered off-handedly, 'tell Lindy about it.'

A little disappointment like this would never disturb him: in any case he talked mainly for himself, perhaps because he liked the sound of his own voice, perhaps because he liked what he was saying. He watched the twirling chain and grinned peaceably, shaking his head as though he could have told you, had you asked, that the chain would first fly this way round, and then that way round, and everything would end precisely as expected. His old voice droned among the noises of the garden. 'You can't get away from it, though,' he was saying cheerfully: 'You think you can, but you can't. Eh, you think you can?' And he shook his head again, tut-tutting gently, so that his smile was almost something you would want to believe in.

'Don't want to get away from it,' Mother murmured, not having listened.

He continued shaking his head in peaceful agreement with himself. 'It's no good, Poppy, you got to face it. This country's finished. Course you can't expect Dook and them to see it – they think we're up 'n coming, don't they?' Even now, in this flower of his peacefulness, he never quite managed to get away from his habit of ending everything with a question: of wanting to suggest, you felt, that he wasn't saying anything, he wasn't really saying anything. 'We got to explain it to 'em. They're here to defend us, ain't they? But it's no good, eh?' He looked at us in turn, his old grey eyebrows raised in their familiar question. 'Well, it ain't. But we got to make the effort, Poppy. Poppy love, we got to make the effort.'

'Okay, Ted, you make it.'

He flung down his arms as though it would be hopeless to try. 'Ah, you're right there, Poppy. You're too right.' He drew out one of his enormous handkerchiefs – practically a scarf, it was so big, and made of red silk – looked at it carefully, fanned himself and returned it to his pocket. 'That's it, all right,' he went on, recommencing with the golden chain: 'An' there's only one thing to do. Get out from under.' He clicked his tongue, screwed up his eyes, wriggled comfortably in the comfortable seat. 'Get out from under before the whole ruddy contraption comes down on your head. Eh, Lindy?' His old brown eyes swivelled between us so that he was comfortably looking at neither Mother nor me. 'Had it, eh, this country? Course you don't see it so long as you're down there in the muck, swimming and splashing for your life. But just you give a man a bit of easy, time to look round for hisself and size it up, and he'll see it soon enough, won't he? Just's I'm tellin you. Rattling at the joints, falling to bits. And what can you do about it? Eh?' He paused reflectively, shaking his head again. 'You can't do a thing about it. You can't because you won't. You ain't so goddam silly. You wasn't born yesterday.'

For hours on end he liked to ramble on, not troubling anyone to listen much, dreaming and bumbling away as he sat in the sun and took his ease. This afternoon he was particularly well into his stride. He even struggled out of his chair at one point and strolled across the lawn and back, thumbs hooked into the armholes of his flapping waistcoat, eventually fetching up in front of us and declaring with a note of fresh discovery: 'We done our best, eh? We've slaved and toiled and tried. And what's the prospect, eh?' He dropped his arms to his sides. 'Nix. Had it. Gone for a Burton.'

'You sound pretty cheerful, though.'

He denied it. 'No Lindy, you can't get away from it. Christ almighty, you have to be sorry for people. All these silly buggers sweatin away and sayin their prayers and livin like it really mattered. When they've had it, eh? When it's collapsin round 'em and they ain't so much as got the sense to notice it, eh?' He ho-ho'd with a special kind of sarcastic laugh that he kept for these occasions of unusual comfort. 'No, they won't do nothing about it. Nothing. You got to be sorry for 'em.'

'That's all right, Ted,' Mother said from far away, 'you be sorry for 'em. They'll like that.'

His voice rose indignantly, 'Like it, will they? Why, they don't even want to know about it. They'll go right on followin their noses till they smash 'em into a brick wall. Yeah, and then they'll curse that bleedin wall for being there.'

I asked: 'What are you really talking about, Ted?'

He spat thoughtfully on the turf and rubbed out the spittle with the toe of his red morocco slipper. 'It ain't no good your takin that line, Lindy. You know it just 's well as I do. You got to sit down 'n consider things. You got to look at the prospect.' He swung away again, his arms flapping, and waddled off across the lawn and back. When he came back again he was more contented than ever.

Bobbing slightly on his toes he stood in front of us, humming a tune from Rock 'n Roll that he could never quite get right. Mother said irritably that he should shut up and sit down, he was putting her off; but he only grinned and went on bobbing, his hands behind his back and his stomach comfortably bulging at his trouser tops. 'Must say,' he began again, 'must say Harry done a good job on this turf.' He bobbed silently for a while and then suddenly slapped his arms against his sides so that even Mother looked up from her magazine, irritably, while he ho-ho'd his curious laughter. 'Never had it better, have we?' he cackled: 'Ain't that what some silly bugger said the other day, one of them politicians? Didn't he say that?'

'For God's sake,' Mother complained. 'I'm reading.'

'Yeah, he did then. He said that. Said we never had it better. And he's right. We *ain't* never had it better.' He spun round on the turf, wobbling as he went, flapping his arms, shouting in a small shrill voice of triumph: 'Jus' look at it, eh. Lovely grass. Lovely sun. Lovely everything. What more you want, eh?'

A car's engine roared and stilled in the road outside. Mother snapped, 'That'll be Dook,' and came brilliantly to life again.

Dook and Butch were pushing through the gate, Dook carrying a flat slim parcel under his arm. 'Got something new,' he shouted.

Mother jumped to her feet, galvanized, electrified, all her motors suddenly in action.

'Hot,' came Dook's good voice across the turf, roaring, shouting: 'You bet it's hot.'

EIGHT 'My dear ol' Transatlantic cousins,' Ted was saying after his fourth or fifth gin, 'I wanna tell you about the prospect for this country. We're all friends here, eh? We're all men of property, eh? So I wanna tell you. An' I want you to listen.'

'I'm a natural listener,' said Butch. 'Where's that gin?'

'You got enough gin. Jus' you listen to me.'

'Hey Dook, gimme that gin, will you?'

'Poppy, where's that gin bottle got to?'

Mother said: 'Go and get another one, Lindy. It's down by the gas cooker there.'

They did good to us, you see, because they took us out of ourselves. They trampled down the boundaries and rooted out the signposts. They made any other way of living than living largely seem absurd. When I returned with the gin they were enjoying a breather after dancing on the grass. Dook was mopping his nice yellow face, puffed and sweating: he winked as I returned just to let me know that all was well and always would be well and never could be anything but well.

'There she is, then, there's the girl with the gin.'

'Hi, Lindy, give us that bottle, will you?'

Dook grinned, mopping his neck and throat. 'That old woman of yours sure likes to dance, Lindy.'

Butch said with a serious face: 'Surprisin, too, in a female of her age.' Everyone grinned. It was good to think of Mother as an old woman: it did good to us all to have her teased, and she not minding in the least. That was their grand and special thing, to make Mother laugh at herself: you could forgive them a lot for being able to do that.

Dook's new hot number was called 'Rock Island Line', a beating rising tumult of a number that caught Mother's fancy and drove her jagging across the turf, at first alone and then with Dook beside her. Watching them, quaking to the music all through his soft body, Butch said: 'It's as good as the other thing, Lindy. Well, almost.'

Everyone knows what Rock 'n Roll can mean. It meant for Mother what gardening meant for Morton, or explaining other people means to Miss Pakeman: it put her right in tune with herself. She danced with Dook as though fighting all the battles of her life and gloriously winning them: she trampled her enemies into the turf and pranced outrageously on them, heels kicking, skirt splitting up her legs, hair flying about her face, eyes and lips and cheeks rigidly strained with a fury of concentration. She leaped up on Dook and rode him with her legs hooked behind his back, her head falling towards the grass, her arms trailing: she caught him with her arms and slithered down again and pounded after him, bottom jerking, shoulders heaving, the whole of herself an endless shake and shudder with the grand machinery of music. She dived over his shoulder and came down on her hands, prancing on her hands, using her arms for legs, using her long firm thighs for arms to clasp his neck, while the rest of us shook with the same fury and clapped and beat our hands and yelled encouragement.

The sound and fury parted for a moment, and Ted was still saying: 'Yeah, I wanna tell you about the prospect for this country.'

'You still playin that disk?' Butch inquired: 'Don't you have another one, you poor old man?'

But Ted was also in his element, right in tune with himself. He lay back in his comfortable seat and let his chequered waistcoat flap across his chest and twirled peacefully the golden chain so that he could watch it glinting in the sun. He needed no attentive audience: he liked to talk aloud, but mainly to himself: he liked to be there and not there. 'It's only when you got property you can see it, though,' he went on, screwing up his eyes, comfortably, so that they need look at nothing and no one in particular: 'It's only when you're safe, see?'

'You safe, Ted? You a safe man?'

'Safe as houses.' He let himself expand and shuffle in the pleasure of his comfort: even his toes in the red leather slippers wiggled in sympathy with his being so safe. 'See all this? It's mine, boy. It's my little stake, see, my stake in this old country.'

'Okay then, get it out of yourself. Let it come up. What is this prospect you're goin on about?'

'I was trying to tell Al there. Couldn't make him see it.'

'Aw, that fellow's a politician. You couldn't make him see anything. Just you tell me, Ted. Tell y'r old friend Butch. I'm *ignorant*.'

'There's more sense in you, Butch, than there's sense in a lot of 'em I've met.'

'Hey, Dook, you hear that? Says I'm a sensible guy. Be sayin his prayers next.'

So Ted went on about the prospect for this country while some of us listened and some of us dozed. Mother was lying with her knees apart and her hands in the lap of her skirt, her head on Dook's shoulder, her eyes closed, enjoying the sunshine and the satisfaction; and Dook was just sitting there, agreeably, and doing us good. I don't remember whether Ted said anything much, or much that he'd not already said a dozen times before: his old brown voice droned on about the prospect for this country, and the gloomier the prospect the more cheerful and comfortable he seemed; and somehow or other, I don't know why, it was a comfort and a pleasure for all of us to know that the prospect was so bad because it came out, or it appeared to come out, that the prospect had no connection with us any longer. Butch said it was like mourning the death of a respected

184

parent you hadn't seen in years: you'd made your life and you were sorry for the poor soul's being stricken down with cancer and sure to die, but then we all had to die in the end; and it wasn't you who'd got the cancer, not this time anyway.

'Ah, you're right there, Butch, you're too right.'

'What, me right again?'

There was a certain majesty in Ted at such moments. He had, you felt, all the answers in the palm of his fat brown hand. 'We're grateful to you, Butch, I wouldn't deny it. We're grateful. You're down there in the shit, fightin for us, defendin us, and you don't mind. You're big hearted. You're doin it for our sakes.'

Butch heard all this with a contented grin. 'Poor old Ted,' he said now and then: 'We're doin it all for you.'

'An' I'm grateful, Butch, I'm grateful. We don't want none of them so-'n-so's here.'

'Aw, politics,' Butch cried disgustedly, 'for chrissake don't get on to politics. We got that with Al as it is.'

'No it ain't politics,' Ted objected calmly, almost buzzing with the goodness and the kindness that you could see he felt, sitting there in the sun: 'It's the facts. Al don't understand the facts. Al keep tellin me we ought to be standin on our own feet. For chrissake, we ain't got no feet to stand on. You know that, Butch, we ain't got no feet to stand on, not any more?'

'You don't want to worry about Al. Al ain't human, not proper, are you Al? Al can't even have a woman without his telling her she ought to be ashamed of herself.'

They nagged on agreeably at each other, and then Mother and Dook danced some more. Afterwards we were sitting in the sun again, beside the grass beneath the fluttering trees, and they were drinking and feeling the goodness and the kindness in them and not even discussing any more; when we looked up and saw a strange man. We saw a strange man coming across the turf from the garden gate. He was strange because none of us knew him; but he was also strange because he came from a world we had gratefully forgotten, a world where men wear grey suits and old shoes and earn their living by going to work from nine till five.

This strange man said in an office voice from Rolcaster: 'Excuse me, but would this be Mr Breldon's place?'

We left him standing on the grass in front of us, a strange man with a small sharp face and a small soft hat cocked a little on one side; and we did not move a muscle.

'What you want?' Ted asked finally.

'Well, I want to speak to Mr Breldon if this is Mr Breldon's place.'

'That's me, Ted Breldon.'

Even the grass had faded.

Ted got up in the end and shook himself and buttoned up his waistcoat.

The stranger said: 'I must apologize for interrupting like this. We all like an afternoon off, I'm sure.' But he looked not in the least apologetic. He watched us with curiously nervous eyes. There was a feel about him of knowing everything we should say and do, considering what he meant to tell us; and of knowing exactly how to deal with it. Perhaps he had said it all before, and was bored with having to say it all again: bored, but also a trifle nervous.

'You better sit down 'n have a drink.'

'Oh no, I won't do that, if you don't mind. Never believe in mixing business with pleasure.'

'You got business here?'

The stranger put a hand into his inner pocket and brought forth a slim long envelope, which he handed to Ted. 'Perhaps you'd be good enough to read that', he said, watching us. 'It may save time in explanations.'

Ted opened the envelope without looking at it. Now we all watched him. There was even a sense in which he read the type-written letter it contained without looking at it. But he did read it, and he appeared to understand it.

'You from the council? You know what this says?'

'Oh yes, of course I know. That's why I came. To explain it if it's not quite clear, you know.'

The comfortable majesty in Ted had altogether sapped away. He said to Mother: 'Letter from the council. Says this cottage is condemned property. Can't be occupied. Say's its been condemned for seven years. Says they're goin to demolish it.'

There was a silence.

Mother said: 'We paid for it, didn't we? We bought it?'

Ted explained: 'I bought it off a Mrs Plum. She didn't say anything about its bein condemned. Though it was a fair pigstye when we got it.'

'She ought to have said something,' the man from the council interrupted genially: 'She ought to have said a great deal. You know' – he allowed himself a little laugh, apologetically – 'you've been had, Mr Breldon.'

Butch said: 'That's a funny way of doin things.'

'It may or may not be funny, my dear sir. It happens to be the way we do things over here, whatever may be done elsewhere. We don't like people living in condemned property.'

Ted exploded: 'But we done it up. Go 'n look for y'rself. We done it up proper. New roof. New timbers.'

'Well, of course I am sorry about that. I am very sorry indeed. Of course there may be some compensation. It does seem that you have been greatly misled, although I understand – of course I only *understand*, you know, it's not our business – that the vendor has since died and I should anticipate – I should *anticipate*, you know, it's not our business at all – that you may have some trouble in getting compensation from her legatees. I say you *may* have some trouble.'

Mother put in coldly: 'Compensation from Gladstone Plum? You're crazy.'

'Well, there is no occasion to make a scene about it, I'm sure.'

'Isn't there?'

'It would do no good, I fear. I say I *fear*. The property was condemned seven years ago which meant, of course, that it could not be placed on the market and sold. Of course there may be a case for reassessment – there *may* be, you understand, I have no authority to say there is – and no doubt you could appeal against it. But of course I do not know if you would find that worthwhile. You should never have bought it in the first place.'

Ted waved the letter. 'It says we've got to clear out. Clear out at our earliest convenience. Well, it ain't convenient. Not now and not at any time.'

I don't know quite how it happened, but they argued for a while and then Ted put himself in the wrong by losing his temper and hitting the man from the council. He hit the man from the council in the face, knocked him down, and then kicked him. Dook ran over and pulled him away and made him sit down, helped the man from the council to find his spectacles in the grass, and said he was sure that there must be some mistake. But the man from the council seemed not in the least surprised, nor even angry. He said that he could well understand everybody's feelings, but they wouldn't get anywhere by becoming violent, and he should report the assault to the council and the council would proceed in the normal way. 'Of course they will send the police. I say I *expect* they will send the police,' he went on pleasantly, even managing a smile: 'The council does not like having its officers treated with violence. Oh yes, I should think they will send the police.' It was the first time, as a matter of fact, that those dismal words were mentioned.

We persuaded him to sit down and have a drink with us while Mother brought basin and flannel and washed the blood from his mouth and Dook gave him a whole packet of Chesterfields, and nobody allowed Ted to utter another word. The man from the council took off his trilby hat, which had somehow stayed in place all through these experiences, and wiped his balding head with a dirty handkerchief, and said it wasn't in the least his fault, there wasn't anything *he* could do about it, he was simply carrying out instructions and he'd better warn us that what they decided upon they usually carried out. They were reasonable people, but they had their regulations and their instructions, and they carried them out. You could take them to law, you could take them to Parliament, you could take them to the House of Lords if you'd a mind to: but you wouldn't get anywhere. The regulations had to take their course. There would be no law and order in the land if they didn't. He grew quite friendly in the end, and even leant over at one point and tapped Ted cheerfully on the knee and said not to mind about having lost his temper, everyone lost their temper sometimes, it was part of John Bull's character, wasn't it?

Ted accepted that with some relief. 'You don't want to go talking like that about the police, though,' he added.

The man from the council laughed agreeably but what he actually said was something different. Fortunately they had the police, he said, for otherwise what should they do in cases like this? 'Oh, I'm sure you will appreciate that, Mr Breldon. You won't hold that against us. I shouldn't be at all surprised if they send the police. I say I shouldn't be *surprised*, you know.' He didn't mind being knocked down and kicked: all in a day's work, wasn't it? And Mr Breldon wouldn't mind if they sent police, would he? Fair enough, wasn't it? The man from the council even allowed himself a merry little laugh at this point.

After a time he went quietly away.

But the letter he had brought he left behind him; and when he had gone we understood that matters remained exactly where they were. The council would act. They would proceed. They would proceed in the normal way. There was never, in my opinion, the smallest chance of preventing them; although Ted declared that nothing in the world should evict him from the cottage. He wasn't going to law, he wasn't going to Parliament, he wasn't going to the perishing House of Lords, not he: he was just going to sit where he was and watch them turn him out if they dared.

Dook rose to his feet unexpectedly and remarked to Butch and to Al that they ought to be going. Butch got up and said the same thing. Al said nothing but was already on his feet.

'You go along, dears,' Mother said sharply, 'you might get into trouble if you stay.'

'That's not fair, Poppy. You know we got to be careful.' But it was quite fair, really, no matter what Dook might say: we all understood that.

'Go on,' Mother said without mercy, 'they'll be sending the police any time now.'

They went without another word. I suppose you could not really blame them.

They left us staring at the new green grass and the neat clipped hedge. 'You know,' began Ted after a while, 'there's something wrong with this world.' An expression of strained astonishment had gathered in his face. 'There's something bloody wrong with it.' I saw that he hadn't even the heart to twirl his golden chain.

Mother said sarcastically: 'You better write and tell the news-papers. They'll always pay for a new idea, won't they?'

'Ah, you're too right there, Poppy. You can't change it, not for better nor for worse, you can't.'

'Now there's a silly thing to say. What about the effort you were telling us about? You make it, Ted, you make the effort. You'll change the world in no time. Got the vote, haven't you?'

'Have I?' And then, for some reason that was neither clear nor spoken, the bewilderment in Ted's face was followed by the slow shadow of a grin that gradually appeared and won the upper hand, edging itself into his puffy lips and cheeks, advancing and retreating, and finally breaking forth. 'That's right,' he said: 'I've got the vote 'n I've got the choice, haven't I? If it's rainin in Brummagem, eh?'

But Mother snapped at him: 'Choice? No, you haven't. We're staying here.'

NOTHING happened for a time. Nothing came of it:
NINE   the council sent no more letters, the police did not
appear, we settled down again. But no, that's saying
too much: we did not really settle down again. We lived through
those weeks, I think, in fits of worry and worse than worry.
There were days when the strain of waiting – just waiting, waiting for bad news – was so bad that I wished it would come at
once. The memory I have of that time of waiting is mostly of
that: that, and another thing too – the memory of some vague
and yet tremendously important argument that none of us could
grasp or understand.

'Nonsense,' Pakeman has said, 'you're dolling it up. You don't
remember any such thing. How could you? There wasn't any
argument.'

There was, as a matter of fact, a violent argument between
those two, between Pakeman and Morton; although I don't
know if this could have caused my own opinion, then, that the
fates were clashing in the skies above us. But I certainly remember this argument, and I remember it very well, partly because
this was the first time, I think, of Pakeman's visiting Morton,
but also because both of them have told me of it separately.
But there were many other arguments as well. There was more
than an argument between Mother and Jacob, mainly because
she suspected him of telling tales on her. There was a steady
grumble from Ted, arguing that they ought not to have the
tarts here any more, they ought to close down the business, they
ought to watch their step. There was an argument with an angry
man from Enfield, who appeared one day with a complaint that
Ted wasn't giving him a fair slice of the cake; and whom Ted,
with a confidence I never saw in him before, actually threw out
of the house. There was an argument with Al, who considered

that Ted was sticking him for too much money, which I expect he was. There were endless arguments about money.

Yet all these arguments seemed oddly unimportant at the time: to me but also, I think, to all of us. Something was going to happen, sudden and inescapable – I think we all knew that. So what did it matter what we said? Or even what we did?

It is odd that what I best remember from this time is the argument between Pakeman and Morton.

TEN

'A BRISK young woman suffering from BO,' Morton complained afterwards to Mr Morton but also to me: 'comes to your door at some ungodly hour of the morning. So you let her in and give her coffee and listen to her. And before you know where you are she is ranting at you like an unsuccessful parliamentary candidate.'

'A lot of people,' said Mr Morton, 'are rather like that, you know.'

'I can't stand seeing people make fools of themselves.'

'A lot of people, you know,' continued Mr Morton in his gentle voice of resignation, 'can't stand anything else.'

He sat beside her while she lay in her favourite position for talking, which was horizontal. She lay on her sofa, a red cushion beneath her head, and smoked from a long slim holder while he sat beside her like a doctor, a little forward in his chair, patiently, listening to the symptoms and not minding much because by now he knew them backwards, and need not worry any longer. Through these months of her kindness to Jacob I had changed my feelings for Morton: I had grown to like her in spite of her symptoms. But Mr Morton loved her, I think, because of them: also, perhaps, because they were symptoms of the same burden that he carried under his sad gay waistcoat back and forth to London every week without its ever seeming to grow lighter.

'Humanity,' he said now with a cheerful sigh, 'is somehow better than it should be. There's that, you know.'

'Give me a sherry, darling, and stop being so godly. You weren't given hell by an ex-hockey captain at ten in the morning. She seemed to have the idea that everyone ought to be doing something about everyone else. She's like a ghost – a pretty solid one, though – out of the nineteen-thirties: she's keen and eager about changing things for the better. Imagine that if you can.'

'I am trying, darling.'

'Arrogance. It's the arrogance I can't bear. Head stuffed with facts and figures, marvellous fluency in the rules and regulations – oh, you can't deny them that, they've got the Bill of Rights off pat – and as much real knowledge, as much real understanding, as you could comfortably stand on the end of a pin. Half this social urge, in any case, is just a way of proving that you're as good as anyone else. Why can't they see that nobody denies it?'

Mr Morton said affectionately: 'Doesn't anybody?'

'No of course not. Nobody that matters.'

'I suppose that's true.' Now that I have seen what London is like I believe they would have gone upon each other's nerves in any place but our village, or another village as quiet as ours: for what they wanted in each other was something shy and silent and hard to hear. They loved each other's weaknesses: you can't do that in a noise.

'Of course it's true. She comes here at ten in the morning and accuses me of what she's pleased to call social abdication. She stands on my hearthrug in shoes she's forgotten to wipe and rants at me about the school lavatories. She infers that I'm a hopeless decadent because I don't believe in progress or whatever it is. She tells me I'm wrong about Jacob. Sentimental patronage, she calls it if you please: the sentimental patronage of the comfortable and well-to-do. You'd think she'd never heard of income-tax.'

'She'll learn,' said Mr Morton gently.

'I doubt it. That's rotten sherry, darling.'

'It's very uneven, this South African stuff.'

'I can't think why we have it.'

'Income-tax, darling.'

'Well, there you are. I gave her some and she said it was very nice. Very nice. She said so.'

'We'll give her Spanish next time. We'll educate her.' But she liked his gentle teasing; perhaps it took the sting from her worries.

'All the same, she's wrong about Jacob. I'm dead sure the only thing to do with that boy is to leave him alone. Not to interfere. Just let him come and go. She calls that abdication.'

'It's a good strong word.'

'Oh, it's part of her idea that humanity is somehow getting better and better. I don't believe that. I don't believe it at all.'

He looked at her curiously, watchfully, as though listening for something beyond the words. 'You think it's getting worse and worse?'

'No, neither worse nor better. Circumstances change, the real problem doesn't. The real problem' – she described circles in the air with the slim long holder, making rings of smoke – 'the problem of living, of managing to live – that doesn't change. That just goes round and round. Progress in drains, yes. Progress in happiness? I wonder.'

'Still, one's happier with decent drains, don't you feel?'

But she had gone back to an earlier thought. 'A youth club, that young woman says. There's what we ought to have for young people like Jacob. Draw them into the community, she says. Well, I won't do it.'

'I don't think you should, darling.'

'I won't do it because I don't believe in all that stuff about the brotherhood of man. They had it all in the 'thirties, and look where it landed them. Everyone's got the same problem – this thing of getting through life as well as you can. Everyone's got to solve it for themselves. You can't help other people. You can just about manage to help yourself.'

Pakeman's story of this argument with Morton is a different one. She told it me only the other day, long afterwards, so perhaps she does not quite remember how it really went: she is convinced she won it, though, and that I am glad she won it.

She was sitting across from me, with her elbows on the table that I have here, and the grey London light falling between us. 'Of course I let her off lightly, you know. One can't just trample on people.' There are times when she seems to forget why I am here.

'Still, I had to let her have one or two things pretty straight. Oh, these pure and elegant people – they're so well-intentioned! And so futile. This country's positively cluttered with them. Lindy, are you listening?' I was offended, as a matter of fact, that she should take my agreement so much for granted.

'They'll never face real situations,' she went on after I had assured her that I was listening.

'All they care about is that whenever something goes wrong it should on no account be possible to say it was *their* fault. So that when something does go wrong – and of course it does – they can be ever so civilized about the mistakes and failings of other people. Of people who do face real situations.'

I asked her: 'But is it true that everyone can get better and better?' ·

She is brisk about this kind of question. She can't see how anyone can doubt it. 'Look at the Chinese,' she said to me then: 'Put things in their full perspective.' But I couldn't look at the Chinese: I could only think of Jacob and me, and of Mother, and wonder for the millionth time what other future there might have been for us.

Morton always made her dreadfully impatient. 'That woman thinks you can do it all by love,' she burst out. 'Well, you can't, that's all. And when I said that to her she answered that you can't do it by hate either. I'm not so sure. Hate's at least a strong emotion.' I couldn't see why it should matter to her what

Morton might think; but somehow it did. Somehow it nagged and worried her.

'Kindness – that woman talks of nothing but kindness. When what she really means is indifference. Despair. You don't cut out a tumour with kindness, you cut it out with a knife.' There is always a little of that about Pakeman – urgency, decision, the distant flashing of a knife. 'This kindness thing – it's a sort of rot eating into us. It's as if we are all sitting in a train that's stopped and won't go on. So there we sit, exhorting each other to keep calm because there's nothing to be done but be kind to the driver, poor worried man. Well, if we all got out and threatened to shoot the driver we might get on a little faster, seems to me.'

But I must have looked my thoughts, for she broke off then and frowned, cross with herself. 'Sorry, Lindy – you're getting so well I'd quite forgotten myself. But that woman – she maddens me. Why couldn't she have *done* something before it was too late?'

ELEVEN

THAT was unfair, of course, for Morton did try to do something before it was too late. She called on Mother and accused her of not looking after us – after Jacob and me – but the only practical result was that Mother suspected Jacob of telling Morton the facts of Ted's business.

It still worries me to think there may have been some truth in that. They hated each other so much by now.

A scrap of conversation haunts me. It occurred a day or so after Morton's row with Mother. I was getting Jacob's supper in their kitchen when Mother came in unexpectedly and threw at Jacob: 'What have you been telling that woman up the road?'

He would not look at her at first. He never looked at her if he could help it. He sat with hunched shoulders at the kitchen table and went on eating the spaghetti I had made for him. Mother seemed ready for another flaming row; but it was less easy to have a row with Jacob than to have a row with Morton – or with anyone else I know. He simply went away from you whenever it suited him: though he might not move a muscle, he could as well have thrown down his fork and gone out of the room for all the change you would get from him. But now he did glance up at her.

'What woman?' The fact is that he could never bear to look at her but with something of the misery of their first disastrous meeting. You felt it was hard for him to look at her at all, hard and somehow shameful: she felt it too. 'What's the matter with me, then?' she had once burst out at him: 'Aren't I fit to look at?'

Now she said bitterly, 'You start messing about with things that don't concern you, and you'll run into something you don't like!'

'What's that then?'

She stood by the table, staring down at him, and said quietly: 'I'll tell you one thing. Once and for all. If I've got to suffer because of you, I'll make damn sure you suffer too.' It is the sort of thing that angry people say without meaning it: even though I heard her very well I did not really understand, although I should have understood.

When we were alone that evening I asked him if it wasn't true that he had told Morton of the tarts at Rolcaster? But he only shrugged his shoulders angrily, and turned away.

People are as they are. You have to love them as they are, or else not love them at all.

PART FOUR

ONE

THAT time of waiting was only a few weeks: looking back, it might have been as many months. Only when it stopped did I realize how much I had been afraid.

It stopped suddenly. Ted and Mother made a run for it. They rushed from one end of our village while the police were asking questions at the other. Afterwards we discovered that the police had not come for them at all; but it made no difference, for Ted and she had gone.

Jacob disbelieved in my fear. When they vanished in the frantic blue of their exhaust Jacob never doubted that we had really escaped: he looked across at me, as we stood in the silent road, and cried: 'Shan't see them again.' Just as when they had waved goodbye and gone pelting down the road, he kept his arms crossed firmly and his head a little forward in a trick he had of staring from under his fringe of hair. Dook had sometimes teased him for copying James Dean, and perhaps there may have been something in it; but there was no doubting that smile of triumph. 'They've gone,' he cried with that rare and joyful smile. 'They won't come back.' I said no word to that for I was glad of his happiness; but all the same I grudged him the triumph that he felt. Only it is true, and I knew it even then, that you have to love people as they are.

And in any case, after we had bid Dook farewell and turned our backs on the road, that morning of their departure, the doors of happiness seemed suddenly flung open. The cottage was foul with dirty glass and crockery. It reeked of gin and vomit and the stink of perfumes that the girls had used. It was sour with a kind of rubbery sickness as though they had thrown rubber on the fire and let the fumes pour over them. But I doubt if we minded any of that. I opened the sitting-room windows to let the fresh air in; and we stayed there for a little while – not for long in case the police should find us – so as to enjoy the simple truth that they had gone and we had stayed. The drink and the sweat and stench of it did not appear to concern us in the least.

After we had done with gathering our things we went away without even bothering to close the door. I was thinking that nothing in the world would ever bring us here again, and so, I think, was he. We crossed the garden at the back and traversed the fields until we had reached the green road that goes out past our village church and dwindles forgotten to the woods.

It was still early in the morning, so early that the distant frontier of the woods lay blurred in purple shadow beneath a silver sky, and darkness still lingered near us in grey thickets. High over the fringe of the woods there were clouds solidifying into light: later they would climb in long arched regiments across the sky and glitter with the summer sun while tractors fired and backfired in Jerman's garage, as Steppins got them ready for work.

We climbed a small rise that carries the green road under Jerman's elms. Looking back from here beyond the grey-metal trunks and blackthorn briars, you could see the dry red roofs of our village among apple trees and poplars. But I did not want to look back.

When we reached our hut in the woods Jacob fetched water from the nearby stream – it joins the Stint past Chudbury – and I cooked breakfast on our Primus stove. I had done this often before, but I did it now like it was the first time. And we passed that first day of our living together, I think, in altogether looking forward: while the kingdoms of this earth, as the Devil showed Jesus, were spread before us, waiting for us, waiting to welcome us and take us in and make us one with themselves. We discussed our way to get there. We counted our money and reckoned for the hundredth time how soon we should be able to leave this place and go to Australia.

That same afternoon, though, a new thing happened to us. We caught the groan and clamour of heavy traffic on our weed-grown airfield. Odd cars would cross it anyway, using the small road from Rolcaster that flowed into the sea of tarmac and out of it again; but now this was a stronger and much larger noise. Jacob thought we should discover what it was, so we went to the edge of our woods and crept beyond the outermost brambles as far as the back of a mound they had heaped together, long ago, to fire their spare bullets into in the war. We climbed the mound on all fours and wormed our way through summer hemlock until we could oversee the runways. They stretched away beneath us like dirty carpets spread on Jerman's fertile land, their frayed lengths fading in the distance through the sunny haze of afternoon until we could barely see their termination. But out of the haze, blundering down those strips of tarmac like stupid animals, there came truck after truck with high-boarded sides and short snub noses, steering past us down toward the empty sheds and hangars that stood away to one side and had not been used since the wartime planes took off, years ago, for the last time.

We lay on the earth and watched them until I was catching my breath with an excitement that I could not understand. I asked Jacob what it meant. When I asked him a second time, pulling at his sleeve, he answered in a flat voice of anger and despair: 'They're coming back to the airfield.'

'Doesn't matter to us, does it?'

He said in his flat withdrawn voice: 'They finished with it when the war stopped, didn't they? Can't you see. They're going to start using it again.'

We were both whispering although we might as well have shouted for all the danger of anyone's overhearing us.

'What shall we do?'

'Get out. Soon as we can.'

I remember the dry orchard scent of that hemlock in my nostrils. It might have belonged to another world.

'But it's all a joke. Dook promised us it was.'

'They'll search the woods.'

I put my face down into the summer grass and felt my stomach heave and tremble with an aching disappointment. We had escaped from Mother and Ted: now it was demanded of us that we should escape from this too. From all this: I could have found no words for it – for these grinding snub-nosed trucks that went blindly steering past us, down there through the summer haze, one after the other, back and forth to the sheds while we watched; and every one of them a proof of our helplessness.

We crawled away and returned silently to the woods. All through the large free weeks that followed we never quite came, I think, from under that shadow: unless perhaps it is only my imagination that this shadow existed of itself, rather than grew secretly out of another shadow, the shadow of Mother's possible returning: the shadow that stood behind all our dreams and all our days together. From this time onward, in any case, Jacob thought of nothing but to save the money to get away, get right away from here. He had always meant to get away: now he wanted nothing else, talked of nothing else, thought of nothing else. It drove him like a madness. And I went behind him, clinging to him, trying to follow.

There are times in our countryside when sunlight rarefies and brightens until the light is very clear, and then, while slate-bound clouds come piling from the sea, you can tell each separate blade of grass as if it stood alone and made its separate claim on life no matter what might follow. Perhaps that is why I remember these large free weeks of our living together with such unforgettable exactness.

TWO

TED and Mother, like I said, were put on the run by a false alarm. After our first day and night of living in the woods and making it really comfortable, Jacob sent me into Chudbury by a long way round so as to discover what was being said. I went to my aunt Pooley's at the old schoolhouse and found her still in her petticoat and nightcap, but full of the news. It doesn't take twenty-four hours for news of that kind to run from our village to Chudbury – nor back again if need be and doubled twice the size in running.

I have always loved my aunt Pooley. That morning I threw my arms about her neck and kissed her face until she was laughing like a young girl. She was delighted to see me but also a little anxious. 'Thought as how you'd 'a gone with 'em,' she said, beaming and nodding and clasping her hands in her lap. 'You two coming over to live here now, ain't you, Lindy?'

I told her that we should be coming over to see her regularly, but that we were living with Mrs Morton now, just because it was easier for school and Jacob had his work in that direction. Besides, there wasn't really enough room at my aunt Pooley's, and then Morton was well-off and my aunt Pooley only had her old-age pension and bits of money she picked up quietly, for charring now and then, without letting the pension people know. She listened disappointedly to these explanations. 'Thought as how you was coming over here to live, Lindy,' she repeated.

There was much in me that wished that too, but I managed not to let her see it and consoled myself with thinking that there really wasn't room. All she had was half the old schoolhouse, a big room partitioned down the middle with my aunt Pooley on one side and Miss Fen on the other. My aunt Pooley and Miss Fen could not abide each other: at the least unusual noise from the other side – and naturally you can hear pretty well every-thing through a thin partition – they would hammer and shout and carry on as though the place had caught fire. We two should have made a lot of extra noise and Miss Fen, apart from hammer-ing and shouting, would have soon walked up the road and complained to the council. That was the last thing we wanted.

'Silly old creature,' grumbled my aunt Pooley, who as a matter of fact was a good deal older than Miss Fen: 'I'd tell her something if she done that.'

'But we'll come and see you twice a week,' I promised.

And yet it was such a welcoming place, this half-room of my aunt Pooley's, that I could not help being sorry for myself. She had done it up with odds and ends of curtain and a bright bit of rag on the bare boards near the black iron stove: and often we had come here on Sundays and had our tea with her, while she rattled on about Chudbury gossip and the people she remem-bered. She remembered many people. She would sit in a straight-backed kitchen chair with her wrinkled hands in her lap and giggle like a young girl and talk as though the years had lost their number: of how she was born in Lowton but never knew her father, and had come long ago to work at Chudbury Grange in Mrs Chamfrey's time there; and of how she had stayed at Chudbury ever after, what with one thing and another, but mainly because of Samson Lewis. Samson was a figure you might have disbelieved in but for there being his photograph on the chest of drawers among her bits of mending and bottles of camphorated oil and the cough mixture that she drank at nights. There among the bottles, and seeming even to smell of cam-phorated oil himself, a dark brownish Samson Lewis peered from above a high white collar and jacket. Whenever she talked of Samson Lewis her old face seemed to return across the years and lose its age until she tossed and giggled, declaring of him at the end of her talk that there could never have been a better man to keep you warm in bed than Samson Lewis was. You might have thought he was a kind of hot water bottle.

206

She got on famously with Jacob. She expected nothing of him, was never surprised, and took whatever he said and did for granted; and this was just right for him. But then she expected nothing of anybody and always took life exactly as it came: she made you think that she had long since got the upper hand of being alive, and was doing life a favour by continuing to live; instead of the other way round, which is the general condition in my experience. Just like me she was begotten on the wrong side of the blanket: just as I'd have done, but for being sent to this place, she went to work as soon as she left school. She had drifted from Lowton to Chudbury and had lived with Samson Lewis whenever Samson happened to be there, which was not by any means often because Samson followed the sea; and after Samson died of cancer and they'd sold off the Grange and sacked the staff she had continued working as she could until they had given her the old age pension and half the school house to live in; and it all looks, writing it down, like nothing at all. Yet she had somehow got the upper hand of life so reassuringly that I never saw her but I got from her, sooner or later, a feeling that one day I might be able to get the upper hand myself.

You could tell her anything and know that it would never shock her. You could go to her and confess your silliest thoughts and fears; and it never made her think the worse of you. I never heard her say a hard or hopeless word against anyone excepting when she lost her temper with Miss Fen next door. 'Run out too quick,' she said with a shining smile on that day after their departure: 'Didn't come for them at all.' She had her hands in her lap and her head cocked a little on one side; and unless you'd known her well you might have thought her a little soft in the head.

I said I couldn't believe that. They'd come in a car, three of them in uniform. Harry had told us.

My aunt Pooley began whispering at the top of her voice, pointing with a terrible frown at the partition beyond which, as she believed, Miss Fen was always listening for her smallest word. As a matter of fact she could never speak softly: it was something to do with Samson's not having had his hearing in good order. She told me she had walked up to Mr Green's: Mr Green was the Chudbury police constable. 'Wasn't after Poppy nor Ted, that lot. They was asking after a car smash over to the by-pass there.'

'Well they've gone,' I said, 'and they aren't coming back for months. Perhaps they aren't ever coming back. They gave us money and said to come and live with you.' But that was not quite true: it was Dook who had given us the money.

She took this as quite in the natural order of things. 'Give you money, Lindy?'

'Twenty pounds.'

Now she was tossing and smiling in her girlish way. 'Easy come easy go,' she judged. 'Lot of goings on, I reckon?' She wouldn't let me talk about that though: she wasn't going to have Miss Fen overhearing it. But she decided: 'Poppy won't go far, that's for sure. There's them as travel up and down the world. Samson was a one for that. And there's them as'll never get away from their own place.'

I said: 'She's going to marry Dook, she says, and go away to America.' It was, at least, something she had once said. It might even possibly be true.

But my aunt Pooley seemed not to have heard me: she rocked in her straightbacked chair and smiled in her foolish girlish way at her hands in her lap, and said to herself: 'Samson was a one for that, always trying to get away.' She nodded and tossed her head and smiled down at her hands.

I'VE been running ahead of my story.

THREE   After the letter from the council Ted had wanted
        to end the village parties and close down the busi-
ness with the tarts, at any rate for the time being: what he had
called 'easing it off' until he should somehow settle with the
council either for withdrawal of the eviction order or else for
compensation and a new house. There would be support for
him in the village, he had said, because everyone knew that
Mrs Plum had properly diddled him; and he talked of calling
on Mr Harold, or asking Thompson to intercede for him with
Mr Harold, so as to get Mr Harold to write a helpful letter to
the council.

'Only I don't see as we can do that, Poppy, so long as we're
carryin on this way.'

'I'll talk to Tommy for you,' Mother offered. It sounded more
like a threat than a promise.

For that Ted came as near to anger as I ever saw him. He
said it wouldn't be a ha'porth of good Mother's talking to
Thompson: Thompson would never dare go to Mr Harold
unless it was all done fair and above board. Couldn't see
she that?

Mother could see nothing of the kind. The letter from the
council worked on Mother in the same way as Thompson's
having sacked her: what is more, she took it for granted that it
was one of her enemies who had gone to the council with news
of Ted's occupation of Mrs Plum's old cottage – for how otherwise could they have found out? – and she made it clear, right
from the beginning, that her enemies should suffer for it.

Ted had muttered and complained against this: he even argued
against it. He went back into that mysterious and threatening
time when Mother had been my age, or not much more, and

worked at Enfield before they had evacuated her in some business that Ted knew a thing or two about, but wouldn't say more – shooting little glances at me, glances that bent and slid and disappeared – because, he said, he wouldn't drag up the past against anyone, let alone against Poppy Wellin, who was his best friend. But the more he talked the more surely he drove her into doing what he least wanted her to do. She was much stronger than he was, and in any case they were after two quite different things. Ted was after a quiet little business in the country: Mother was after revenge.

He had often talked of this quiet little business in the country, and now he talked of it continually. He wanted, he said, to settle down. He was tired of battling and wrestling. 'You want to understand that, Poppy,' he declared one Sunday afternoon: 'There's two sides to business.' Tisn't only going out and gatherin it in. It's retiring, too, and livin respectable off of it.'

Mother had always let him talk, though she had seldom listened. 'You want to understand, Poppy, them Yankee-doodles won't be here for ever. They'll get tired of it and go home one o' these days, sudden like, from one day to the next I shouldn't wonder. They'll wake up one morning and they'll say what the bloody 'ell we doing here anyway, payin out a lot o' dough and gettin nothing out of it? They'll do that, see? Yeah, but where will you be then, eh?' He waved his cigar at us and continued in his gravest manner. 'You got to pervide for the future, see? That's what business means, see? I reckon everyone knows that. You makes a lot of dough but then you consolidates. You puts your money into something respectable 'n safe as houses, and then you lives off the proceeds. You becomes a pillar of the realm.'

'That what you're going to be, Ted?'

Ted replied gravely: 'Ah, you don't want to make a mistake, Poppy. You got to pervide for the future.'

'Any ideas, Ted?'

'Poppy love, that's one thing you couldn't say against Ted

Breldon. Never short of a good idea, Ted wasn't.' He spoke of himself as being somehow in the past: he often did that – it was part, I think, of the fading process, of his never seeming altogether real. 'At this rate, Poppy, we'll chuck it in next year. And I know what I'll do, eh? All right, I'll tell you. Notice anything about Rolcaster ever?' He looked carefully at each of us in turn and paused for a puff at his cigar. 'Nice little dump, but there's one thing it don't have. It don't have a launderette.'

'A what?'

Ted explained: a shop, he said, where you put in half a dozen of these new automatic washing machines and charged people a regular fee for letting them come and do their washing in comfort. 'I got ideas. I seen one of 'em. They got one over to Enfield, last year, big one with a dozen o' them machines and a coffee bar with soft chairs so's you sit 'n wait while your stuff's in the machine. I seen it. Owner got a wife dressed up fit to kill, 'n a new Austin 90, 'n a couple of kids that do the work.' He slid a look in my direction. 'Nice job for you, Lindy. Five quid a week 'n all you do is stand around and talk to the customers and serve 'em coffee at ninepence a cup. Small cup too. There's dough in cups o' coffee.'

Mother let him talk: you could never be sure she listened to him. I listened if only because Ted's ideas grew so oddly out of his talking: the more he talked the larger and lovelier they would grow. 'Stands to reason, Poppy. One of them launderettes in Rolcaster: that's solid, see. That's respectable. And you wouldn't stop there, eh? You'd fit a couple o' them machines into a van 'n you'd come round the villages 'n get the women to use 'em instead o' havin their arms in the washtub Mondays, wouldn't you? Reckon it up y'rself. Over to Chudbury, now, there's fifty women if there's one that hates the livin thought o' Monday, don't they? So up you comes with them machines 'n you charge 'em half a crown a go an' you're quids in 'fore you know it. You sit in that van 'n you're big 'n generous enough to let 'em pay for usin them machines, aren't you?'

'It's wonderful, Ted.'

'Of course it's wonderful, Lindy. It's business. It's what put England out in front of all them wogs 'n frogs. It's what they do in America, eh? Breldon Laundries, there you are. Once you got the dough it's easy. It's dough you want, eh?'

'Now how did you guess that, Ted?'

'All right, Poppy, so it's dough you want. So you got the dough now, eh? Yeah, but it won't last. It'll last another year – maybe. An' I tell you what we do. We close down the business over to Rolcaster 'n we send them girls back where they come from and we put the dough into a bank 'n we're respectable. Can't be touched, eh? Breldon Laundries.' He threw the stump of his cigar into the empty fireplace and sagged like a man who has really done a power of work.

But Mother, I suppose, was sure she could win by her own way. Through the whirl and bustle of all the weeks that followed, and all the parties that followed, Breldon Laundries seemed forgotten. She was not in the least after settling down: she was after something quite different. And when the letter from the council was confirmed by another letter – an eviction order this time – she thought, so far as I could tell, of practically nothing else. Ted argued with her; but for a long while he argued in vain.

On the day that the eviction order came he told her that the Americans would never stand for trouble, 'They got problems, too, Poppy. Dook ain't going along with us if it don't suit him, eh?'

'I'll look after Dook.' She had a meanness in her voice when she was angry with you: a meanness that seemed to enjoy hurting you even if it should hurt her too. I think she enjoyed hurting herself.

Ordinarily he would never have taken the argument any further, but the worry of it drove him. 'I got to say it,' he went on indignantly, speaking in a small high voice of anger that took him as near as he ever came to saying what he really thought. 'You think those boys need you, eh? All right, so you give 'em joy 'n comfort, I ain't sayin you don't. But you're losing sight

212

of another thing, see. How much they need you is nothing to how much you need them – nothing at all, eh?' Mother was smiling her crooked smile and was going to reply but Ted would not let her. ''Swhat none of them clever guys can grasp, eh? We got to have 'em. We can't afford not to have 'em. But Christ they ain't got to have us, have they? They c'n go off 'n live with them wogs 'n frogs if they want. You know bloody well they can. An' that's just what they'll do if we ain't careful.' He struggled out of his comfortable chair and ruffled himself in front of the empty fireplace. 'Was a lot of silly buggers in the pub last week, over to Rolcaster. Talkin about the Yanks this 'n the Yanks that. Christ I wanted to tell 'em a thing or two. Ought to go down on their knees 'n thank Christ they got the Yanks.'

Mother went on filing her nails, letting him talk. He turned on her angrily: 'You sit there 'n say nothing. All right then. But I'm tellin you the facks, see.'

'So what?' Mother replied without looking up. I could see that she was losing patience with him.

I doubt if Ted could see it. He was really troubled. He'd changed a great deal since those days of poverty and begging when he'd first come to us: he'd grown fat and comfortable. He wanted to be respectable. I don't see how you could blame him for that.

'I'll tell you what,' he rushed on. 'You go on like this, and you'll make it too hot for 'em. Yeah, they'll get a nice little word from the coppers, over to the Base, 'n 'fore you know where you are they'll have this village out o' bounds. Yeah, 'n then they'll get on to the Rolcaster end, 'n they'll put a stopper on that too. And then what?' He was almost shrieking at her. 'You'll have the coppers on the doorstep quick enough – askin who the bloody 'ell you think you are, with a knockin shop in Rolcaster?'

'Of course they don't know about it already,' Mother said sarcastically. 'They got to allow it, you said it yourself.'

'S'right they'll allow it so long's there ain't no fuss 'n trouble, see? But you start makin fuss 'n trouble and they'll be down on you quicker'n you know. They'll tip a word to the officers over to the Base, 'n they'll be down on you the day after.' He said disgustedly. 'You think I don't know? Christ I seen it.' He shouted suddenly: 'Why you think I left the last place, eh? Jus' for fun? Well you listen to me, Poppy Wellin – I ain't going to have it a second time. I ain't going to have it.' But it was useless; and I suppose we all knew, even then, that it was useless.

All the same, nothing came of Ted's worries – not even another letter from the council; and the parties continued. They continued and grew wilder. The only thing to increase Ted's worries was a brief conversation with Morton. She stopped him in the road one day and lectured him on what was wrong with his treatment of Jacob – and I think, though I never got this quite clear, on what was wrong with Mother's treatment of me. 'Said to me,' Ted reported, 'that she couldn't stand by 'n see that boy abandoned to a life of – I dunno what it was. Said he couldn't read. I dunno. Lindy, can he read?'

I shook my head.

Ted was indignant. 'What they been teachin him then, all them years? *My* fault if he can't read, is it? Didn't I teach him *meself* to read, eh?'

But Ted's feelings about Jacob would never take him far: he regarded Jacob, you would have thought, as someone on a level of age with himself. 'Make 'is own way,' he had said once, 'doesn't want me to hold 'is hand.' That was Ted's opinion on Jacob; and I'm not sure it wasn't rather a sensible one.

But in any case it was not what Morton had said about Jacob and me that increased his worries. She had also mentioned that 'certain things' were coming to her ears. Ted guyed that in telling us of it: he minced ridiculously and thrust out his bottom and tried to imitate Morton's careful way of speaking. But he quit doing that after a while and remarked to Mother in his ordinary voice: 'So it's like I said, eh?'

Mother played dumb over that: she'd already had her own row with Morton. Then she grew angry, when Ted insisted, and demanded to know who it was that told Morton what went on.

'Doesn't have to be anybody that tells her. You can hear the row half way to Rolcaster, I s'd think.'

'Shall I tell you who it is then?'

Ted was quick enough when it suited him. 'I'll belt that boy if I catch him,' he said, retreating.

He never did it, of course; and I doubt if he could have done it. But from that time onwards we all knew that Mother had made up her mind on whom to blame in case of trouble. She could scarcely bear to have him in the same room with her now, not even for the time it took him to eat his meals. But the parties nevertheless continued. They became the talk and scandal and amazement of the village, of Chudbury and surrounding villages, practically of our whole countryside. It was only after the shock of Mrs Thompson's actually coming to plead with her that Mother showed much sign of relenting. She agreed then that perhaps they were going a bit too far and a bit too fast: only by that time, as it seems, it was also a bit too late.

FOUR I SOMETIMES wonder how things might have turned out if only the last big party had gone off without trouble and Mother had then stuck to her agreement to have no more. For Ted in the end managed to convince her that she really was ruining the business at Rolcaster, as well as making more enemies in our countryside than anyone could easily have counted; but one last party, she declared, she must and would have. It should be the best and biggest of all her parties. For the last time they would dance and racket into the small hours and after that there should be no more. She had her generous side, and perhaps she meant it.

Nobody was more relieved, I think, than Dook. Over these weeks he had grown irritable and nervous, just as Ted had done: more than once I had overheard him complaining to Mother that they would run smack into trouble if they didn't mind out. He did not want to run smack into trouble: he didn't want to run into trouble in any way at all. Mother had sneered at him for that, although once when she flung at him that he could run away at once if he wanted, I thought that she might not be so far, herself, from losing her nerve. There was that in her too: she might kick everybody out of the way, regardless of the consequences, and then suddenly break down – just as on that first day of letting Thompson make up to her, and at other such times that I can still remember.

'It's the party to end all parties, isn't it?' Dook cried on arrival with Butch and Al that summer's afternoon. 'So we brought a couple of bottles.' In fact they had brought a couple of cases stacked high with various drinks. They staggered back and forth with them between their cars and the cottage.

Ted was in his strongest mood, which meant that he talked a great deal. He talked all the time. Perhaps because it was to be the last, this party seemed to have a special excitement in it right from the beginning: even the girls whom Ted fetched from the station later on became noisier than usual, although you might have thought it scarcely possible.

Before fetching the girls Ted decided they should have a little drink, just to celebrate. 'The best party of 'em all,' he explained '*and* the last. Right, Poppy?' Mother nodded easily: even she, now it came to the point, seemed glad enough to agree with this.

'To the queen of East Anglia,' Ted proposed. She enjoyed that. Everyone drank to the queen of East Anglia.

Ted got into his stride. He wanted, he said, to develop a few ideas. They let him talk, sprawling round the empty fireplace while he ruffled himself in front of it and developed his ideas.

The pleasant summer sun came across the room and danced in beams of dust. From where I was sitting, tucked into a corner, Ted seemed far away and varnished with respectability and time. It is one of my firm memories of him: of a fat and comfortable man, fat and comfortable and safe, developing his ideas while the sunlight filled and faded between us, and age lost all importance. He might have been, then, a young man of long ago; or even a young man in years ahead. But can it possibly be the same in years ahead?

Hands across the sea: he was off on a familiar line about hands across the sea. I don't quite know what that may have meant, except that there might be Dook on one side of the sea and Ted on the other, and they were England and America extending to each other the hand of friendship. This may seem ridiculous, but then a great many things *are* ridiculous; and if Ted enjoyed seeing himself as England shaking hands with America, I don't really see why he shouldn't have done so. It was not a crime.

Mother perhaps thought that she had gone quite far enough in reason and respectability, and took at once the other point of view. Nobody minded that, of course: it would be too much that Mother should be reasonable and respectable for long, or over more than one thing at a time. Besides, she was especially handsome that afternoon. She wore a flaring scarlet skirt and wide purple blouse of clinging silk material that came low over her shoulders and chest and showed a great deal of what they all wished to see: not because she much cared, I believe, whether they saw it or not, but because she was proud of her figure and thought it well worth looking at. There was nothing dishonestly coy about her. What she had she showed you that she had: Dook was fond of saying that she 'had it all.' Her black hair swept back over her handsome ears and fell in long curls upon the nape of her neck: round her throat she wore a necklace of sparkling diamonds that Dook had discovered at the PX, and another cluster of diamonds in the sudden parting of her bosom.

Currents of emotion seemed to run out from her and return again. She had no lack of sex appeal.

Ted was the only man, so far as I know, who was never in the least affected by her sex appeal. I do not know what it was, in the way of sex, that mattered with Ted: something he did not want enough to dare, perhaps, or did not dare enough to want. He liked to fiddle with himself while he stood with his back to the fire and his hands in his pockets, developing ideas; but he never offered me any harm.

He was developing his ideas about the launderette at Rolcaster. 'What we're doin for you now,' he was saying, 'is all right. I ain't saying nothing against it. But it's not solid, eh? It's not solid, and Poppy 'n me don't get any younger.' They grinned at the notion of Poppy and Ted being in any way a pair; but he continued without bothering with that, for talking was his real love. There was, he said, another thing.

'Watch it,' Butch called.

'Ah, Butch, you want to be careful now. We're doin you a service, eh? An' we're glad to be doin it. Here's you havin to leave your hearth 'n home and come over to poor ol' England, eh? We got to do something in return, stands to reason.'

'Stands to reason,' chorused Butch.

'The spirit of old England,' said Dook.

'In person,' agreed Butch.

'Yeah, but it ain't solid,' Ted continued, addressing someone far away above their heads. 'An' it costs you a pile of dough. Them girls never stop askin for more dough, and it's my guess they never will. That's the nature of wages, seems like. Well, don't you get to thinkin all that dough goes into my pocket, see?'

They all had a good laugh over that.

'Now I wouldn't say as Poppy there don't like a new dress every so often, and it don't come free. But it ain't solid,' he went on, 'It ain't a proper basis for you 'n us, sittin here and being friends and needin each other. Yeah, and defendin each other.' He ruffled himself and took a long pull at the glass of whisky in his hand. 'It ain't a proper basis, say what you like. I been thinking.' And then he was off on his notion of the launderette.

'They rents you these machines, see? But they don't make a limit to the amount you can use 'em, once you got 'em, see?' He looked round craftily. 'Now,' he said, sending the tip of his tongue round his fat red lips: 'Now supposin you boys was to come in on a launderette, eh?'

'Come in?' asked Dook innocently.

'Take a share in it. Invest in it.'

Butch groaned in mock dismay, settled down in his chair, pushed his pork-pie cap over his face and pretended to snore.

Al asked: 'We sitting here all day and jawing?'

But Ted was not to be defeated by a little criticism of that kind. He was fairly into his strongest mood. 'I ain't content with doing you a service, see. That's on'y natural, like, you defendin us and us defendin you, eh? But it don't stop there. We got to stick together, we got to help each other.' He ruffled himself in front of the empty fireplace and wiggled his toes and regarded the rest of us with care. 'We got to get you to invest. Capital 'n interest. You come up with the capital and we come up with the interest.' There was after all a deal of pleasure in listening to Ted: come what may, you felt, Ted would always wriggle through. So far as he was real at all, Ted would always survive.

Dook made a show of hauling out his wallet and counting imaginary notes. 'Okay Ted,' he agreed, 'how much was it you said? Ten thousand do for a start?'

Al repeated: 'We sitting here all day and jawing?'

'Just going, just going,' Ted reassured him, waving a hand in his direction: 'They'll be on the five seven, no sense going beforehand.' He was really pleased with himself. 'Partnership,' he declared suddenly, coming as near to anything sharp and definite as he would easily get himself. 'That's what we want, don't we? Partnership. We can't do without you, so we got to make sure you can't do without us. And how we do that, eh?

Service. Service all along the line. So you're the big guys with the capital 'n I'm the little guy with the interest, ain't I? Ain't I now?'

I have no idea where Ted may be now; but wherever he is I like to think of him standing in front of somebody's fireplace with his thumbs hooked into the armholes of his waistcoat and an old smile varnished on his face, drawing out of himself a plan that is always new, always hopeful. It rises into the sunlight like a gleaming silver bubble, and you watch it with a precious hope of security and comfort, somewhere far away; and then it bursts, noiseless, placeless, as though it had never been. And when it bursts, when it vanishes upon the summer air, Ted is disappointed and nods his head in disapproval and begins all over again. And you let him begin all over again. Somehow or other it is desperately important that he should begin all over again, for it matters not at all how often the bubble should burst: what matters is that Ted should blow another one.

In the comfort of that particular bubble we strolled into the summer garden while Dook opened cans of beer and brought them on a tray with glasses. It would be too hot for dancing, Mother decided, so instead of the gramophone we had the portable wireless on the clipped new turf. Altogether it was a quiet and comfortable beginning to what Dook had called the party to end all parties.

FIVE   TOWARDS six o'clock Ted returned from the station with Suzy and Mary. Those girls came softly through the gate with their little wooden faces painted red and black, and their little square boxes with handles on the top: the one, I thought scornfully, as empty as the other. They came in very quietly and walked up the path and not across the grass, one behind the other, and gingerly sat on the edge of the chairs that Al and Butch made empty for them; and all they could say, to begin with, was hallo.

Mother called: 'Give them a drink, Dook, they've seen a cow.'

'Very funny,' said Mary.

I must have looked my thoughts, for Butch said teasingly: 'Hi Lindy, where's y'r lipstick?' He squatted on his heels in front of me. 'You ever thought how you was throwin y'rself away on a lot of hicks?'

He blinked up at me with the sunlight in his chubby face. I put out a toe and shoved him gently over. He lay on his back and roared for help, thrashing his short fat legs. This cracked the ice a little, and Butch broke it altogether by sliding out a hand and catching Suzy's ankle while she was taking a drink from Dook. Suzy pitched down beside him; and at that, like a signal, the whole tremendous machinery was in motion. Suddenly we were shouting at each other, easy and relaxed, and having a high old time: suddenly it was a party.

They began to dance for all its being too hot. Ted brought out the gramophone and some records while Mother flung off her shoes and bullied Dook into dancing with her, although it was Al who really loved to dance: Al followed with Mary and took it seriously, making her take it seriously as well. Then you forgot, and possibly Al forgot it too, that Al was homesick and unhappy: he swayed across our neat clipped turf with the bright sun slanting in his eyes, and his long arms and legs joined and fitted to him properly at last, while Mary, far beneath him, was only a small fat doll. I was sorry for her then because Al tired of her and took Mother away from Dook. The others stopped dancing and watched Al and Mother. We all watched. Even Ted sat up and watched while Al and Mother shook and stood, and moved again, frantically, furiously, as the trumpets moaned and the drums beat distantly upon our neat clipped turf.

Seeing us like this, happy together in this party to end all parties, you might have been reminded of Dook's big car: large and long from bashed-in bonnet to upward-jutting tailfins, with

room for everyone, and everyone suddenly twice the size of
their natural selves, and twice as loud, and twice as confident.
'The old wagon,' Dook would say, slapping the wheel, 'what
the hell.' I don't think that Dook, any more than Ted, ever had
this idea of mine that the future and the past really happen
together, in the present: he went from one day to the next as if
each day was a little farther on – farther on to where I do not
know, except that Dook consumed time as cars consume petrol.
He drove on time through the weeks and the months and appeared quite sure that he was moving all the while. This made
him cheerful to be with; but it also made you feel that he was
with you, and you with him, only in the way you knew that
scenery was with you while you steered along our country roads
in the front seat of Dook's big car, and laughed at the comic
things and people that you saw.

They danced a great deal and they drank between times while
the sun grew hotter and came still closer to the earth, and the
earth swung and heaved in space until we were dazzled and
drunk with the heat and light and movement of it. The summer
evening, long and warm and brilliant, seemed to promise that
darkness would never fall. People came and went, I'm not sure
who: others lingered on the road and gaped through the neat
clipped hedge, and two or three lay fondling under the silent
ash trees or dozed and rested. I cannot remember who was
there and who was not: I was filled with light and warmth and
the assurance that we were moving rapidly from one place to
another place, so that the new must be altogether different from
the old, and consequently better. Two or three more came from
the Base, I think, and one or two from Chudbury; some of them
had girls and some had not. I doubt if Thompson came: perhaps
he came later, or intended to come later. But Morton came.

Mother had sent me in to cut sandwiches. I opened tins of
spam and boiled two dozen eggs and sliced loaves of bread and
buttered them, while Dook opened cans of beer that foamed
deliciously at triangles which he cut into their lids. He thrust his

sweating head beneath the cold tap and came over and put his arm round me in sheer friendliness. I remember the filmy blueness of his eyes and the small bulbs of water on his leathery skin and the drenching smell of his body close to mine. When I carried out a loaded tray of beer and sandwiches I went into the circling swaying crowd of them while the trumpets moaned and the drums were thudding on our turf, thudding in my head, and life was powerful and frantic. Then I saw Morton, in purple trousers and canary yellow sweater, dancing with Butch; and I knew in my astonishment that we had certainly moved from one place to another place, an altogether better place, and left the wearisome old world behind. I ran my tray into Mr Morton's wide green waistcoat and looked up and caught a glance in his smiling eyes, and the glance confirmed that Mr Morton thought the same as I thought. I shouted to him and it is even possible he shouted back. Just for a moment or so we were alone together in all that swaying shouting mob, and he seemed not to mind in the least that I should know what he thought. 'Quite a party, isn't it?' he said, looking over to where Morton danced with Butch: 'I really think she's enjoying it, you know.' But I suppose it was saying more than one person may easily admit to another, especially if that person is Mr Morton, who shuts away his sadness and his hopes, if he has any, behind a patient smile and a wide green waistcoat with cheerful buttons. He said quickly: 'Here, Lindy, let me help you with that tray.' And took it from me and pushed cheerfully through the crowd to where we had the table for drinks. 'Make way, make way,' he called to everyone. He seemed to have forgotten the differences and that was just as well, for everyone treated him as a funny waiter who ought to hurry up or else he'd lose his job. They shouted for sandwiches and beer. 'Coming, coming,' he shouted back.

By this stage, at one of our parties, you would not expect to know what should happen next: you were steering through the fun as though you navigated on the wide free ocean, and you came upon the things that happened next as sailors of the olden time had come upon goddesses and griffins and men whose heads did grow beneath their shoulders. By this stage too, our parties would have grown not only in numbers but also in a way which is hard to describe – in a way which made them larger in shape and circumstance. They spread. They went on in different parts of the garden. They caused dancing on the turf and drinking on the edge of the turf and dozing and fondling under the trees. By this stage the girls had taken off their dresses and were stripped to beach suits; one or two had floppy hats that grew like enormous mushrooms on the lawn. The men had taken off their shirts and danced in their singlets and tight trousers, crane-like with crew-cut heads pushed forward on their shoulders, their arms flailing, their knees wobbling, while drums beat distantly to the happy moan of trumpets on the neat clipped turf. By this time we were coasting in top gear across the wide free ocean and as likely as not we should be doing this for ever.

I am not sure what time it was that I caught sight of Jacob. He was skirting the edge of the grass, his hands in his pockets and his shoulders drawn together, his face turned away from us. I felt a twinge of irritation and dismay: I wished he could be like the rest of us and enjoy himself and forget for once the troubles that drove him along his own way that was no one else's way. No one else's but mine. He had come in quietly through the gate and pricked the silver bubble that blurred and glimmered and contained us all. Butch saw him too and shouted to him, attracting attention so that others looked; and then I wanted to rush to his defence and was ashamed of my disloyalty.

Butch yelled through the din of drums and trumpets: 'Hi, there's Cheerful Charlie. C'm on over 'n have a drink, Charlie.'

It was Butch's notion of being friendly and welcoming, but Jacob could never take it in that way. He refused to answer Butch's call, and kept on doggedly round the edge of the grass towards the door; but many had seen him now, although really they were laughing not to make him look silly but to welcome him. Only he would never see it like this: I knew it would take me hours to wheedle him out of the mood they were driving him into just as surely as a hammer drives a nail. I was angry with them but I was also angry with him; and that was a new sensation. For the first time it was as if he were also refusing to answer me: perhaps it was then that I fully understood how far he would go from them – how far I should need to go too. I didn't want to go then: I wanted to stay and make him stay. But I started pushing through the crowd towards him, and it was like the beginning of a long journey: along his way, not along mine: not steering across the wide free ocean but steering deviously, doggedly, with the wind in your face all the way, going much farther than you ever meant, and having to follow where you should have led, and having to continue when you should have stopped. This was the day, perhaps, when I slammed the last door on being a child.

Butch managed to get there first. 'Hi Charlie,' Butch was saying, 'C'm on over 'n have a drink.' He had put himself in Jacob's way so that Jacob had stopped and was looking at Butch through his fringe of hair like a trapped animal; and he wasn't copying James Dean either. I looked round wildly for Mr Morton; but Mr Morton was nowhere to be seen. I caught Butch's arm. 'He's hot and tired, Butch. He wants to wash. You'll come out later, won't you, Jacob?'

That made it worse: he thought that I was taking sides against him. He would not look at me. I ran to him and took his hand, but he flung it away. 'Hi Charlie,' Butch was saying, 'you can't do that to a lady.' He caught hold of Jacob's shirt neck. Jacob put down his head and thrust it sharply into Butch's stomach so that Butch gasped and let go; but people were crowding up and had surrounded us until Jacob could no longer escape. Suddenly Morton was there too; and Mother as well.

Mother was furious. There was never much required to make her furious with Jacob, nor he with her; and now the fury of enjoyment seemed to spark off in her the whole train of quarrels they had bickered in for months, so that she positively glowed and flashed with the fact of being able to hate him, and feel her hatred, and have it strong and solid in her hands, as it were, so that she could use it properly against him at last. You would not have understood this without knowing how we had lived together. Several of the men and girls, crowding about us, thought that Jacob had assaulted Mother instead of Butch, and piled their anger on top of hers. He stood unyielding amongst them, ragged and bedraggled, an unwanted stranger who had spoilt their gaiety and fun.

Nothing much came of it, though, or nothing that could easily be seen. Butch turned away in disgust and pushed off into the crowd; the crowd drifted away after him, throwing questions to each other but quickly losing interest. Someone put on a new record. Only the four of us were left; and then Jacob walked away, leaving Mother and Morton and me.

Morton said: 'Forgive me saying so, Mrs Wellin, but I don't think you ought to talk to him like that. It sounds, I mean, as though you really meant it.' Mr Morton was somehow with us now, distracting her, catching at her arm; but he was just too late. Mother appeared to notice Morton for the first time.

'And you're another,' she began furiously, exactly as though Morton were Jacob, and she hated the one as much as the other.

Mr Morton was saying: 'Oh I say, now, Mrs Wellin –' But she was driven by her anger now, and more than Mr Morton's gentle voice would have been required to stop her, even though the drums were thudding on the turf and the whole party suddenly returned to life again.

From what this quarrel led to you might have thought that they said a great deal to each other. I don't remember their having said very much. It seemed to come out that they were quarrelling over Jacob, and that Morton was trying to protect him. At any rate she did her best. 'I'm not going to have that boy bullied and bear-led,' I heard her say: 'I've told you that before.' Mother

226

began to swear at her; and with every word Morton's face seemed to take a wooden slap and lose something of itself, as though Mother was dismantling her, taking piece from piece, the high-arched pencilled eyebrows, the clear unruffled forehead, the prominently staring eyes, the carefully arranged lips; and Morton, through all this, terribly unable to defend herself. I looked past her at Mr Morton: he was bending forward a little, gazing at Mother with a serious fixed stare like a man who goes through pain he cannot bear, he simply cannot bear.

Morton said: 'That's more than enough, Mrs Wellin.' Her whole face and bearing seemed terribly deranged. Her voice came sharply out of a soft blurred face. 'I thought these parties were harmless but I see I was wrong. They're nasty and indecent as I've been told.'

'You've been told, have you? Bet I know who told you. Don't you think he won't pay for it.'

Morton saw the danger now, but once again it was too late. 'I'd like to make it clear that Jacob has told me nothing.'

'Hasn't he?' Mother jeered. She could never manage to show mercy when she was winning.

But that let Morton off. 'Oh it's common property, Mrs Wellin. After all,' she laughed abruptly, pressing back against Mr Morton's green waistcoat and pointing a finger-nail, sharp and polished, towards the rest of them: 'you can't be surprised, can you?'

Mother ignored that. 'If anything gets done against me,' she said in a cold slow voice, 'if anything gets done, I'll know exactly who's to blame. And I'll see it gets done to him too.' All the strength and fury that were in her went into those words: they struck firm and clear and unforgettable: they were like a black line ruled thick beneath a long account so that you knew the sum, no matter how often you might add it up, from top to bottom or from bottom to top, must always be the same.

Mr Morton got them away from each other after that. It wasn't so difficult, in fact, because there seemed strangely nothing left to say. Morton did say something, though; and Mother replied.

'I shall inform the police.'

'Do what you bloody well like.'

The two of them began walking out across the turf towards the gate and a shocked silence ought to have gone with them; but instead of that there was the beating of the drums and the moaning of the trumpets and the clink of bottles and the rising flood of alcohol. They went out like people who have sinned and ought to feel shame; and I ran after them, not wanting them to go like that. It was difficult to go along the pathway to the gate. On the edge of the sunlight Butch and Suzy lay across it with two others just beside them a little farther on. Al was propped against a bush, a bottle in one hand and a strange look of pain twisting through his face while a girl sat in front of him and screamed at him. I came up with the Mortons just as Mr Morton tripped over her outflung arm: or perhaps he stepped on her hand, for I do not think he looked where he was going. But even then he paused, and I heard him saying something properly apologetic – it was natural for him to apologize, I think, at all moments of misfortune in his life: whereupon that girl stopped screaming at Al and began screaming at Mr Morton, reeling somehow to her feet and wriggling her mostly naked body in his face. And the strange thing was that it was he, and not this silly screaming female, who appeared ridiculous: it was he who appeared in the wrong. But I ran past her and shouted at her, feeling ridiculous myself, 'You want to dress yourself'; and caught up with them just as they passed through the gate.

I gasped out words of apology, catching at his arm; but he looked at me distractedly and shook away my hand from his arm. 'Mary, my dear,' he was saying to her; and then I could not hear any more, except that he appeared to be telling her that it was his fault, entirely his fault. He walked away with her, his head close to hers, his shoulders bent like those of an old man.

I went back not through the garden but round the hedge

into the cottage through the kitchen window. He was eating bread and jam in wolf-hungry mouthfuls. I said hopelessly: 'You angry with me?' I felt exactly as though I was Mr Morton.

I didn't expect much from that and I got nothing at all. But he let me sit with him while he stripped to the waist and scrubbed the chalk white skin of his chest and neck until it grew flushed and rough. I brought him a clean shirt and he took it from me, not thanking me but letting me give it to him, so that I knew that somewhere inside him, as yet beyond reach, he was ready to forgive me and make it up. I smiled at him to make this easier; and he gave me an angry little word of thanks. It was a good deal in the circumstances.

Later on we slipped out through the kitchen window and across the weeds at the back, through the hedge, and into the long quiet fields. Behind us those trumpets moaned to the hollow twilight, no longer filling the world but giving forth only a small noise that you could limit and enclose. We left it behind us. We walked together into the still evening where clouds and woods reached to one another with grey curving arms, until, far away on the skyline, they met at last and married and were lost in the advancing night. We walked through the elm coppice and heard the last of the trumpets far behind us, sarcastically calling; but now we heard the other callings too, the comfortable yapping of the Sealyhams at Mannerses and a lone crow honking as it passed above us. I took Jacob's hand and we had after all escaped.

SIX   WE returned to the cottage at about ten o'clock the next morning, for it was a Sunday and we meant to collect things we should need. We had decided to get ready to move altogether into the woods, at any rate until the end of the summer; and after that, no doubt, we should go to

Australia. By ten o'clock, we thought, everyone but Mother and Ted would be gone.

We got in through the kitchen window and found the kitchen empty, as we had expected, and the sitting-room too. I noticed an envelope on the kitchen table. It was addressed to me.

I took it up and read it, standing there among the bottles and the glasses and the mess of the night they had made of it. I called to Jacob and read it aloud to him. It was in Mother's writing, but Ted had signed it too. It said that they had got to go away for a time. They'd got to go at once, we'd find out why soon enough and we'd better keep out of the way. I was to go and live with my aunt Pooley, and Jacob had better not be seen at our cottage or Ted's either. They would be back again before long, *when things have gone a bit quiet*; and within the envelope, although the letter said nothing of this, there were twenty new pound notes. Its postscript said in Ted's writing *you better burn this*, so I put it on the gas burner, lit the gas, and watched it flake away to crumpled ash.

Suddenly Jacob called to me: 'Look, they're still here.'

Ted was returning up the path. He waved his arms at us when we ran to the door: unshaven, uncombed, tieless, even his long brown shoelaces dragging on the ground, he crowded us back into the cottage. 'Coppers,' he said, breathless. 'Can't wait. You got that letter we wrote?'

He stared through us and round us. There was an unfamiliar stillness in his bleary eyes that seemed to make it possible for him to let us regard him without his wavering or blinking. I noticed that his brown eyes stood within rings of grey vaporous stuff and was surprised, even while I listened to what he said, that I had never noticed it before. He appeared to me, then, as being at last quite real: as real as when I had found him on the airfield long ago. You might have thought just then, but for his being so dirty and unshaven and breathless, that nothing out of the way had occurred – that he was rather satisfied with the situation, and, just possibly, even glad of it.

What he said, more or less, was that Harry had appeared and told them that the police were down at the other end of the village, inquiring at Miss Wixty's after a Buick that was wanted. Harry had managed to discover this from Miss Wixty's companion-help, a London woman who never mixed with the village but whom Harry happened to know quite well. Afterwards, as my aunt Pooley told us, it turned out that Miss Wixty's farmer, the one who came at weekends, owned a Buick in his own place and had driven into another car on the Cambridge by-pass, causing an accident. But Ted thought at once that it must be his Buick that was wanted: and wanted because Ted was also wanted.

They had already thrown things into the car. A trail of odds and ends went dribbling down the path, a slipper and a dressing-gown cord and a bottle of stomach pills. Ted caught up a last handful of clothes and rushed off to the gate again; we followed him.

Dook was still there. 'Here they are,' he said, straightening himself and giving us a wry smile.

Mother muttered something and seized the clothes that Ted carried, stuffing them into the boot. I was astonished to see that she too was in the same breathless condition as Ted: only there was a difference, for Ted looked as though it was only natural and to be expected, this sudden departure, while Mother did not look in the least like that.

Ted cried: 'I told 'em, Poppy. They say it's all right.'

Mother said sharply, not looking at us: 'It's got to be all right.'

Dook put his hand on her shoulder, forcing her to stand up. He said roughly, not asking her but telling her: 'You say goodbye to them properly.'

I was even more astonished when she stood up and turned to us. She was wild with anger: yes, but not with the furious conquering anger we had always lived with.

'Go on,' Dook said, a bit grimly, 'you say goodbye to them properly.'

She might have been ten years older. That is something often said of people when fear and trouble overtake them; but it was true of her then. Her cheeks and mouth had lost their firm full roundness, their blooming blossoming roundness: I thought that time had suddenly run ahead of itself, so that her cheeks and mouth and the lines of her face were sunk within themselves, deepened in shadow, turned sour and ugly. I saw her suddenly old and spiteful; and beaten. I tried to think of something comforting to say; and there was nothing.

She said nothing to me either, for all Dook's telling her; but she did speak to Jacob: 'You've done this, haven't you? I'll get even with you.'

Jacob frowned. I think he was almost as surprised as I was.

Perhaps she was a bit hysterical. Even now, looking back, I am not sure why it should have hit her so badly. She said: 'You stay and I go, is that it? We'll see.'

They were useless silly words. Even Jacob saw that, for he made no answer to them. Meanwhile Ted was in the car and had started the engine. Dook slammed down the boot. We followed him round to the front of the car. Mother got in and Ted leaned out of the driver's window.

With him, though, the months and years might have gone for nothing. I could scarcely believe my eyes: he looked almost happy. He grinned at Jacob and me. 'If it's rainin in Brummagem,' he said with a wink, 'why, you got the choice haven't you? You always got the choice.' He thrust up a hand and gave Jacob's arm a friendly shake. 'You take care of yourselves, you two. We'll be writin and we'll be sendin money, I shouldn't be surprised. Who knows – may even be back before long, eh?' I looked past him at Mother; but she kept her face turned stubbornly away.

Somewhere in the distance a car changed gear. Ted gave a shout: 'Mind y'rself! We got to be goin, eh?'

They vanished into the dust of their wheels, into the frantic blue of their exhaust. It was suddenly quiet.

But Dook was still there. 'You'd better be going too,' I said to him.

He nodded quietly, looking at us without a smile. 'Guess that's right,' he said slowly. 'Tell me, you get that money I left?'

'What money?'

'That twenty pounds I gave them for you.'

'Was that your money, Dook?'

'Well, it ain't much, but I'll send you some more. You won't see a cent out of those two.' He said it with a slow and final bitterness.

'They had to go.'

'Did they?'

He gathered me in his arms as I buried my face in his shirt, clinging to him. I heard him saying to me: 'You going to be all right, you two?'

'So long as they don't come back.'

'They won't.'

'Then we'll be all right.'

He pushed me gently from him and got out a notebook and the stub of a pencil from one of his hip-pockets, tore away a sheet and wrote on it his name and address in America. 'It's time I got out of this place,' he said briefly, bitterly: 'It's time I got home. But you two write an' tell me if you need money or anything.'

'You aren't taking Mother there?'

'I'm not taking her anywhere.'

'But you'll be seeing her again?'

'Not if I can help it. Sorry, Lindy, but that's how it is.' He looked puzzled, shaken. 'She's crazy, just crazy. As for him –' he jerked his head contemptuously: 'The spirit of old England, Jesus aren't you lucky.' He broke into a rueful smile: 'There it is, Lindy. Just a mistake. Just one great big mistake, the whole damned issue.' I didn't really understand that.

But he turned quickly to Jacob and seized his hand, shook it tremendously and at once got into his car and started the engine,

I waved to him sadly, miserably, as he drove off down the road, and Jacob cried, 'Shan't see them again!'; but I couldn't share his gladness. I was overwhelmed, I don't know why, with a sense of helpless waste and disappointment: as though – yes, as though nothing that Dook had brought us and meant to us could ever possibly be any good. I expect that's silly: I expect I was only wretched with familiar misery.

We spent a little time in the cottage after that, although there was no need to wonder what we should do next. We collected all the cans of food and household stores that remained, and these we carried in sacks through the back garden and over Jerman's field to the verge of the woods. We had to make two journeys of it. We stumbled among bottles and glasses and the drenching tide of misery; and when we had collected the last of what we should need we left that place of fury and despair.

SEVEN   YET the misery departed too: for as soon as we had lived three or four weeks at our hut in the woods it came to seem that we had lived there practically for ever. We told no one but my aunt Pooley: the village thought that we were living with her, at Chudbury, and Chudbury thought – if it thought of us at all – that we were living at Morton's. The only one to be hurt by this arrangement was Mick Lissard.

He stopped me in Chudbury one day when I was coming from my aunt Pooley's. There is a narrow humped bridge at Chudbury that goes over a mill stream; Mick was waiting there so that I should not be able to avoid him. I didn't want to avoid him.

He said anxiously: 'I know where you're staying, you an' Jacob.'

'You won't tell, Mick.'

'Course I won't tell. But –' he hesitated.

I said quickly: 'I'll let Jacob know. Only you can't come and see us.'

'Why can't I?'

I knew the answer to that, but I could not say it to him. I could scarcely bear to say it to myself. Jacob had even refused to allow my aunt Pooley to visit us.

'Well, we're just not having visitors.'

'Doesn't seem like Jake wanted any friends, Lindy.'

'Yes he does,' I lied, 'you mustn't take it that way.'

We were sitting beside each other on the coping of the bridge. I gave him a kiss and made him promise neither to visit us nor look for us nor tell others what he knew; and promised in return that I would try and persuade Jacob to let him visit us. I was getting wiser: I was growing up. Perhaps it was just in time, or perhaps it was just too late – perhaps I ought to have braved his anger and let my aunt Pooley and Mick and others come and visit us in the woods whether he liked it or no.

EIGHT   But I never did that. I kept them all away. And it is true that Jacob, so long as he was on his own, seemed happier now. The more he felt we had escaped, really escaped, the easier and gentler he became. Life grew calm again.

He continued to work for one of Mr Harold's tenants on the road to Lowton, keeping his bicycle in a tumbled barn on the edge of our woods. After breakfast, which I cooked on our Primus, I used to walk with him to the barn and sometimes across the fields to the road, one of the pleasantest walks you could imagine. From where the hut lay hidden among bracken and bramble and thorn we had to scramble upwards through a sloping pinewood where many rabbits had their burrows – or used to have them before the rabbit sickness killed them off – and the going was difficult because once you raised your eyes to the sloping pine tops and the clear sky above them you were as likely as not to go tripping into a burrow, and fall on your face among the bluebell shoots that grew there. But after you had climbed for a while like this you crested the hill and came suddenly close to the sky; and here the pine wood stopped at a low stone wall with a field of wheat beyond it and, beyond that again, there was the small road to Rolcaster. Usually I stood on this wall while he wheeled his bicycle through the young wheat to the road beyond, and waved to him until he was out of sight. Then I went back to the hut, washed up the breakfast things, and made our beds and put things straight. The rest of the day I had usually to myself: sometimes I went to my aunt Pooley's or now and then to Morton's, skirting the airfield on these expeditions because they had people busy on it now and going across it was for-bidden; but often enough I would just stay by myself in the hut and read or sew or daydream about the life we should have together once we had got away from here and travelled to Australia. Towards six o'clock, or soon after, Jacob would come home again.

He talked of getting away whenever he talked of anything. Calmer though our life might be, we still lived in a wildness of impatience to get away. And as the airfield came slowly into use again and occasional jets began screaming overhead, his worrying and impatience grew worse: he seemed then to have it firmly in his mind that unless we got away soon we should never get away. We decided that once we had a hundred and twenty pounds we should take the bus to London and buy our tickets for the steamer. By the beginning of harvest we had seventy-five pounds or thereabouts, so that we should certainly be able to get away before winter made living in the hut impossible; for earnings in harvest time would be heavier than usual, and now that I was not at school I ought to be able to earn as well. Yet his worrying continued.

Those unending talks we had about Australia, its certain welcome and its certain sunshine and its altogether different and better life, are entangled in memories of our own summer countryside. Day after day the sun of that warm summer came out of a sky that was clear and creamy blue but for the high white clouds that always sail across our skyline. At night the stars shone down in winking clusters until the darkness between them glowed like soft velvet: then the wheat on Jerman's land, as we came from Chudbury, gleamed in a silver sea through the time of full moon until our woods, long low shapes of darkness, were tall ships at anchor out there, waiting only for the ocean tide. Small night breezes rippled that silver sea as we came down the small road from Rolcaster so that it seemed, whenever we turned off into our pathway through the wheat, that we embarked on a good new voyage to the ultimate ends of the earth. Owls called to one another. Gulls flew in from the coast and fled about in half-lit mystery above our heads. And as we crossed the last beaches of that silver sea and came within the shadow of our woods we had the scent of honeysuckle to greet and please us: we entered our woods like travellers landing on a distant shore. We closed the shadowy doors behind us and felt that we were safe.

Morning after morning of that summer the sun rose into a pallid mist that gave sure promise of light and warmth, and through all these weeks the promise stayed unbroken. If I went to Chudbury then and turned to regard our woods they were like ships no longer but were softly filled clouds that barely swept the ground, one after another with the sight of far fields in between until they were lost in the morning distance. I was too happy to notice how the days swept by.

'Such sensible children,' Morton said. 'I must go across to Chudbury one day and thank Miss Pooley.' She was basking, as we were, in the quietness of our village now.

I BEGAN to teach Jacob to read. Of course he would
NINE be able to read in Australia – it went without saying:
        but I thought it was a fine and happy thing that he
should trust me enough to let me begin to teach him now, before
we got there. After starting on space comics I fetched a reader
from Mick Lissard's place, not telling Mick why I needed it
(though he must have guessed: he loved Jacob too): and within
a week he was reading the small words without help, and spelling
out the longer ones without minding that he could not read them
yet. The days slipped by uncounted.

On Sundays we would generally stay at home and make the
hut still more difficult to find: now it was arranged so that leaves
and creepers matched together with the darkish green paint he
had used on the outside planks until no one could have found it,
I think, but for knowing beforehand where it was. All this, we
said, was just for the time being: yet we worked at it so that it
might have been for ever. It might have been already in
Australia: once we were safely in our hut, lying on our beds and
talking of the altogether different life we should have in
Australia, we thought of ourselves and of other people in an
altogether different way. We should be just the same as everyone
else in Australia: we should be living in an ordinary house in a
row of houses and with friendly neighbours – neighbours who
took shape for me, nearly always, as the white-haired woman in
a mauve hat who had stopped her car for us, long ago, on the
winter road to Thaxted. We should be like the others. We should
be married.

That was how we came to making love. I am not ashamed of
this, no matter what was said later; but I am not going to tell
much about it. I had never felt about Jacob in that way, although
I had grown up out of my childishness and knew I was a woman:

we used to undress in front of each other without thinking twice about it, for we had never thought twice about it. Then one evening, taking off my petticoat, I knew that he wanted to look at me and I felt myself blush for it. I thought: in Australia we'll be married, in Australia we'll make love. And quite suddenly I wanted not to wait till we should get to Australia.

Like mother like daughter, the magistrate said afterwards: she said it kindly, wishing to explain and not to hurt. And it did not hurt, because it simply was not true. Mother wanted that for herself, to prove something to herself: I wanted it for both of us, but mainly I wanted it for Jacob. I wanted it for him in the same way that I wanted him to be able to read: I wanted to make him like myself, like everyone. I loved him too.

So I went on taking off my petticoat that evening, and all my clothes, and stood by the window that he had made for us, and looked into warm green leaves where our sheltering blackthorn grew. It was the slow resting moment when twilight flickers into darkness. I blushed at fearing that he would find me awkward and disagreeable to look at. My stomach trembled: I remember thinking that nothing in any case could be quite the same after this. But I took courage, for I wanted life to change: there was nothing I wanted more. After a while I managed to look across at him and understood that it might after all be harder for him than for me. So I went to him and took his hand and put it to my breast: I sat beside him in the summer twilight and explained to him that we should be married in Australia. He could not bring himself to say anything to that: he was still fighting a difficult and distant battle. He let his hand stay where I held it but kept his head turned from me: I was afraid for a while of having touched the hidden perversity and anger that could rise in a moment and shut you from him altogether. I began talking to him. He could not do me any harm, I told him: nothing but going away from me, staying away from me, could do me any harm. Above me I could not see the sky but I could imagine it, star-clustered there beyond our flimsy roof: I peered up into the darkness and knew the scent of honeysuckle and the bitterness of ivy and the sweat of his body against mine. The world was very close to me then. I pulled down his head and put his shy face between my breasts. I felt his fingers moving on me. I was not much afraid.

Perhaps he held it against me afterwards. I think he did. Even though he wanted me he nursed a secret grudge for it – as though his coming into me was also a defeat, a lessening of the fact of his escape. I do not really know; the warmth and love of being together were more than this grudge, much more. I scarcely noticed it.

WE made love properly on Sundays when there were
TEN long hours for lying together and dreaming and enjoy-
ment. At other times he came into me quickly, furiously, grudgingly, so that there was no pleasure for me and none for him either, I should think, but the bare satisfaction of desire. Yet I was wonderfully happy for most of the time.

Even the new jets rocketing overhead with a din that seemed to paralyse the brain could not spoil our peace and pleasure in that long summer and its harvest. Mr Harold had informed Oliver it was the best year he well remembered: one of the heaviest, according to his father's books, that they had reaped at Jerman's for a good fifty years, ever since old Jeffreys and Mr Harold's father had marched away to the Boer War and only old Jeffreys had returned. Not being pressed by the weather they let the corn turn golden to the last ear: they let it stand upon our fields until it glowed in the sun like golden mirrors and swayed in the starlit night like a silver sea. Regularly, every time we saw him – and we saw him pretty often – Oliver Chamfrey clicked his tongue against his teeth and sucked on his whiskers and wrung his hands with satisfaction in the field of corn he'd persuaded Mrs Chamfrey to allow him to sow that year. There was good money in it, Oliver considered: and you could practically see the good money in it, silver and golden money, solid standing corn across the acres of our countryside.

Mr Harold borrowed Jacob for the work at harvest time; and so it came about that he was set to helping in the home fields with Mr Harold's combine, a monstrous red machine with a crooked spout above it whence beaten corn hissed down in crackling richness. They put Jacob to driving the tractor which pulled the corn truck, moving alongside the combine, into which the combine poured its harvest. I was more than ever grateful now to my aunt Pooley, for she kept up the old habit of gleaning – not because the combine left anything much behind it, but because it was a habit she enjoyed. I always went with her; and occasionally two or three other women would join us for a while. For day after day we moved across the new stubble, coming behind the combine and its corn truck with the scent of corn about our heads until we felt as though half-smothered in a haze of golden dust. Those golden days seemed half a lifetime.

They were good days for making money too. Driving the tractor for the corn wagon, Jacob seldom put in less than ten hours a day and sometimes more, starting at six in the morning and going on often till it was nearly dusk; so that his week's pay went up by several pounds in spite of the fact that he was not yet seventeen. Then Australia seemed to glimmer nearer during the minutes that we lay in bed together, before going to sleep, and thought of our pound notes piled upon each other in the tin beneath the floor of the hut. Sometimes we would make love for all that we were tired, and then the difficult grudge he had against me, for coming into me, seemed altogether gone. I held him in my arms and felt that nothing could matter so long as we should never part.

My aunt Pooley kept our secret, as Mick Lissard did; and I do not think that anyone else so much as bothered to inquire. Whenever I saw Morton I was careful to speak of Chudbury and our living there; and Morton, watching us at work together in the fields and understanding it was promotion for Jacob that he drove the corn-wagon tractor, had only kind words for us. She did ask once or twice if there were any news of Mother; but there never was, and we were all made comfortable by that. Day after day we harvested, traipsing long miles behind the slow combine with its spout erect and fruitful against the high white clouds of summer.

I used to go with Jacob soon after half past five through our dawn-lit woods to the barn where we kept his bicycle: there I would pack his breakfast thermos and an early sandwich into the carrier basket and walk with him while he wheeled his bike through the last of the woods and across our field to the small road beyond: then we waved goodbye to each other across the scented stubble, and an hour or so later I would tie my hair into a handkerchief and take our lunchtime sandwiches and another thermos of tea, and go by the same path and the same road to the village, or else straight to the place where the work went on that day. Sometimes I would call first for my aunt Pooley and go together with her to the fields.

I did this whenever I especially wanted her to myself. I told her everything that happened to us. I doubled the joy I had in telling her.

'You goin to have a baby if you don't mind out,' she said, her old blue eyes dancing with the happiness that I wanted her to share.

'I don't care.'

'Don't care, don't care,' she said, her voice rising to its familiar shriek: 'You got to care, seem like to me. That Jacob'll care. He'll care.'

'We're going to be married.'

But she went on shaking her head. 'Don't care,' she repeated, nodding and shaking, 'you got to care.' She did not really mean this, though: secretly she loved me the more for giving myself to Jacob. I knew that well enough. 'You got to live the way you're set,' she'd said once: 'No good runnin out from that.' She had wanted to have a baby from Samson Lewis, I knew that too, only Samson had somehow failed to give her one.

Then we came to the rim of the wide flat-curving field where the combine worked that day and joined the others, and went across the stubble to the distant place where the combine was, its muffled engine chattering behind a veil of dust, its thin spout tall above the shadow of the woods. I scarcely spoke to Jacob all day except when we stopped for tea and sandwiches, or once or twice when Harry had to fix or settle something in the combine: otherwise he would come driving by on his tractor, hauling a wagon-load of corn to Jerman's yards or returning with it empty, his thin shoulders tensed forward over the jerking wheel, his whole body keen and sharp with the skill of mastering that difficult machine. At night I would hold his trembling hands and try to soothe them until he could relax and go to sleep.

Unless the men had decided to continue working until dusk we would walk home with my aunt Pooley, going through the village and along the road to Chudbury with the scent of corn and the dust of harvest like a golden cloud upon our heads. We stopped occasionally at the *Wheelwright* for Jacob to slake his thirst: he could go in there now and drink with the others on a level with them, and it did him a world of good. He could even put his hand to his purse and stand my aunt Pooley a drink when she fancied one, which wasn't often.

Once he even said to her, sitting in the bar with the others: 'You coming to Australia with us, Aunt Pooley?' And when she did not seem to hear what he said he repeated the question.

'You coming to Australia with us?'

She looked suddenly severe. 'Samson was always one for gettin up 'n going away,' she said. 'Reckon you've got to live the way you're set, though.'

Then it happened that Oliver made an interruption. 'You doing nicely, Miss Pooley?'

As though she had forgotten what Jacob had said and what she had replied she cried to Oliver: 'Got to be, haven't I?'

'Ah, that's right, I expect,' Oliver replied.

'Course it's right,' said my aunt Pooley.

But mostly we discussed the weather and the chances of its staying dry until the rest of the corn was in; while the men drank their satisfaction and Oliver would hover round, drawing pints, and nervously wonder if the weather could possibly allow him to wait with his own field until Jerman's combine could be hired. He wondered this merely out of nervous habit, not bothering anyone, for everyone knew that the weather would not break. 'Be thunder when she do,' commented old Jeffreys, 'but she won't break now, Oliver, an' you can lay to it.' We sat amid the comfort of their sweat and the scent of corn, and listened in content.

If Jacob and the others had decided to work until dusk I used to walk back to Chudbury with my aunt Pooley and rest with her until past eight o'clock and then return to the fields for Jacob. We would go home by way of the pub, just the same; but without my aunt Pooley he would not stay there long. After his pint we strolled off along the road until we were free of the village and as far as the edge of the stubble. Now it shone no longer like a silver sea: it lay fine cut and sharp beneath our feet, and across its desolation our shadows went separately upon the ground. Everything comes to an end.

ELEVEN   MOTHER's letter reached me after the harvest, when Jacob had returned to work at his old place on the Lowton road. I think it may have been getting into September: I know that we had packed more than a hundred pounds into the tin beneath the floor, and talked of making our trip to London, for buying tickets, at almost any time now. I was spending most of my days with my aunt at Chudbury, for it seemed barely worth while looking for work because we should be gone so soon. Jacob could read the papers pretty well now: he could even write a little too. The summer was nearly over.

My aunt Pooley received the letter. It was addressed to her, although it was written to me, and it came from Rolcaster. Mother was lying in hospital there. 'Seem like she's pretty bad,' declared my aunt Pooley, holding the letter in her lap before giving it to me to read. I took the letter and read it then; and each single doubt of our ever getting away rose up and hemmed me in. Mother's handwriting was more of a scrawl than ever: it wandered along the lines, rising and falling, and words were terribly mis-spelt. It had never struck me that Mother was less educated even than I was: she was not much better than Jacob, I saw that now, in the matter of spelling and writing. There was little enough in that letter, though: only three things – that she was ill, that she wanted me to visit her at once, that she was without a penny.

I caught the bus that morning. In my purse there was five pounds that I had taken from Jacob's tin.

Afterwards, when I tried to make him understand why I had taken it, I found there was nothing more to say but what was in her letter: that she was ill, and wanting me, and without a penny. But he couldn't see that it made any difference: he was always one for snapping the chains that held him. Even taking the money, for him, was the lesser part of what I'd done.

From the bus station at Rolcaster I asked my way to the hospital and walked there. It was a long walk. The hospital stood in one of those endless roads they have at Rolcaster where many people live whom you can never see nor ever want to see: an old tall greyish building behind iron gates. I had to wait in the hospital smell while my legs caught their old fit of trembling that I'd lately dared to think was gone for ever; but the only chairs were occupied by other people who also waited. A nursing sister asked me whom I wanted and went away without a word. I waited. Another sister came and asked the same thing. This one said, 'Who? Mrs Wellin?' looked at me sharply and also went away. I continued to wait. At last a third sister came and asked again, but replied: 'Oh, you can see her, I think. Come along then.' No doubt they were very busy.

She went along a corridor and up a flight of stairs and along another corridor, walking so fast that I was trotting after her, and turned quickly through a pair of swing doors. Now the smells were stronger than before. We entered a ward. 'She's over there,' the sister said impatiently. 'There's nothing much wrong with her, you know.' I looked at the women in the beds, one after another, and one after another they looked back at me, sadly, ashamedly, as though I must be the carrier of evil news. I could not see Mother among them. I stared into one sad face after another and at last into Mother's face, staring back at me. It was like a meeting of strangers.

I walked to her bed at the far end of the ward. She spoke my name and put out her hand. I kissed her on the forehead. She smelt of sawdust death. I thought, this is what it comes to, this is what it all comes to. I sat down breathless on the empty chair by her bed.

'You didn't bring me any flowers, Lindy. Aren't there any flowers in the garden?'

'There isn't any garden.'

I ought to have felt sorry for her. Perhaps I should have done so, once I had recovered from this fact of being held fast again; but she was never one for having mercy. She smiled her crooked little smile, just as in the old days, and said: 'False alarm, Lindy. They thought it was cancer, but now they say it's just exhaustion.'

'Exhaustion?' I asked. I felt numb and frozen.

'I don't mind telling you, I suppose.' Her voice had altered little but for its being huskier than before; yet otherwise she had altered a great deal, although I think that I felt this more than saw it. I think she was thinner and sharper in the face: what I most remember – but I don't remember much – were the lines and shadows in her face; for they were still there, just as I had first seen them on the morning she had left us. She wasn't beautiful, lying there in that bed: she was a tired woman in middle age who had lived stupidly. I could have looked at her without pity, but mostly I looked at the red hospital blanket that covered her bed. Stupid, I kept thinking, stupid stupid stupid.

'You've changed, Lindy. You've grown up. We'll be better with each other now, shan't we?'

'Are you coming back?'

'I don't mind telling you,' she repeated sharply, 'though there's no reason why I should. I'm still your mother, aren't I?' But she did mind telling me: it was as bad, I saw, as playing on this beaten nerve that was somewhere broken in her. I don't remember all she said: it was hard to pay attention. She and Ted had got clean away: they'd never seen Dook again: they'd gone to Southend or somewhere in that direction – I'm not sure exactly where – and lived in a big hotel until the money had given out. Then one morning Ted had pushed off in the car, not saying a word, and left her with the bills unpaid. She'd met a man in the bar: more than one man in the bar: somehow or other the bills were paid. I didn't really listen. It was as though the beaten nerve was inside me instead of her.

'You coming back?' I asked her.

Then I knew how much she had tricked me. She grew angry. 'Coming back? Of course I'm coming back.' Perhaps she had also tricked herself: perhaps she had imagined, until she saw me and how little I wanted her back, that she was really beaten. Perhaps it was true about the fear of cancer.

'Tommy'll give me a job, won't he? I've still got my cottage, haven't I?'

She talked a great deal. I sat beside her in dumb misery. Every word made a new rivet in this chain that held me to her. I saw then that you can never break a chain like this: you have to live with it, you have to let it wither from you. I knew that Jacob would never understand this.

'Where you living?'

'At auntie's.'

'With him there too?'

'Yes.'

She began to swear at him. It might have been that all the filth and sickness in her were bottled in her swearing at him. She poured out her filthy language, and seemed to grow strong and well. Her stone brown eyes lost their dullness. Her face became less lined and yellow.

I said: 'We're going away.'

'Not with him, you're not. I'll watch that. Wasn't for him, nothing of this would have happened.' The poison seemed to run out of her: the strength seemed to flow back into her.

I said foolishly. 'We've saved up. We've got a hundred pounds. We're going to Australia.'

I opened my purse. The thought I had then, a silly thought, was that I could somehow buy her off. I took out the five pound notes that Jacob had sweated for, and gave them to her. She held them in her hand, and I knew that I had not bought her off, I had only sold myself. I did and thought all this as though I stood outside myself and watched in a trance.

She was pleased with the money. 'That'll do for a start,' she said presently with her crooked smile, 'that's something on account, isn't it?'

'It's his money. Our money.'

'He know you took it?'

I wanted to say yes; but she knew me too well. She said quickly: 'Don't you tell him, Lindy. He'll never notice, with all that money. A hundred pounds, what's he want with a hundred pounds? We'll borrow his hundred pounds.'

'We're going to Australia.'

'He can go to the North Pole for all I care.' Now there was energy in her again, a fearful warning energy: she flicked the pound notes through her fingers. 'You and me, Lindy, we'll start again. Ted went off without a word to me. All right, we'll say finish to that. He was never any good anyway. I'm coming back to the dairy. I'm going to look after you better than I did before.'

I managed to say: 'I don't want anything to do with you.'

'Don't care too much what you want if it comes to *that*.' She was almost enjoying herself now; but then, I suppose, she remembered where she was. 'The idea – me lying in hospital and you coming and telling me what you want and don't want.' Now she was so near shouting that other women round us heard and rustled in their beds to mind what we were saying. There were tears in her eyes; but I think they were tears of anger. I should have been sorry for her: to go through life and have nothing but anger and hatred at the end of it: to come down to this, to have nothing but this. I didn't care if she lived or died.

She caught at my wrist when I rose to go. Her face blurred with sudden weeping, but I regarded her without shame. I was past shame: I was past hope, I thought of the long bus journey home, and of what I should have to tell Jacob at the end of it. Her bitter words drummed into me. She'd come soon. She'd settle us. She'd pay him out for turning me against her. She'd have me back if it was the last thing she did.

Somehow I got away from her. But the words were in my head and I could not get away from them. They drummed at me in the motors of the bus through that endless journey home: they screamed in the telephone wire while I walked from Chudbury bus stop along the small road from Rolcaster, going to the woods: they called in the yapping chorus of the Sealyhams at Mannerses: they came at me from Jerman's rookery. It was dusk when I reached the path where Jacob and I had always left the road. I set foot upon the empty stubble.

The stubble lay desolate and useless, fit for the plough and nothing more. I walked across it in the falling light. It seemed that I had never been this way before.

He was waiting for me at the edge of the wood. I saw him

stand up and come towards me. I remember screaming: I remember the pain of his hand as it split across my face.

Afterwards he was sorry for hitting me and tried to comfort me, asking me over and over what he could do to make it up. I told him he could get me a bowl of fresh water from the stream so that I could wash my bleeding lips; and when I had done that I told him to think no more of it. I said it was my fault for taking the money: I oughtn't to have taken it.

'I saw you'd taken it,' he muttered, 'your auntie told me where you'd gone.'

I looked into his strange sharp face, into his eyes that were hard and unforgiving. I made him turn his face and look at me too.

'I'm sorry, Jacob. She tricked me. She said she was very ill. She isn't. I'm sorry, I didn't mean to hurt you.'

'No,' he said.

'We'll go away if she comes back.'

He flung off from me, his shoulders hunched together, his hands in his pockets as though he feared to bring them out. His voice was also hard and unforgiving. He wouldn't stand for her coming back: he wouldn't, he wouldn't.

I went after him into the woods, trailing after him. I was crushed between these two, locked between their anger and their hatred. The whole of life was there between them, all that could ever be mine I thought, the mean and narrow boundaries that contained it all. I went after him hopelessly. I couldn't get away. I did not want to get away.

TWELVE SHE returned on a Wednesday morning. She left the bus at Chudbury and went straight to my aunt Pooley's at the old schoolhouse, and my aunt Pooley told her we were living at Morton's. It all came out afterwards. She walked down to our village then, and because it was the middle of the morning no one seems to have noticed her: she got to Morton's, apparently without even stopping at our old cottage on the way, and found Morton in her dressing-gown. Morton told her we were living at Miss Pooley's. Mother said it was a dirty lie – she'd just come from there; whereupon Morton tried to shut the door in her face. She forced the door open and got inside.

Morton told her that if Miss Pooley had refused to give her any information then she could be sure that she, Morton, would not give her any either. Why had Mother come back at all? She had abandoned her daughter in the most callous way, but she, Morton, could tell her that everyone in the village was in fact a great deal the happier for it. She could tell her that her daughter was in good hands. Mother had better go away again. In any case she had better leave this house at once because otherwise she, Morton, would telephone for the police.

'That's what you did before, isn't it? It's all you can think of, the police.'

'No, I have never done it before, though perhaps I should have.'

'And there's another dirty lie.'

Morton became frightened of what Mother might do. She changed her tone and pleaded with Mother to go away. She promised to write to Mother and tell her everything she knew about me. Only Mother should go away.

Mother said to her: 'There's nowhere for me to go.'

THIRTEEN I USED to wash the breakfast things in a slow stream that runs through the woods where we lived and joins the Stint near Chudbury. It is much too small for fishing and yet it broadens here and there into muddy bays and shallows: below one of these we had built a dam of stones so as to have several inches of clear water in a pool, and this was where we washed our dishes and ourselves. The roots of a smooth beech gave us a good dry place on the bank, and blackthorn thickets made a screen so that we could take our clothes off, when we wanted to wash properly, and soap ourselves all over, standing in the pool we had made and letting the suds and bubbles float away gently down stream. In that boiling summer weather it was cool and quiet here, cool and green within the beech leaves that made a sunlit canopy above our heads, and silent but for the leaves and birds and buzzing creatures.

After I had washed the breakfast things that morning I took off all my clothes and washed myself, as much for the pleasure of it as anything else, for even then the air was clear and warm and sunlit, and time was slow as the clamour of sultry weather in September. There was time for everything: there would always be time for everything. I tied up my long yellow locks that were growing softer and losing their brittle nastiness, and soaped myself gently and slowly, enjoying the feel of my cool hard hands, enjoying the sight of my small fat stomach and its tuft of woman's hair and my breasts that were a woman's breasts, enjoying the slow rich unrolling of my life and his life.

I could not imagine life without him; and I do not believe that he could have imagined life without me. He would forgive me for letting him come into me, for making him come into me: I was certain of it then. I soaped my naked body and was glad that I could give myself to him and was sure that once we were away from here he would lose his fear of being with me, would throw away his grudge for being with me: and then we should have each other always, whenever we desired, and never care for anyone else. Then the world would be close to him as well as to me: and happiness would also be for us. Somehow or other I had won this battle. I knew it then for sure. I knew that I had got the better of the evil fates and that the victory could be mine – in the end could always be mine. Sunlit water sprinkled from my hand in the smoky summer air that fell and filtered through beech leaves above me: the reflection of my body in the tea-brown water, when I looked down along myself, was plump and pale and trembling in the pool. But I did not tremble: I sang and slapped myself with gladness at my firm untrembling body.

It must have been my singing that gave me away. I was holding my breasts, measuring again their woman's fullness, when I got the feeling that someone watched me. I snatched for my towel, lying on the beech root. I looked up and she was leaning against the trunk.

'It's only me, Lindy.'

Her voice at least had scarcely changed: it was much the same thick vibrant voice, a little husky, a little harsh, strong and slow and hard. It brought her back to me with a sickening determination. I wrapped the towel round my body and saw her clearly through the dusty sunlight: otherwise she was not the same. She wore the same summer dress that she had gone away in, a brilliant saffron silky thing; but that was faded now and shabby, and she had no stockings, and her suede shoes were fouled with mud. I noticed every smallest thing about her: she had not even bothered to shave the crisp black hair on her calves. She wore no lipstick nor other make-up. There was a pinkish puffiness beneath her eyes that I have never seen before. She was not handsome now: she was old and used.

She was trying to smile pleasantly. She said: 'It's no shame having a daughter with a figure like yours, Lindy. To think what a funny kid you were.'

I was no longer afraid of her. Being with Jacob, being in love with Jacob, had ended that for good: I recognized it even while I stared at her. But I wished that I was afraid of her; for in place of fear there came something else that was still more difficult to bear. She began coughing: she had always coughed a little, from the cigarettes she smoked, but now she coughed with a dry hopeless retching that seemed to pump her of breath, and leave her without strength to resist it. She crouched down on the beech root and got off her shoes and put her soiled feet into our pool;

253

and there was nothing I could say or do to stop her. I pulled off my towel and gave it to her: she bent over her soiled feet and washed them with our soap and then she washed her lined face and dried herself and gave me back the towel and put the soap on the ground beside her.

'It's mucky there,' I said, 'give it to me.'

She gave it to me. 'How strong you're getting, Lindy. It's you who'll be looking after me now.'

'No, we're going away.'

'All right, you're going away. Ted went away. Dook went away. Everyone goes away.' There seemed no strength in her. 'But we can get along together till you do, can't we? I've come home for good. It'll be different. I'm going down to Jerman's for a job. They can't refuse me a job, can they?'

I was fighting with pity and wishing it were fear. Then she stood up slowly, taking her time, and began unbuttoning her dress. I said sharply: 'What are you doing?'

'Can have a bath, can't I, Lindy?'

'It's our pool.'

'Is it? But it's running water.' She was strong enough to be sarcastic. Now she had taken off her dress and her petticoat and was loosening her hair.

'You can't,' I said foolishly, helplessly, 'it's our pool.'

But she pulled down the rest of her clothes and stepped naked into our pool. 'My, it's cold, but it's just what I need.'

I had to watch her. You will think it foolish of me, and perhaps you will not understand it; but the sight of her nakedness as she went down on her knees in our pool and scooped up the water and threw it over herself turned my victory into defeat. 'It's wonderful, Lindy,' she cried, shuddering and shivering and splashing. And then it was simply that she was strong and I was weak: as I helplessly watched her there in the middle of our pool, in this pool that was secretly ours and ours only, where we had gazed at each other without shame and loved each other, it was like all these months had gone for nothing.

'Where is he?' she called to me.

'Working.'

'All right, you can come back to the cottage with me and help me put it straight.'

'I'm living here now.'

'I know you are. She lied to me over there, but I knew where I'd find you all right. But you can come, can't you, and help me put the cottage straight?'

I finished drying myself and began to dress. She came splashing out of the pool and took the towel from me. 'Haven't a bit of money you can let me have, Lindy?'

'No. It's his money.'

'But he doesn't need it all. Not right away. We'll pay back.'

'No. I shouldn't have given you any in the first place.'

'Did he cuss you for it? Mean about money, is he?'

Even now, wheedling, coughing, she had the power to paralyse with her questions. She knew the places that would hurt. She worked at them, carefully, wearily, like the peeling of plaster from a wound. 'Never mind about that now, then. We'll see later. I'll borrow from old Pooley.'

'She doesn't have any.'

'Oh she's always got the odd pound note stuffed into her mattress. Old bag of bones, she doesn't need it.'

I finished dressing. I watched her while she dressed.

'That's better. That's a lot better. Feel almost human again,' she cried gaily. 'You'll come over to the cottage, won't you?'

I could have said no. I could have turned about and walked to my aunt Pooley's without another word. But chains like this one are not to be broken: I knew it then even if I forgot it afterwards. I went across the glade as far as our sheltering blackthorn while she came close behind me, and called to her to wait while I put my towel away.

She came in after me. She came into our hut just as she had walked into our pool, and the effect on me was pretty much the same. She came in and poked about and was loud in her admiration of what we'd made of it. 'Proper little home, isn't it,' she said coolly. I knew she was prying into everything. I had forgotten that the board under which we kept the tin with the money had loosened so much, with use, that you could easily see it in the floor. She saw it and suddenly stooped and picked it out. I called to her; but already she had her hands on the tin. She opened it and shouted her delight: and I could not stop her. 'Another ten quid or so won't notice, Lindy,' she shouted, and began counting notes into her hand. And still I knew the chain could not be broken.

'You've got to put it back.'

'Come off that, Lindy. It's only a loan.'

She glanced up at me with her crooked smile. 'Tell you what, Lindy, I'll only take a fiver on condition you'll come with me now and help me set the cottage straight. And I'll give him an IOU for it too.' She took a stub of pencil out of her handbag and tore a corner from a comic that was lying on the table. When she had scribbled on it she showed it to me – *IOU a fiver Poppy Wellin* – and put it into the tin, returned the tin to its hold and the piece of boarding after it, and stamped on the floor.

We went out of the woods together, while she talked as though nothing had changed between us, as though nothing could ever change between us. I trailed after her through the weeds of the garden and into the cottage that smelt of damp and desolation. The old life caught at me chokingly.

FOURTEEN ALL through that day, as we set the cottage to rights, I kept saying to myself that tomorrow this would be yesterday, past and gone: I should have finished with it, I should be free. I ticked off the hours until six o'clock when I meant to leave her: if I left her then I should still be able to reach home before him. She had spent none of the money, for there had been no time to spend any; and I meant to take it from her bag before I left.

I suppose I meant these things. I suppose they were true. Another truth grew alongside them, though: it was this, in the end, that made me fail. It grew in me secretly: it flowered full-grown. We were carrying carpets into the garden so as to throw them across the hedge and beat them: we had worked hard all day, scarcely stopping for so much as a glass of water, she and I with our hair tied into handkerchiefs and our sleeves rolled back and our faces bright with sweat and blurred with dust by turns, cleaning, sweeping, polishing, till we had almost made a new home in that decaying place.

Carrying those rags of carpet we bumped into each other at the door. They slid and tottered to the ground and we on top of them.

We looked at each other and burst out laughing.

'Lindy, you're filthy!'

'Look at yourself, then,' I shouted back. And we were laughing with the sheer pleasure and relief of it. Her face had lost its shadowed misery, its sick meanness. It was almost strong again.

She got up and began dragging those bits of carpet into the garden: but I was frightened of myself then.

I went straight to her bag and wrenched it open to take the money from her while I could. There was nothing else in its soiled silk lining except a dirty slip of lace handkerchief and a tarnished lipstick holder and a stub of pencil: that was all she had. I took the pound notes out of her bag, but I also put them back again. I watched my hand put them back again. I couldn't take that money from her then: I simply couldn't take it.

I even argued with myself. Why should I take it, I argued: she needs it more than we do, doesn't she? Five pounds can't make any difference if you're going to Australia: besides, she'll get a job and pay it back. We don't have to go at once: we can wait a while can't we?

I heard her vigorous beating of the carpets.

She wandered into the cottage again; but I had thrust the bag beneath its cushion on the sofa.

'I need a drink,' she cried from the door: 'let's go over to the *Wheelwright.*'

From that, though, I managed to dissuade her; for if I couldn't take the money from her, I couldn't let her spend it either. I told her she'd be the better for a good night's sleep: she could meet the village tomorrow.

'Oh, I don't know,' she said, undecided, ready to listen to reason: 'My, it's nice to be working at your own place again. Nice to have you too, Lindy. Even if it's only for a few weeks, eh?' She was standing between me and the window, her back to the light. She put up her arms and yawned with noisy contentment. I could not properly see her face: she might have been young and strong again.

'Well,' I said, 'I don't see why we can't stay a few weeks.'

'That's right. Try it out, eh?' She was even making fun of me, so easy were we now together. 'Never know, do you – might even like it.' I thought then that this was the first time in our lives that she had ever really wanted me, depended on me. I was flattered by that: yes, I was also glad of it.

I didn't see it as a hopeless betrayal; although hopelessness did have something to do with it. Ever since she'd taken off her shoes and bathed her soiled feet in our pool, hopelessness had grown in me. And then the habit of being with her while she happily worked: habit had done the rest. Habit: it's another name for cowardice. I know that now.

Yet there was something else that mattered more. I thought to myself, I kept thinking: don't run away, don't let him run away either, don't try and break this chain. Stay a few weeks – she'll have to loosen it herself then. Just a few weeks. Then we'll really be free.

I'm not pretending there was anything good in this. I only wanted to have life straight and clean behind us. I wanted never to have to look behind us: never again. We should go to Australia: there'd be nothing, nothing at all, to drag behind us into our lives together. Nothing at all.

I said to her as she came over to me: 'Well, we don't have to go for a bit.'

When she took my head between my hands I let her kiss me. I put my arms round her and embraced her. I kissed her back.

She said admiringly: 'My, you've grown up. That was a proper kiss.'

He found us like this. We heard his voice calling to us from beyond the window. I wrenched myself away from her even before I saw the look in his face.

'What's that?' Mother asked stupidly.

He was leaning on the sill, his hunched shoulders shutting half the light from us. Pointing at us in one hand, steadied by the other, he had his pistol.

'What do you want?' she asked, not angrily but weakly, stupidly.

'The money.'

'What money?' I think she had really forgotten the pound notes she had taken.

He said, not looking at me: 'You can have Lindy. I've finished with her.'

I could not seem to get my mouth open. I heard Mother saying, 'Decent of you.' It was after all she who recovered first.

'All right, the money then.'

Mother put her hands on her hips. 'And if I keep it?'

'I'll kill you.'

'Think I'm afraid? 'Tisn't loaded anyway.'

'Isn't it?' There was a shattering crack: the bullet must have hit the wall behind us. 'There's five more like that.'

Then at last I got my voice. I shouted at him: 'Jacob, I'm coming with you.'

'No, you're not.'

But I turned and pushed her out of the way, seized her bag and wrenched it open and recovered the money. I was running for the door when she came at me and caught my dress. The shooting had somehow set us free: now we were both desperate. She began slapping me about the head, shouting at me that she would never let me go. I got away from her, struggling towards the door: she came after me, overwhelmed me, had me on the floor with her knees in my chest, her hands beating at my face. I remember the choking smell of dust.

There was another explosion and I was free of her. She had fallen back against the sofa. I got up and looked at her: I thought that she was dead.

But she wasn't dead. She wasn't even hurt. In that long deaf silence while we stared at her she said: 'Well, that's finished it for you. They'll get you for this.' And slowly she sat up then, one arm caught across her chest. We looked at her while she pulled that arm away from herself: there was not even any blood on it. She said stupidly: 'Went between me.'

I screamed: 'It won't next time, so you leave us alone. We're going. We'll never come back.'

Slamming the door behind me, I ran to him and pulled him away from the window. He looked at me as stupidly as she had done. But I shouted: 'She's all right. You can't kill her. Nobody can.' I was pulling at his arm, shouting at him: 'Come on, we can go. We can go.' I simply lost my head: that is how I try to forgive myself now.

He let me pull him away from there. He let me pull him into a run. We ran out of the garden and fled away down the road.

We ran as far as Morton's and past Morton's into the first belt of woodland. Only there we slowed at last into a walk. It appears to me now that I was quite clear in the head. I knew exactly what to do: it was I, not he, who decided this. When we reached the edge of the airfield I stopped and said I wanted to explain the events of all that day.

'Doesn't matter.' Wonderfully, there was no bitterness left in his voice: he was not even angry with me any more.

'Still I want to tell you.'

He was gentle with me while I told him. 'Doesn't matter,' he repeated. 'Wasn't your fault.'

'Give me a kiss, Jacob.' He embraced me. When I felt his body come ungrudgingly against mine, it seemed to me that everything was clear once more and always must be clear. I had snapped the chain: it was broken and gone for good. We should never be stopped.

I clung to him and he let me cling to him, his face close to mine, his eyes steadily regarding me. 'Let's go home quickly,' I whispered, 'or as far as the woods.'

'Yes.'

I knew then that his grudge against me was absolutely gone: I knew it with a calm and simple joy – that after all these things, that after all this terrible day, none the less we were together and should never more be parted. That was what I thought: that is what was in my mind. Perhaps we had to pay this price in order to know it, both of us. There is no sense now in asking whether it was worth the price: if I blame myself to the end of time there will never be an answer.

The minutes passed: they might have been as many hours. I didn't count them. I said: 'There's no one to see us here.' I lay down on the stubble, sharp and warning though it was, and pulled him down to me.

The minutes passed: I used to bang my head whenever I thought of how they passed. But then, that evening, I wanted never to let him go. We lay there on the edge of the forbidden airfield, close in each other's arm, with his body hard upon me and the stubble sharp beneath; and then it was the threshold of another journey, of a journey so long and so complete that it would never end: a journey we should go upon together, equally together. I knew that he really loved me then. I knew that we were truly and equally together. I knew that the world would be for both of us: for both of us together.

That is what happened. Presently he said: 'We ought to go,

Lindy, it's not safe here,' and got to his feet. I looked up past him as he stood above me; and beyond him the sky was tipped with orange like distant woods on fire, and all the kingdoms of this earth waited only that we should knock and enter.

And then, really, it was over. Far away, down towards the hangars and the sheds, a jet threw out a sudden screaming wail and we had to shout our words. As suddenly its engine stilled again, and the silence seemed to wail at us instead. I pulled down my clothes and got up quickly.

'We can go to London tomorrow, and get the tickets.'

'There's a Rolcaster bus at half seven.'

'Shall we catch that one? Tomorrow morning?'

'Yes, that one.'

I said happily: 'Well, I hope I'll wake up in time, that's all.'

He put his arms on my shoulders and kissed me on the lips. Nothing can destroy that fact.

'Let's go home now, Jacob.' There was happiness even in the saying of his name.

He flung back his head and let his hands drop gently from my shoulders. He was really at peace then. I knew it from his face, from his glowing eyes, from his voice and the ringing clearness of it. 'We'll cut across the tarmac, Lindy. It's quicker that way.'

We stepped on the tarmac. Appallingly, the jet began again with its screaming.

I shouted: 'They'll kill a person one of these days.'

'No, they're not flying from here yet. Only testing or something. We'll be away before they're flying from here.'

We got out on the runway. We began walking quickly, for it was strictly forbidden to be here at all. We were far across the runway when we heard their warning shouts behind us.

They were running towards us over the tarmac: two or three of them, American servicemen, with Mother among them.

Jacob cried: 'Run, Lindy!' We began to run across the remainder of the tarmac, a narrow strip of darkness with the darker woods already tall and sheltering in our eyes. We ran for the woods.

We never reached them. We reached the far edge of the runway and jumped clear of it. But there I tripped and fell, my ankle twisted. He came back and pulled me to my feet. I tried to run on my twisted ankle. But I could not do that. I shouted into the gathering darkness that he should go without me; but he would not go without me. He stopped with me and put his arm round my waist, helping me along.

They caught us up: they were bound to catch us up. Only then, as they came quite near us and their shouting was hard in our ears, he dropped his hand and let me go and turned back to them.

I turned back with him; and for a moment all of us were like figures in a waxworks, like figures dumped in the basement of a waxworks, set against each other in strange attitudes, suddenly frozen.

One of the servicemen said: 'Put that pistol down.'

The other serviceman moved up a hand to unsling the short squat gun that he carried over his shoulder. Jacob said: 'Don't you move.' The serviceman dropped his hand again.

'Okay, son, but you're out of bounds on this airfield.' He said it patiently, humorously. He looked quite an old man.

Jacob said: 'We'll get off it, and we'll never come back to it. Only don't you follow us, see. Don't you let her follow us.'

Mother was somehow off to one side, and near to me, nearer to me.

The servicemen seemed amused. One of them laughed easily, boastfully. 'Okay, but how do we know you won't come back?'

'I promise we won't.'

'You do?' The older one went on patiently: 'Well, okay then. Guess it's our fault anyway. We got to get more wire in here.' He turned away, beckoned to the other one.

Jacob lowered his pistol, and that was the breathless second when Mother sprang at him. That was my fault too: I want to be honest, and that was my fault too. I should have seen her creeping nearer.

She sprang at him, shouting, and they crashed to the ground together. There was another explosion. Then, in the hush of that explosion, Mother got up slowly, and Jacob stayed on the ground.

One of the servicemen said: 'Christ, she's shot him.'

Mother said: 'It went off. It hit him.'

I knew what had happened: I never had the least doubt of it.

The older serviceman, who had knelt beside him, looked up after a while. 'That's it, then,' he said.

Time passed in blackness. After a while there were ambulance men and policemen. They took me with them. They took me to Rolcaster.

THERE is really nothing more to tell.

FIFTEEN   Months ago I was brought to this place of bricks and mortar so as to be looked after. Pakeman often comes to see me and so does my aunt Pooley whenever she can pay the fare (or Mr Morton gives it to her) and Mr and Mrs Morton also come to see me. Everyone has been very kind to me, and really I am quite all right again. I shall be let out quite soon now.

There is one thing, though, that I should like to tell, because it has meant very much to me. It came about during my appearance at the juvenile court before I was sent here. Pakeman led me to a chair standing by itself in an island of bare floor: beyond the floor was a railing, and beyond the railing there were faces staring at me.

A woman's voice spoke to me. Pakeman whispered: 'Lindy, the magistrate is telling you to look at her and pay attention.'

When I looked up at her I saw she was the same polite woman

with white hair who had stopped her car for us on the winter road to Thaxted. She was even wearing the same kind of flat velvet bonnet only now it was a red one and not a mauve one. She spoke to me in the same sensible inquiring voice.

'Now, Lindy, we've got to see what's best for you, haven't we?' For a moment I thought she would recognize me, but she looked down again at papers on her table.

Mother was also somewhere there, but I never really saw her. Practically everything that was said has gone from my mind: Pakeman has told me what was said and of the judgment that the magistrate made. I was not to go back to Mother again. I was to be found a place to live with someone else. It seems that Mother said nothing to this, neither for nor against it. All that, in any case, is finished: there is no sense in going over it again.

But I heard something of what the magistrate said; and whenever I let my eyes look up from the bare island of floor I looked at her. She said to Pakeman: 'I understand there is an offer of guardianship that is suitable, Miss Pakeman?'

'Yes, from Mr Ralph Morton.'

'Is he here?'

He got up from among the people beyond the railing. I saw the others then – my aunt Pooley and Mrs Thompson and Mrs Steppins and the elder Miss Titheram and some from Chudbury as well. They were sitting all together beyond the railing like people who belong to one another. I can remember thinking how extraordinary it was.

The magistrate said: 'Perhaps you could tell us what you intend?'

But it was Morton herself who answered that.

The clerk had to write down particulars.

'Mary Wolstonecraft Morton,' he repeated after her.

She was dressed in an ordinary way, wearing a brown tweed coat and skirt and a pale yellow scarf; but these ordinary clothes did not suit her. They gave her a pinched and humble look, they made her appear awkward and unimportant.

They talked a great deal of what should become of me. I remember little of it.

'I imagine you've room for an extra member of your family?' Yes, they had room: of course they had room.

'And Miss Pakeman – tell me, do I understand that the mother will not be returning to the neighbourhood? After being released, I mean?' No, she would not: Pakeman had ascertained that. Mrs Wellin would confirm it. I suppose that Mother did confirm it. I can't remember.

I can't remember that, or much else beside, because it seemed to me, however unlikely you may think it, that through all this time the magistrate and I were on one side, and all the rest of them were on the other side. They were all there together, beyond the railing: and beyond them there were the others too – Oliver and old Jeffreys and Thompson with his tiny head and his lusting after Mother when he shouldn't, and even Mr Harold Jerman himself, somewhere in the sky beyond. It was they, I thought, who had to be here in the courtroom, not I: it was they who were on trial. It was they who were having to answer the questions they had never asked. At one point I even stood up to get a better look at them.

The magistrate said to me: 'Lindy, sit down when you are not answering questions, will you? Just sit down and be a sensible girl. I am sure you can be if you try.' No doubt because she smiled at me it was the only time, in all that day, when I came near to crying.

SIXTEEN   THIS morning, while they were both here to see me, there was another argument between Pakeman and Morton.

Pakeman began it, I suppose, by saying in a way that was meant to be kind that after all it was a thoroughly good thing that I had never managed to go to Australia. Pakeman is sure that I have quite recovered: she believes in 'bringing things out into the open,' as she says. She tries to make me talk about Jacob.

'After all, you can't escape reality by running away from it.'

Morton took the other side: she is the only one of them all who has never said a word against Jacob – except for Mr Morton and my aunt Pooley, who never say a word against anyone. Now she told Pakeman that she and Mr Morton had themselves actually thought of selling up their cottage and moving right away: they weren't sure they might not do it still.

'Well, you can move to another village. No need to go to Australia, is there?'

'I never said we were going to Australia.'

They were cross with each other for having come on the same day.

'But Ralph and I think that on the whole we shall stay where we are. Perhaps we shall all get over it the sooner. It was really for Lindy's sake –'

'Oh, you can't export despair, if that's what you mean.'

'My dear Miss Pakeman, I'd forgotten about you. But we shan't all make wild and glorious revolutions.' They go upon each other's nerves until it is painful to be with them. 'Some of us are glad enough just to survive. And survivors don't need to be heroic, you know – they've gone through too much. They just want to survive.' She gets a little breathless when she argues with Pakeman; but she cannot bring herself not to do it. 'There's a good in survival, you know, even if it isn't the good that you admire.'

Mr Morton put his hand on her arm, gently, protectively. She turned to me nervously: 'So now it's just up to you and us, Lindy, pottering along together, patching it up somehow, muddling into the future.' She gave Pakeman a challenging look as though daring her to contradict. But Pakeman can sometimes manage to allow for other people: she said nothing more then.

But I said: 'It's very kind of you.'

After the Mortons had gone I repeated that to Pakeman. 'It is very kind of them, isn't it?'

She had to say: 'Yes, of course it is.' But then she had to go on: 'Kindness – if that's what you want?'

She sat down with me again. I thought she was looking tired, though perhaps it was only because she frowned. 'Wasn't thinking of you, Lindy. You'll be all right, kindness or no kindness. You're the stuff that lets humanity evolve.' It is something she keeps saying to me: it seems to give her some kind of answer to herself. 'But for them –' she broke out irritably: 'Oh, I don't know. Pity and kindness – they're a sort of death too, aren't they? They're flags of surrender.'

'I think it's kind.'

We have come to know each other quite well. She looked up at me then with a quick smile: 'You don't mind going back to the village?'

'No, I don't mind.' Perhaps I should have said it anyway – it was nothing that I said it: only I knew then that it was true. I looked past her into the tired London day and knew that I was not afraid of going back. I was not afraid of anything.

I shall be going to Morton's in three weeks' time, and I am glad to be going there. I shall stay with them for a while. After that I shall strike out on my own. I shall continue with my life.